The Experiencers
The Valiant
Chronicles: Book I

Val Tobin

This is a work of fiction and any resemblance to persons living or dead, or places, events or locales is purely coincidental. The names, characters, places, and incidents are products of the author's imagination or are used fictitiously. Readers familiar with the Newmarket/Aurora area might note, correctly, that no hospital exists in Aurora. That change was deliberately made for the story.

DEDICATION

To Bob, Jenn, Mark, Chanelle, Savannah, and Jack.

ACKNOWLEDGMENTS

Editing by Alan Annand (Sextile) sextile.com and Kelly Hartigan (XterraWeb) editing.xterraweb.com. Thank you, Alan and Kelly.

Thanks to Patti Roberts of Paradox (paradoxbooktrailerproductions.blogspot.com.au/) for the amazing cover.

Thanks also to Andrea Holmes, Val Cseh, Amanda David, Judy Flinn, Tania Gabor, Michelle Legere, Julie Marsh, Moses Leal, Peter Wolf, Sheila Trecartin, Kathy Rinaldo, Jennifer Fasciano, Bruce Greenaway, Dr. Maral, Sharon Reesor, Anne Collins, Angel Morgan, Erika Wolf, Diane King, Angela Swift, Jeff McQueen, Arla King, Blair Weeks, Tara VanderMeulen, Karen Stephenson, Kevin Barnum, Jim Smith, Dr. Alis B. Kennedy, Heather Tobin, James Borg, Joe Ryan, Brad Jones, staff at Algonquin Park, Archangel Michael, Archangel Gabriel, and my spirit guides.

CHAPTER 1

Michael "Mick" Valiant checked his watch and realized he was going to finish work early. The upside was he'd be home for dinner; the downside was he'd be home for dinner. He cringed. The thought of going home reminded him he might be getting separated soon, perhaps even the next time he was home long enough to see his wife before she went to bed. Jessica had something on her mind lately, and he suspected it was divorce.

He pulled his thoughts away from his marriage and refocused on the job. Michael sat behind the driver's seat in the back of a white van displaying a cable company logo on the side. The video monitor before him showed the inside of the sprawling brick bungalow across the street. His target, Patty Richards, was inside the house.

Aside from the stats he needed for the job, Michael knew little about Richards. He knew her only as a threat to the Extraterrestrial Alliance Project, or ETAP, as those involved referred to it, and any threat to the Project had to go.

Michael glanced over at his partner, Gerry "Torque" Muniz, who sat next to Michael, also staring at the monitor. Judging from the vacant look in Torque's eyes, he wasn't seeing what was there. Sweat beaded on his broad forehead. Hair around his bald spot spiked up, reminding Michael of a porcupine with tiny black and grey quills.

"Why don't you take off that jacket?" Michael asked. "You're drenched."

Torque shook his head, eyes still unfocused. He continued to sit and stare, brows furrowed. Finally, he spoke. "I hate leaving them alive."

He meant Ralph Drummond. They'd forced him into a psychiatric institution to silence him. It hadn't been their typical job. As if they hadn't had this conversation numerous times since they'd been handed Drummond's dossier, Michael said, "Then why did we?"

1

"Have you looked at the rest of the targets?"

This was new. In previous conversations, at this point, Torque would say, "I don't know," to which Michael would reply, "Then why worry about it?"

Michael did a job, following orders precisely, and then forgot about it. It helped him maintain his detachment and his sanity. The Drummond job had been no exception though his initial gut reaction to it had been different.

When he'd first read the file on Drummond, he'd felt uneasy, like something was off. He'd ignored it and carried on. With the reminder of Drummond and his file, the uneasiness returned.

He gave his partner a puzzled stare. "I've read the list."

"No," Torque said. "Have you looked at it in detail?"

"What's your point?"

"I figured out why we didn't kill him and why we won't kill the other two either."

"Okay," Michael said. "Why?"

"They're abductees, and killing them would interfere with the experiments."

"Where did it say that?"

"It didn't. Not explicitly. They're all members of the same UFO group, except this next target. The ones we can't terminate are flagged as 'catch and release.' The aliens want them for their experiments. We have to get creative if we want to silence them. Drummond goes to the mental hospital; the other two are disappeared to the Agency."

"Why didn't I see that?"

"You wouldn't have noticed if you weren't looking for it."

"Carolyn Fairchild and Arnie Griffen. I saw they weren't to be terminated."

Michael didn't have the other files, but he picked up the Richards file and opened it. Torque was right. Nothing in the file indicated she belonged to the same UFO group as the others. In fact, she wasn't a member of any UFO group. Her schedule showed that tonight she planned to attend a concert at her daughter's school. He felt a twinge. She'd be dead by then.

A note in the file stated Richards was Drummond's associate, maintained a blog, and travelled around North America doing speaking engagements.

"What's the blog about?" he asked.

Torque shrugged. "Doesn't matter."

Michael nodded, understanding. He removed his weapon from a pouch at his side and marvelled, not for the first time, at how something so small could be so deadly. The size and shape of a penlight or laser pointer, the weapon discharged a microwave beam that could penetrate walls and kill a person from over twenty metres away. Soon, when he deemed the time right, Richards's heart would stop, and the coroner would list it as natural causes.

In no hurry, he waited and watched. He ran his hand through his hair, an absent-minded gesture he'd repeat often when he waited to kill. He glanced at Torque, expecting a remark, but his partner had returned to staring vacantly at the screen and didn't notice.

Michael looked up when the door to the house opened. Two teenagers stepped onto the porch. Their light and jovial voices carried through the open windows of the van. The girl was Patty's daughter, Michelle. The male would be Ian, the daughter's boyfriend.

Ian said something too low to make out, but it must've been funny because the girl burst out laughing. The hearty laugh jarred Torque out of his stupor, and he shifted his gaze from the monitor to Michael.

Michael continued to wait.

The two teens scampered down the porch steps and jumped into a black Volkswagen Jetta parked in the driveway. Sleek and shiny, the car couldn't have been more than a few months old. Had to be the kid's father's car, but perhaps not. Kids these days were spoiled. The car could very well be his.

Michael checked the clock on the dashboard and waited for the kids to pull out of the driveway. He'd have an hour before the husband returned, which gave them plenty of time. Most of the neighbours were also at work.

The Jetta eased onto the road, the back end swinging past the van. Michael glimpsed Ian's face as the kid straightened the wheel and then accelerated the car down the street. Neither kid spared the van a glance.

Michael changed the view on the monitor to the kitchen, and both men watched the screen.

Richards, her long hair tied back in a ponytail, stood in front of the kitchen island, stirring something in a bowl. She resembled her daughter. It would be easy to mistake them for sisters even though Patty was more than twice her daughter's age.

Michael realized he was holding his breath and exhaled. Sweat trickled down his back, and he checked the thermometer: twenty-two Celsius. Hot, for the end of April in Southern Ontario, but not hot enough to make them roll up the windows and turn on the air conditioning. Fortunately, a light breeze drifted through, easing the humidity in the air.

He started to lift the weapon, but paused. His hand drifted back to rest on his thigh. This looked wrong. It felt wrong. Yet he had the right target. All the information he had bore that out, the clincher being the carefully installed surveillance equipment the grunts from the Agency had placed inside the house. Michael felt another twinge. This reminded him of the Drummond job—like someone had made a mistake and he was silencing the wrong person.

"What are you waiting for?" Torque's voice startled Michael, but he didn't flinch.

He cleared his head and focused. Lifting his weapon, he pointed the business end of it in the direction that put the Richards woman in its path. He clicked a button and locked it into place, keeping the weapon on and trained at her.

On the monitor, Richards swayed. She turned off the mixer, but before she could set it down, she collapsed, dragging bowl and mixer down with her.

The bowl shattered when it hit the floor. Batter and glass sprayed everywhere. The mixer plug yanked free of the outlet, the cord snaking down on top of her.

Michael waited.

She jittered and thrashed. Then she was still.

He waited.

She didn't move.

He removed his cell phone from his jacket, which hung on the back of the passenger seat behind him, and speed-dialled his boss, Jim Cornell. After a click, Cornell's voicemail kicked in.

When the beep sounded, Michael cleared his throat and spoke. "Valiant here. We're done at the job site and on our way back."

He ended the call and returned the phone to his jacket.

A glance at the monitor verified Richards remained motionless. Michael stuck the weapon back into the pouch at his side. Mindful of the low ceiling, he climbed into the driver's seat. He started the van, anxious to leave, but waited while Torque shut down the equipment and climbed into the passenger seat.

When they reached the south end of Richmond Hill, Michael's cell phone rang. He punched the speaker button.

"Valiant here."

"Got your message. Good job," Cornell said.

"I've gotta ask, Jim: what did these people do? They don't seem like our typical targets."

"You can ask, but trust me, they're a threat. And this isn't something we discuss over a cell phone."

"Right." He ended the call, but his doubts continued.

"I wouldn't question Cornell if I were you," said Torque. "If you want to ask someone anything, ask me. If I don't know the answer, it's because we're not supposed to know. Are we clear?"

Michael nodded, keeping his eyes on the road. Torque was right, but

Michael persisted. "Don't you think it's odd we're targeting housewives now?"

"Maybe they aren't just housewives. It's not our job to verify that the targets are correct. What's up with you? I've never known you to question an assignment."

"This feels different."

Torque stared at him, one eyebrow raised, his lips pursed.

"You going all new-agey on me? Have you been spending too much time on Carolyn Fairchild's file?"

Carolyn Fairchild, one of their catch-and-release targets, was a psychic medium running a holistic practice from her home.

Michael laughed, shaking his head. "Thanks for that. I needed a good chuckle."

"Let it go, Mick. Don't worry about if they've been properly vetted. You can be sure they have. Whoever the Agency targets, they no doubt earned the recognition."

Michael didn't reply. He exhaled, releasing tension. These were career-limiting thoughts. He needed to get over them, or risk, at the least, his career, at the most, his life and perhaps even Jessie's life.

Two hours later, Michael pulled the van into a reserved spot in a parking garage in downtown Toronto.

Torque scanned the vehicle. "Don't forget your jacket."

Michael retrieved his jacket and picked up his files. He locked the van and walked around to where his partner, who already had his ID badge clipped to his lapel, waited. Michael pulled his own badge out of his pocket and pinned it on.

"Have time for a drink after we report to Cornell?" Michael asked.

"Still avoiding the home front?"

"I guess. I have to make it up to her, but I don't know how." Even as he said it, Michael knew he wouldn't have that drink with Torque, he wouldn't be home for dinner, and he wouldn't let it drop. He'd hole up in his office and do a little digging on the UFO group.

He mentally reviewed the list of remaining targets: John and Carolyn Fairchild, Shelly and Steven Rudolph, and Arnold Griffen. First, he would find out why Ralph Drummond and Patty Richards were considered such threats they'd had to be silenced immediately.

CHAPTER 2

B efore settling in at his desk, Michael delivered a hurried verbal report to Jim Cornell, who seemed by turns complacent and suspicious. When Michael tried to ask again about some background information on the targets, he swore Torque and Cornell exchanged looks. Michael knew he was pushing it, but somehow, the words kept spilling from his mouth.

It was the way Richards had twitched on the floor, batter and glass speckling her body, and the sight of her daughter, who'd never again have her mother watch her in a school recital. A visceral need to know why compelled him to continue talking about it.

At first, there was stunned silence while Michael sputtered about hitting the wrong target. Then Cornell asked Michael to leave the room.

Now he hunched over the computer at his desk, Patty Richards's blog open on the screen. He scrolled through the page.

Richards referenced Ralph Drummond often, and they frequently collaborated on speaking engagements. While Richards wasn't listed as a member of any UFO groups, she was often a guest speaker. Michael clicked on a link to see on what topic she'd last spoken.

The Government Conspiracy with Extraterrestrials to Plan the End of the World

Well, she wasn't far off the mark. He understood why it would attract attention. Where had she found her information? He checked her schedule. She'd spent the last four months touring North America and was slated to present more talks in early May. Obviously, it was too soon for the websites to be updated with information on her death.

Michael opened up a popular video site and searched for anything that might show one of her talks. He found a large collection, clicked on one, and let it play, immersing himself in it.

Ten minutes later, he heard someone in the outer office. He paused the recording and toggled the screen to a document with his report to Cornell.

Torque stuck his head in the door. "What are you doing here, Mick? I thought you were going home for dinner."

"I stayed to finish some things."

"Such as?"

"Writing up that report for Cornell." He tried to sound bored. "I thought I'd wrap this up tonight."

"You mean you thought you'd avoid Jess tonight."

Michael flushed and averted his eyes. He glanced at the time. It was 7:00 PM. If he dropped everything and left now, it would take him at least an hour to get home. Jess would've had her dinner already, and he'd eat alone, but he wasn't leaving yet. At this point, he wouldn't get home tonight until after she was in bed.

Torque stepped into the office and shut the door.

"Listen. Cornell asked me to make sure you fall in line. This isn't a threat—yet. We've worked together a long time. You're doing well. Never mind what the targets are up to or why they were selected. Leave it alone. If you don't, you could find yourself on the list, no questions asked by anyone about why you're on it. Go home. We have more jobs to do, and I expect you to carry them out the way you've always done. Will you do that?"

Without missing a beat, Michael said, "Sure. No worries. Did Cornell leave yet?"

"Yeah. Anything I can do?"

"No. I'll catch him in the morning."

Torque frowned. "Just remember what I said." He left, closing the door behind him.

Michael waited for a few moments, making sure his partner was gone, before he flipped back to the paused video and clicked "play." Richards's voice, impassioned, floated up.

"The facts I've presented point clearly to a coming catastrophe. Sadly, our government is orchestrating and accelerating the entire thing, and they aren't alone in this. They're joined by covert agencies from the governments of other countries: The United States. The UK and member states of the European Union. Australia. The conspiracy is far-reaching, but it includes only a select number who will survive what comes."

Michael paused the video. He'd heard enough. Where had she found her information? She was right, up to a point. The conspiracy existed, the earth was in trouble, but the Agency wasn't accelerating the damage.

He had a horrifying thought. As far as he knew, the Agency wasn't accelerating it. Was that why they'd killed Richards? Was she exposing something even those who thought they were in on it didn't know?

He searched for Ralph Drummond's blog. When he found it, he saw where Richards had gotten her information. Drummond was vocal. He also had links to videos of his talks about the conspiracy and the coming catastrophe, but he was talking as if he had first-hand knowledge.

Do we have a leak in one of the agencies? In this one?

No wonder Drummond had been silenced, and it made sense they wouldn't want Richards to keep talking. Was their source one of the others on the list? No. If the source were known, he or she would've been the first to go.

Drummond must've had evidence at his home, but the Agency would've removed it all. His house was also bugged and loaded with hidden cameras. Drummond was paranoid—but he was one of the few paranoids who had a valid reason to be.

Michael opened a drawer in his desk and pulled Drummond's file. Included in the dossier were the addresses of his home and a cottage he and his wife owned. It was possible Drummond stored backups of whatever he had at his home, but the Agency would've thought of that.

Only Ralph Drummond could say, but he wouldn't willingly talk to Michael. Ralph would be suspicious of anyone trying to get information from him—particularly one of the men who'd helped lock him up. Perhaps the wife, Beth, would be helpful, but if Michael approached her, then Torque and Cornell would know he hadn't let it go.

The Agency might have what he needed. Anything retrieved from the Drummond house would be in the evidence room in the basement. Michael had access, but only on Cornell's authority. However, it would be empty of employees right now. The room had security cameras, but no one would have any reason to review the footage if he left no evidence of tampering.

Michael slipped a lock-picking tool case and roll of packing tape into his briefcase. After verifying his digital camera and netbook were in there, he shut down his computer.

Ten minutes later, he was jimmying the lock on the storage room door, careful not to do any damage. Once inside, he switched on the lights and locked the door.

An orange couch rested along the left wall, and two matching orange armchairs sat along the right wall. The furniture in here always reminded him of a hippy commune in the 1960s—not that he was old enough to have seen one. But he'd never seen furniture more outdated and garish in his life, and it out-gassed a musty odour, like salvage from a flooded basement. The art wasn't any better. Dogs playing poker hung above the couch, and a velvet matador challenged a bull above the chairs.

An attendant usually sat behind the reception counter. A bulletproof glass pane, drawn across the counter, sealed off the space. When an agent came to retrieve something from storage, he or she would hold the requisition form and ID up to the window. If everything checked out, the attendant would open the door on the right of the counter to let the agent through.

Michael went directly to the door and jimmied the lock, again taking care not to damage the locking mechanism. After switching on the light in that room, he turned off the lights in the main reception area. He returned to the storage area and locked the door behind him.

A long table against the wall on the right, across from the attendant's desk, held the latest evidence to be catalogued and stored. With luck, whatever had been retrieved from Drummond still sat on this table and not on one of the hundreds of shelving units that filled the 700 square metres of the storage room. He didn't want to have to crack into the database to find it.

Michael started with the boxes brought in two days before and worked his way down the table. The third set of four boxes looked likely. One box contained a laptop, external hard drive, and a few memory sticks. The others contained a digital camera, file folders with papers, and larger documents rolled up and secured with elastics.

He set his netbook on the table. As it booted up, he opened one of the file folders. When he spotted Drummond's name, he knew he'd found what he came for. The folder he held contained copies of Patty Richards's blog posts. He returned it to the box. Even if the site was shut down, and he expected it would be, he could still find copies online through an archiving website.

While files transferred from the memory sticks, he unrolled the scrolled documents. Maps. He flattened them onto the table, using nearby boxes to keep them from curling back up. A detail map of Algonquin Park, showing canoe routes, caught his eye.

A black, oval mark in an area near the centre of the park, north of Highway 60, indicated an alien underground base. He'd never seen this base before, and he was sure he'd been made privy to all the ones located in Ontario. Michael photographed everything but put the map with the base into his briefcase. The other maps returned to the boxes.

He picked up the next folder and opened it.

The next time he looked up, it was 9:00 PM. Surprised he hadn't heard from Jess yet, he reached for his cell phone but realized he wouldn't have service down here. He'd have to retrieve any messages from Jess when he left. It also meant he wouldn't be able to call to let her know he'd been delayed. She'd just have to understand.

By the time he'd reviewed half the folders in the box, he'd copied everything from the memory sticks and had cracked the login to the laptop and hard drive. Drummond didn't store files on the laptop. That left only the external hard drive, so he started transferring the files over to his netbook.

Twenty file folders remained. It shouldn't take him long to go through all this since he wasn't reading everything. Whenever he found something he thought would be useful, he took a photo of it to review later. He removed the next folder and opened it.

When he saw what was there, he wished he'd listened to Torque and gone home. He closed his eyes as if to try to un-see it.

CHAPTER 3

J essica Valiant turned off the television and stared at the dirty dinner plate on the coffee table—another meal eaten alone in front of the TV with no word from Michael. Jess picked up her plate and took it to the kitchen. When her bare feet hit the cold linoleum of the kitchen floor, a shiver went through her.

It had felt good to strip down to the bare minimum when she'd first arrived home, hot and sweaty from her commute on the bus from Toronto, but now she felt chilly after sitting in the air-conditioned house. She checked the clock on the stove. It was already after nine.

She rinsed her plate and cutlery and put them in the dishwasher. Jess looked around the kitchen, wondering what to do next. She'd already tried calling Michael, but all she got was his voicemail. She'd left one message. The other two times she'd hung up. Frustration welled up.

They'd spent five years in Canada, and no matter how much Michael promised her things would be different up here, nothing changed. Her routine still consisted of coming home from work to an empty house, eating dinner alone, and then going to bed alone.

Her friends and family thought she was crazy for putting up with it. Most of them told her to get a life. There seemed to be an even split between those who told her to get a hobby and those who told her to get a divorce. She didn't want to get a hobby.

Jess was afraid if she went out and joined something, she'd meet someone else. She didn't want anyone else. She wanted Michael, but, like her friend Sarah said, it didn't look as if he wanted her as much as she wanted him. Still, she wasn't ready to leave him. She wanted to be with him. She loved him.

To be fair, he had a demanding job. An expert in climate change, the issues of the world consumed him. His concerns weren't limited to what happened locally. He wasn't having an affair—not with a woman. His

11

job was his mistress.

When they'd first met, she too had been passionate about her work and spent all her time focusing on her career. It made them a perfect match, especially since she also was a scientist. Her specialty was nutritional research, and she was a formulator for one of the top vitamin manufacturers in North America.

Sometime over the last five years, Jess decided she needed more in her life, and reneged on a promise she'd made to Michael when they'd first married. She brought up the subject of having a baby. He balked, of course. He'd made it clear to her he didn't want to have children.

His work made him pessimistic about the future of the planet, and she understood how that might make him cautious about bringing a child into this world. She was sure, though, that they could manage no matter what happened. Shouldn't life go on with optimism? So Jess decided to do what she wanted and hope for the best.

She'd stopped taking the pill a few months ago, but her opportunities to entice Michael into bed were rare. In what she concluded was masterful manipulation on her part, she'd inveigled her sister to let them use her cottage for a long weekend the month before. She'd calculated her most likely time to be fertile, insisted he take the break from work, and lured him out to the cottage.

He'd kicked and screamed about it but had gone along, and they'd had a wonderful time. They spent cool but sunny afternoons on the dock, Michael nursing a beer, Jess sipping a glass of red wine. They laughed a lot. Michael's dry sense of humour came out to play, and he'd made her laugh until her stomach hurt, as he used to when they were first dating.

When the sun went down, they retired to the cabin and snuggled by the fire. Jess made sure the snuggling escalated into something more. From sundown to well past sunup, they spent most of their time in bed. She'd had her Michael back and knew they were meant for each other. The ulterior plan had worked—she'd received verification a week ago that she was pregnant—but she still hadn't told Michael.

Her inability to share the news with him had made the last few days tense and unbearable. She didn't want to tell him when he came home late at night while she was half-asleep and feeling resentful. She couldn't say anything about it while they rushed to leave for work in the morning. The weekend was coming up, but he'd be working. He was on some kind of new assignment, and it was consuming him. Again.

When she'd suggested to him she wanted some time together to talk, he'd promised to give her that. So far, it hadn't materialized. If anything, he was away even more, and she sensed he was avoiding her. She snatched up the phone and called his cell. It went to voicemail. She hung up, slamming the receiver down a little harder than she'd intended.

She looked around the kitchen for something else to do. Everything looked spotless. Of course—she had nothing to do but clean. Jess wandered back into the spotless living room, eyed the novel she was currently reading, picked it up, and put it down. She was in no mood to read about romance that was so obviously missing from her own life. Sometimes that sufficed, but not now.

She could call her mom. They hadn't spoken in ages, and she was dying to talk about her pregnancy. It would only be just after six o'clock in California, but Mom would've finished her dinner.

Jess picked up the phone again and punched in her mom's number. She settled into the corner of the couch and curled her legs up, draping the quilt from the back of the couch over her lap.

Her mother answered on the second ring and sounded as if she was in a good mood, chattering on about her latest shopping spree and the good use she'd made of her seniors' discount.

Jess smiled. Her mother could justify shopping under any circumstances. Most of the time, all she needed to defend a purchase was her seniors' discount.

"That's great, Mom. I have some news I'd like to share. Don't tell anyone, okay? Just Dad?"

"I promise," her mother said quickly. "What is it? Is everything all right? You're not getting a divorce, are you?"

Always the optimist, huh, Mom? "No. I'm not getting a divorce. I'm going to have a baby." She paused to let it sink in.

"Oh, Jessica. That's wonderful. What does Michael say? He doesn't want you to have an abortion, does he?"

"Perhaps you could've stopped at 'that's wonderful,' " Jess said, thinking she'd made a mistake. It was a pattern she'd followed all her life. She wanted to share exciting news with her mother, and her mother turned it into a catastrophe. Yet Jess continued to try to share good news with her. She was her mother, damn it. Couldn't she just once share her happiness, excitement, or enthusiasm?

"Oh, sweetie, I'm just worried about you two. You both always said you wanted to focus on your careers. You never told me you'd changed your mind. Of course I'm excited to be a grandma again. I love my grandkids, but your sisters always wanted kids and so did their husbands. What made you two decide to have a baby?"

How much should she tell her mother about what she'd done? Probably not much. She'd at least have to admit Michael didn't know she was pregnant. She didn't want her mother blurting it out to him—not that she was likely to be talking to him anytime soon.

"Jessie?"

"I'm here. Michael doesn't know yet. I only found out a few days

13

ago, but he's been too busy at work for me to tell him."

"Was this an accident? I thought you were on the pill."

"I stopped a few months ago. Then we went to Angela's cottage, and, well, now I'm pregnant."

"What changed your minds?"

"I want more in my life than just work. I want to be a mother."

"And Michael? What made him change his mind? I know how adamant he was about not having children. He wasn't shy about sharing his views on that."

Jess didn't know what to say. She didn't want to lie, but she certainly didn't want to tell her mother the truth.

"Well," she said at last, "I guess he's doing it for me." That, she decided, was probably going to be the truth—or so she hoped.

CHAPTER 4

Michael stared at the reports in the folder, the shock of what he saw sending a wave of nausea through his gut. These reports, originating from agencies all over the world, were so highly classified that he'd never seen them. How in hell had Drummond gotten hold of them? Michael reviewed them again. Each one by itself was damning. Collectively, they were lethal and terrifying.

They were proof that the environment was deteriorating to the point where it would no longer sustain life, and the Agency actively contributed to it. The wealthy group of elite and the covert government arm funding the Agency were investing in biotechnology, fuel oils, vaccines, big agribusiness, and similar industries, with the awareness that they were putting financial gain above humanity's survival.

In their quest for more money, power, and self-preservation, they wantonly destroyed the environment, contaminated the global food supply, indiscriminately killed species necessary for food production, and introduced DNA-mutating elements into the system.

Michael tried to process this. A crisis loomed. This wasn't news to him, but he'd thought that, at the very least, they were all working to slow it down. That they weren't, that what they were doing was destroying everything to acquire wealth, seemed insane. Why? Then it hit him. They behaved like property owners who don't care if they trash their home because they know it's going to be demolished.

They knew the earth was beyond the point of no return, and they wanted to cash in the maximum before going underground. Their goal wasn't to speed things up; they simply wanted to suck up as many resources as possible before the end. The acceleration was a by-product, and they considered it just another cost of doing business.

He still didn't know where the aliens fit in. Did they condone this, or did they not care what happened to the earth so long as they had their supply of humans for experimentation? Or were they about to expropriate the earth the way the government expropriated land to build new infrastructure? He photographed the reports, set them aside, and picked up the next folder.

When Michael checked his watch again, it was 11:30 P.M. Jess would already be in bed, and he'd forgotten to eat dinner. He rummaged around in his briefcase, hoping for a protein bar to tide him over until he could get home and spotted one in one of the pockets. He grabbed for it but froze when he heard someone at the outer door.

If the security guard caught him, he'd have no reasonable explanation for being here. He turned off the light, lowered the top of his netbook, and faced it toward the wall. He closed his briefcase to make it seem part of the evidence stash.

Michael crouched in front of the door. The netbook gave off a faint glow from the crack of screen left open so it would continue to transfer files, but with luck, the guard wouldn't get suspicious.

The light in the reception area went on. A flashlight beam shone through the window.

Michael flattened himself against the door.

The beam of light paused at the table with the boxes, shining on the netbook. It sat there for what seemed an eternity.

He realized he was holding his breath and let it out slowly.

The light scoured the room once more and vanished.

He listened for the sound of a key in the lock or the outer door closing. Light from the waiting room illuminated the reception desk and the floor behind it, adding a soft glow to the surrounding area. Michael heard some shuffling and then nothing for an interminable time.

He stood. The light from the reception area was still on, so he was sure whoever had entered hadn't slipped out. He felt an urge to throw open the door. It was like staring into the rushing waters of Niagara Falls and wanting to jump in. He squashed it.

He craned his head so he could see through the window. To his amazement, Frank, one of the security guards, lay on the couch. He was on his side, his back facing out. The guy had come in here to have a nap.

Son of a bitch. Now what?

He was stuck here until Frank finished his nap, and he'd have to go through the rest of the files in the dark. Turning on a light was out of the question. He didn't even want to risk opening his damn protein bar in case Frankie boy was still awake or a light sleeper.

Michael sank to the floor. He'd have to be careful to stay awake. Falling asleep would be the perfect end to his day—or rather, the perfect start to his tomorrow. He hoped Frank's partner would look for him soon. What if Frank slept the whole night away? Michael didn't think it'd be possible on that smelly old couch, especially with the light on, but maybe Frank was used to it. Michael fought the urge to pack up and leave and decided to at least complete the file transfer.

He hadn't touched Drummond's digital camera and left whatever was on it alone. He opened the next file folder, setting it and its contents on the floor in the light spilling in from the reception area. Most of it was conspiracy stuff that Michael discarded, either because it was ridiculous or because it had nothing to do with the Agency or ETAP. He'd probably get through the rest of the folders quickly if they were all like this.

In this way, he examined eight more folders. When he opened the next folder and started reading, he knew Drummond had found a keg of dynamite and lit the fuse with his big mouth. The first printout mentioned not only ETAP, but also Jim Cornell by name, and referenced agents who worked under Cornell by description. Michael recognized himself. He'd have to read this carefully.

He rose, squashed himself against the door, and peered out the window.

Frank lay on his back, snoring.

Michael looked down at the floor, considering. He didn't want to take out his camera and start taking pictures. It was bad enough he was rustling the odd paper though he tried to be silent. A camera click and flash might do him in. He lowered himself to the floor and closed the folder.

There were no labels other than what Drummond had stuck on it. Since it came from a box on the table, he knew it hadn't been examined and catalogued. He was sure no one would notice it missing.

Removing everything from the folder, he set it all in his briefcase. Then, in case someone had counted the folders, he took some of the documents from the previous folder and put them into the empty one. He placed the folder back in its box. Ten folders remained. He opened the first one.

The next time he looked up, he was on the last folder. His legs cramped, and he had to piss. The hard drive was silent. The file transfer had finished—he hadn't noticed when. He flipped through the last folder, dismissed its contents, and returned it to the box. He disconnected the hard drive from his netbook and put everything away.

With luck, Frank wouldn't notice the rearrangement, but it needed to be in order for the person arriving in the morning. Michael checked his watch. It was 2:00 AM. He wondered if Jess was asleep. It would be better for him if she was unaware he still hadn't come home.

The outer door opened. A male voice spoke, gentle and low.

"Frank, hey, Frank. Get up."

Finally. Hopefully, Frank's buddy would wake him and the two would go away so Michael could leave.

"Frank, get up. It's my turn."

Oh, for God's sake. Now the other guy is going to have a nap? Are they kidding?

For a moment, Michael considered shooting them both and going home.

Frank yawned, sounding like he was giving himself a good stretch.

"Hey, Joe. I'm up. Thanks for covering. I'm starving. Want to grab a bite before your nap? I brought some extra dessert. Mary made some of her butter tarts. We could make coffee. What do you say?"

Michael couldn't believe what he was hearing. He hoped Joe thought Mary's butter tarts were irresistible.

"I don't think I should have coffee. It might keep me up."

Michael thought again about shooting those dumbasses. If his situation weren't so dire, he could at least go out there and knock their heads together. He hoped they'd cut him a break and leave.

"Skip the nap. Keep me company. We could play some cards after we do our rounds again."

"I guess I can't resist Mary's butter tarts. Okay."

Michael wanted to cheer. He waited while Frank got up from the couch and left with Joe. They turned off the lights on the way out, and Michael stood in the darkness, giving them a few minutes to get to the elevator. When he was sure they were gone, he turned on the lights in the storage area and verified everything was back the way he'd found it.

He scanned the place one more time. All clear. He picked up the roll of packing tape he'd use to relock the deadbolts and closed the briefcase. For the first time in a long time, he looked forward to getting home.

CHAPTER 5

By the time Shelly Rudolph wriggled out from under Steve, her husband, she'd already decided her affair with their friend, Arnie Griffen, would have to end. Lately, her conscience had been pricking her more than Arnie was. At no point had she thought that Steve deserved the betrayal, or that she didn't consider herself happily married. It was more that she deserved the fun, and Arnie made it so easy.

Shelly turned to face Steve, who was watching her, and said, "I'm going to have a quick shower before we leave for tonight's sky watch. Want to join me? I'm sure Arnie will be late since it's a workday, and he's the one with the equipment."

She meant camera equipment, of course. The sky watch tonight, at the home of their friends, John and Carolyn Fairchild, was part of their UFO group activities. Arnie owned the camera and scope they'd use to view and record it, but she giggled to herself.

Steve smiled in response. "Sounds great."

Shelly headed to the bathroom, thinking how lucky she was Steve had never found out about her fling. It would've killed their marriage, plus his friendship with Arnie, though Arnie was used to that. He'd killed a few marriages and friendships by sleeping with a buddy's wife. The guy couldn't seem to keep it in his pants.

In the bathroom, Shelly turned on the water in the tub and let it run over her hand, adjusting the temperature. She let her mind wander and wondered was now the time to start a family? Steve had broached the topic recently, and she'd hedged again. She'd always wanted kids but refused to commit to it.

Maybe she'd take that step now. If she put this fling with Arnie behind her, perhaps she'd settle down at last and be a mother. Steve would be excited, and it would be a sure-fire way to kill the affair with Arnie.

But was she ready to get fat? She tried to imagine her stomach round and heavy, sticking out in front like she'd swallowed a watermelon whole. She thrust her pelvis forward, practicing her pregnant-lady stance. Perhaps she could handle it.

Shelly slid the shower curtain aside and braced her hands on the wall as she stepped into the tub. While she washed her hair, she thought about tonight. They were having more sky watches lately. With Ralph Drummond now in a psychiatric hospital, Arnie insisted on it. She still couldn't believe it. Ralph had seemed so stable the last time she'd seen him.

Arnie maintained Ralph had been coerced, and Ralph's wife, Beth, wasn't talking about it. She'd cut them off from the family and told them not to contact Ralph. It was surreal.

Would the government force someone into the nut house just for talking about UFOs?

The shower curtain parted, and Steve stepped into the bathtub. Shelly smiled at him.

"Welcome aboard, sailor." She lathered him with soap, pleased she'd given him a fun afternoon in bed. She couldn't remember the last time they'd taken a whole afternoon like this.

Fifteen minutes later, Shelly was dressed in denim shorts and a T-shirt that read, "Someone went to Salem, Massachusetts, and all I got was this bewitching T-shirt." A gift from herself.

She checked to see what he was wearing. A green polo shirt and khaki golf shorts.

Thank God. Not the shirt with the horizontal stripes. She hated that stupid shirt. Didn't he know how fat he looked in it? Suddenly, she wanted like hell to get out of there.

"Let's go," she said, trying to keep the irritation out of her voice. "Carolyn said to be there for six o'clock and it's already five."

Steve glanced at the time and then gave her a slantwise stare. "Sure."

He was wondering why she sounded on edge, but she noted he wasn't curious enough about it to ask. They left the apartment together, and Shelly locked the door. In the hallway, she felt another twinge of guilt and took his hand.

"I love you," she said, meaning it.

He gazed down at her, his affection showing in his eyes. "I love you, too."

She thought about seeing Arnie at Carolyn's tonight. Steve was so oblivious.

Or really trusting. He trusts you and you screw around on him. You really are a ho.

She tried to clear those thoughts from her mind. She'd end it soon and tell him they could have a baby. Not tonight though. First, she needed to talk to Arnie alone, in person, somewhere no one would overhear the conversation in case it didn't go well.

Shelly wished the affair were behind her so she could get on with her life, doing penance for her transgression. She'd make it up to Steve even if he never knew about it. If only he hadn't gained all that weight, or at least dressed better, maybe she wouldn't have cheated on him.

She dropped his hand when they stepped out into the parking garage. As they walked to the car, he took her hand again.

"Is everything all right?"

"I'm fine. Sorry. I hate running late, and if we stop to pick up the munchies I promised to bring, we're going to be late," she replied, deflecting.

"Relax. We'll call Carolyn on the road so she'll know we're on our way. We won't be more than fifteen minutes late, tops. It's just a sky watch, not a formal dinner."

"You're right. It'll be nice to have an evening with the group, especially after having the whole day to ourselves. It was good, right?"

"It was great. We should do stuff like that more often. I've been working too many hours and haven't spent much time with you lately. I can change that," he said.

She cringed at the prospect. She'd grown used to having a lot of time to herself. How would she cope if he started hanging around?

"Well, your job's pretty important. You got that promotion, and they need you there more. I understand. We'll do what we did today. Take a day off work sometimes and be together? You have tomorrow off too. How rare is that, even for a Saturday? And our vacation's coming up in a few months. That'll be fun." Was she rambling? She thought she was rambling.

They got in the car, both silent, and drove from the parking garage. On the road, she caught him glancing in her direction.

She back-pedalled. "I didn't mean I don't want you around. I'm worried it'll affect your career when you're starting to move up. When you're settled, you'll spend more time at home."

"Sure." He fell silent again.

Shelly stared ahead. Her mind was on Arnie. Perhaps she would sleep with him just one more time and then break it off.

CHAPTER 6

A rnie Griffen inspected the open case that held his scope and camera equipment, readying it for his UFO group's sky watch at Carolyn and John Fairchild's. He was sure he had everything, but he double-checked for the power inverter. He'd forgotten it once, and recording the sky watch had been cut short when the battery died. The others were good sports about it, but since then, Arnie obsessed about his equipment.

It hadn't been entirely a wash. He and Shelly Rudolph had stayed up late that night, and it was the first time they'd locked lips and made with the hot and heavy. He'd craved her almost from the time they'd met, but she was the wife of one of his friends, so he'd tried to control himself. As usual, that never lasted.

This time, though, he'd been able to hold out for over fifteen years. He was proud of that, but that night, Shelly had flirted with him all evening. When everyone else packed it in and went to their tents, he and Shelly were left alone, sitting by the fire, stargazing. Shelly moved in on him almost from the moment they heard Steve snoring like a hibernating bear in the tent he shared with Shelly.

Shelly sat close to Arnie—almost on top of him. There was no mistaking what she wanted. He no longer remembered what they'd talked about, but he would never forget what they did. She raised her lips, inviting his kisses. He didn't need to be asked twice. He dropped his mouth over hers, exploring with his tongue. She took his hand and stuck it under her shirt.

Arnie pulled away, grabbed her hand, and led her to the kitchen tent where they'd have privacy. He was naked and holding a condom in his hand by the time she zipped the netting closed. Her clothes hit the dirt right after. She ripped the tablecloth off the picnic table and spread it out on the ground. He pressed her down on it and kneeled between her open

22

thighs.

She clawed at him while he fumbled to put on the condom, and her nails raked his biceps. He bit his lip to stifle a moan, but when he shoved into her, he couldn't hold back, and he groaned, not caring if the whole park heard him. Shelly writhed under him, and her hungry gaze roved over his body.

That his friend, her husband, slept nearby did cross Arnie's mind, but he soon let it go. It's not as if he'd had to talk her into it, and what a woman did behind her husband's back was up to her. That platitude had served him well for years, though it had earned him a few black eyes, too. After that, they got together whenever Shelly could get away and he wasn't working. He'd been banging her for almost two years now. She was a sweet ride.

Arnie took out his cell phone and made sure there were no messages. He wasn't on call this evening, but they still sometimes called him anyway. As a senior developer for a company that created and sold custom software for insurance companies, he knew more about the product than anyone else.

He loved programming but hated the stress of the long hours. Sometimes, he'd found himself still at the office at two-thirty in the morning. It was during those times he'd had some of his UFO abduction experiences. Most people were abducted from their beds. Arnie was abducted from his office.

Not today, thanks. I gave at the office. Ha, ha, ha.

He checked the time. He should leave soon. The drive to Carolyn and John's was going to take him about half an hour, and he wanted to get there a little early. He closed the camera case and picked it up. It was heavy, but he was used to lugging it around.

The antithesis of the computer nerd, he worked out and bulked up, though not to steroidal extremes. He didn't need glasses. He towered over most men. His blond hair, the light fuzz on his chin and cheeks, straight nose, and perfect teeth made him a woman beacon. Arnie had won the gene pool lottery.

He first realized girls were attracted to him in grade one when twin sisters in his class fought over him. They each claimed him as a boyfriend, and one grabbed one arm, the other grabbed the other arm, and he was sure he'd be split like a turkey wishbone until the teacher on yard duty intervened.

The girls got a lecture; Arnie got a lesson in charisma. He decided they could both be his girlfriends and added a couple more to his entourage before the year was out. Of course, at that age, when they played doctor, it was with a toy stethoscope and kept their clothes on. He didn't graduate to gynecology until he was fifteen.

Arnie carried his case to the door of his condo. He then went to check on his mother, who was living in his spare bedroom, and no, she didn't cramp his style. The ladies he brought home grew more infatuated with him when they saw he was taking care of his mother. It made him feel like a hero.

His mother didn't comment on anything he did. She simply sat, day after day, in her armchair, with her knitting needles and her television going, and the occasional cognac to cheer her up. Arnie had Beverly, a nurse, come in to tend to Mom's basic needs—he slept with the nurse at the end of her shift most times—and made sure his mother never lacked for anything. If she disapproved of her son's sexploits, she didn't say so.

Mom looked up from her knitting when he stuck his head in her room. She paused, her needles poised mid-clack and hovering expectantly over the sock she was making. The socks-in-progress were lime green and neon, and he'd wear them around the apartment when they were done.

"I'm going," he said.

"Okay, Arnold." Only his mom called him by his full name. He hated his name. It was his one feature that screamed "nerd."

"Do you want me to get you anything before I leave?"

"A tea might be nice. Thank you. And maybe some of those cookies with the chocolate on them?" Mom liked her sweets. Arnie was surprised she wasn't diabetic. She wasn't even pre-diabetic. Her blood sugar consistently tested normal. He counted his blessings. By the time his father had passed away, he'd been on a whole pharmacopeia of drugs, including insulin. Arnie had no wish to deal with all that again.

He went into the kitchen and got the kettle going. He put some cookies on a plate, setting the plate on a round, red tray with snowmen and children painted on it, a souvenir from his childhood. His mother had bought it when his kindergarten class had a fundraiser. Thirty-five years ago.

A sugar bowl, saucer, teaspoon, and small pitcher of milk went onto the tray, and he carried it to his mother's room. She smiled her thanks when he set it on the table next to her.

He returned to the kitchen as the kettle clicked off. Arnie poured the water directly onto the tea bag in the mug. Tea grannies everywhere would've fainted to see how he made tea, but he couldn't be bothered using a teapot, and he sure as hell wouldn't let his mother try to pour herself a cup of tea from a full, hot pot. He took the mug of tea into his mother's room and set it on the tray.

"I could call the nurse back. She'd come and stay the night."

"I'm fine. You don't need to pay someone to look after me. If I want to use the washroom, I'll go slowly. I got time. It's all I've got left." Mom smiled, but it wasn't bitter.

He made up his mind. He'd never enjoy the sky watch if he left her alone. Arnie picked up his cell phone. His mother's big, brown puppy eyes of reproach watched him while he talked to Beverly, who assured him she'd be right over.

"Don't start. Okay?" he said. "I'd be as irresponsible to leave you here alone as you'd have been to leave me at home alone when I was five." The moment he said it, he could tell it had been the wrong thing to say.

"I'm not five," she said.

The indignant tone brought another stab of guilt. "I know, Mom. I'm only saying it would be hard for you to manage all night here alone." He tried not to sound like he was talking to a five year old. He thought it worked. "She's on her way. Be nice."

"When am I not nice?"

He sighed. "If you don't want her to keep you company, tell her to hang out in the living room. Don't worry about the money. I have it to spend."

"You go," she said. "That nurse will sit here doing nothing, and you can pay for it. If it makes you feel better, then make yourself feel better. Who needs to save money when you have it to throw around? Your father was never so wasteful."

"It's not wasteful, but you're welcome anyway." Sometimes, being a hero was tough. Arnie leaned over, kissed her wrinkled cheek, and gave her bony shoulders a hug. "I'll see you tomorrow."

She nodded.

He left the room, and she called after him, "You're a good boy, Arnold."

He grinned. "Thanks, Mom."

At least one woman thinks so.

He picked up his case, opened the condo door, and stepped into the hallway. He couldn't wait to get to Carolyn's and kick back for a while. A nice, relaxing sky watch was what he needed to get away from it all. He whistled as he walked to the elevator.

CHAPTER 7

Carolyn and John Fairchild lived inside the southeast limits of the town of Newmarket in a two-story century home nestled in a valley on a one-acre chunk of land complete with duck pond and forest. The forest stretched out beyond the boundaries of their property, and it was in the forest that Michael "Mick" Valiant set up his post.

Close to the property line he picked a spot with an ideal view of the backyard and balcony. He'd barely settled in when his cell phone vibrated. He answered it, keeping his voice low.

"Yes?"

"It's Torque. Where are you?"

"Out. What's up?"

"Seriously, Mick, where are you?"

"That UFO group is having a sky watch tonight. They're going to get buzzed, and I want to see it."

"That's against protocol. Cornell is losing patience with you—says you're not much of a team player these days. You're not supposed to spy on these people yourself. That's what we have field grunts for."

"I have some thoughts on that."

"You don't get paid to think. You'll cause trouble for both of us. Spend the weekend with your wife. We're having this conversation too often."

"Relax. I won't interfere. I'll talk to you tomorrow." He hung up.

Michael considered leaving, but only for a second. He refused to let Torque drive him away. Perhaps he wasn't much of a team player these days, but lately, he hadn't been feeling much like part of the team. Torque and Cornell were both acting cagey, freezing him out. And what he saw made no sense.

When he observed these people, he didn't understand why the Agency watched them, followed their blog posts, tapped their phone lines, and bugged their homes. They were no different than any other group of UFO enthusiasts, though Ralph Drummond and Patty Richards had definitely known more of the truth than most UFO nuts, and he suspected Arnold Griffen also knew more. The group as a whole seemed innocuous enough, particularly the two couples, the Fairchilds and the Rudolphs. They gathered for sky watches, read books about UFOs, attended conventions, searched the Internet for information on UFOs, reported a few incidents to the Mutual UFO Network (or MUFON, as it was more commonly known), and generally played around with the idea that there were extraterrestrials visiting Earth. They also had, as most UFO groups did, a few members who claimed they were abductees, and who, Michael knew, were experiencing what they claimed to experience.

He'd seen his share of spies and terrorists, and this group didn't fit the profile. Arnie Griffen was the closest to a loose cannon the group had right now. He screamed "conspiracy" like the Internet town crier, but even Arnie didn't seem to have the inside scoop on the Project itself.

The information Michael had stolen from the evidence room was devastating to the Agency and for Michael. If Drummond had gone public with it, they'd have been terminated, of that Michael had no doubt. He agreed with Torque it would've been better to silence Ralph permanently except for one thing: if what he'd found in Ralph's files was true, then Drummond wasn't the enemy—the Agency was. Michael vowed to get to the bottom of it before more people died.

Using binoculars, he scanned the balcony. No activity yet. He'd packed himself a thermos of coffee, a bottle of water, and some snacks. He'd almost left the coffee at home, considering how hot it was. The beginning of May was usually still cool, but a heat wave had settled in— the second one this spring. It reminded him how quickly the end was coming. Michael poured himself some coffee and settled down to wait.

***

Inside the house, Carolyn Fairchild took a pizza from the oven and set it on the counter. "John. Pizza's ready. Did you find the laser pointer?"

He appeared at the kitchen door holding up the pointer. "When is everyone supposed to arrive?"

She glanced at the clock on the stove. "Any minute."

He angled toward the pizza and gave an exaggerated sniff. "If they don't hurry, I'll eat it myself."

She smiled, snatched the laser pointer from his hand, and handed him the pizza cutter. "You can cut it up for me, but that's all."

John gave her his best pouty face but set about cutting the pizza into squares. A knock sounded on the front door, and she went to answer it.

Arnie stood on the porch, a large case next to his feet. She gazed into his eyes. They were his best feature, of many great features, and, like most women, she was drawn to them. Unlike most women, though, she knew better than to keep gazing. Arnie was one of her best friends because she'd been able to resist his charms. Admittedly, it had taken an effort of will and a stubborn commitment to her marriage on her part.

Arnie smiled his magic smile, which always reached his eyes.

"That looks heavy." She nodded at his case.

"It's okay," he replied.

John appeared from the kitchen door and waved. "Do we need to be up on the balcony or down on the lawn?"

Carolyn waited, trying to be patient while Arnie pondered. A car zoomed by on the street, hidden from view by trees and shrubs and their long, winding drive. She scanned the floor to make sure Fox, their cat, wasn't around. Finally, fear of feline escape got the better of her.

"Step inside so the cat doesn't get out."

He picked up his case and entered, bumping the umbrella stand as he did. She reached out to steady it as his hand caught it. When their fingers touched, an impression of an owl flashed into her mind, followed by an image of Arnie screaming in terror. Startled, she pressed her hand over his and stared into his eyes. Her mouth went dry and her gut gave a lurch of fear.

"What's that look for?" Arnie said.

"I have a terrible feeling." She slowly released his hand. *Angels and guides, please clarify this message for me.* "What are you up to?"

"Nothing." Arnie took her hand again.

Fear crept through her, lodging in her solar plexus.

Don't let him set up his camera.

"Don't set up your video camera."

"You're joking, right?" He frowned, irritation in his voice.

Over the years, Arnie had acknowledged Carolyn sometimes had accurate hunches, but he preferred to believe they were coincidence.

"I wouldn't joke like that," she said.

A knock on the door silenced her. Carolyn opened it, and Shelly, oblivious to the tension in the air, stepped in, her big voice preceding her.

"Steve is getting the stuff from the car. I hope you don't mind some junk food. I had a craving for chips and licorice. Weird combination, right? Probably PMS—what?" she said, finally taking notice.

No one spoke.

Then John said, "Carolyn thinks we shouldn't use the equipment tonight."

Steve appeared, carrying a box of drinks and food. Everyone shifted to let him in the house, and Shelly closed the door. Carolyn led them into the living room and sat down on the sectional sofa. The others followed, gathering around the coffee table. Shelly sat next to Carolyn.

"What did you see, Carr?" Arnie asked.

She told them and then said, "I'm uneasy about setting up the recording equipment tonight and using it to sky watch." How to explain that sense of impending doom? She had to make them understand.

They all stared at her.

"Maybe you're interpreting it wrong," Shelly suggested.

Carolyn's eyes widened, and her mouth dropped open. Had she heard correctly? Shelly usually backed her up without question, trusting that if Carolyn sensed something, then it was accurate. In some ways, Shelly was too much of a believer, never questioning, always jumping to the paranormal explanation.

Now she decides to become a skeptic?

"I'm not interpreting it incorrectly," Carolyn said. "I know what I feel. It's only one night. Let's skip it."

"I'm sure it'll be fine. What might happen? Arnie, it won't blow up or anything, right? It's only a camera." Steve was using his reasonable voice and sounded patronizing.

You don't know, Steve.

"It'll be bad," she insisted.

"What if we set it up on the balcony? It'll be off the grass, close to the house," Arnie said.

"Carr, you think this was a warning, but seriously, where's the harm? We're going to view the sky and record what's there. The laser pointer's more dangerous. If you point it at a plane, you could bring it down. We won't use it," John said.

Carolyn considered the pointer. "It's not that."

"We're not harming anyone, the equipment isn't hazardous, and we're not going to play loud music, have a fire, or do anything that could cause trouble. We'll take it easy, and if it looks like there'll be a problem, we'll put everything away. Does that sound reasonable?" John said.

Everyone but Carolyn nodded. All eyes turned to her. Reluctantly, she agreed. "I don't feel comfortable with this, but if you all want to go ahead anyway, I won't stop you."

"You have our permission to say 'I told you so' if something happens," Arnie replied.

It'll be too late then. At that thought, she almost protested again. *They're not saying it, but they think I'm being ridiculous.*

She looked over at John. His expression was neutral. She stared at him for a moment and then turned to face Arnie. He was already halfway up the stairs.

CHAPTER 8

W hile Arnie, John, and Steve went upstairs to get the TV and set up the equipment, Carolyn and Shelly went into the kitchen, Shelly carrying the box of food and drinks.

"Would you like a hand?" Carolyn asked.

"I'll be okay," Shelly said. She set the box on the counter and took out the snacks.

"Doesn't it bother you I had a premonition?" Carolyn couldn't help asking. Of all people, Shelly should know what that meant. Friends since high school, Shelly had heard Carolyn predict many things.

"I thought you'd back me on this."

"I'm sorry, but I don't understand how anything can go wrong." Shelly at least had the decency to look apologetic.

"Others never get how it can go wrong. I'm frustrated no one will listen to me," Carolyn said.

"We're listening. We'll be careful. I'm sure if his equipment gets broken or something, then he'll get it fixed."

"You're assuming. It feels bad. Not just camera-knocked-over-and-smashed bad, but someone-getting-hurt bad, or all of us getting hurt."

Shelly looked away, raised a hand to touch the back of her head, and then scratched her neck. Carolyn could almost hear the debate going on in her friend's head. Then Shelly firmed her resolve.

"It'll be fine. I think you don't realize the times you get it wrong. You only note the times when you're right."

Carolyn was stunned. "Is this how you've always felt?"

"No, I trust you, but I think it's not as bad as you imagine."

"I'm not imagining."

"I don't mean to imply you're making this up. The problem is it's rarely anything concrete. I can't constantly live in fear of something happening."

Carolyn sighed and gave up. She arranged slices of pizza on a plate.

"Not to change the subject," Shelly said, "but can I ask you something?"

Carolyn looked up. "Sure."

"I'm thinking about telling Steve I'm ready to have a baby."

"Oh, that's wonderful." Carolyn went to her friend and hugged her.

"Don't say anything, especially to Steve. I'm only thinking about it. I keep waiting for the right time, but I've been thinking we should just do it."

"It wasn't perfect for us when we had Samantha, but we managed."

"How long did it take you to get pregnant after you started trying?"

"Almost a year. Some people get pregnant the first time."

"Is that why you only had one child?"

Carolyn was silent for a moment. She'd never talked to anyone about this before.

"No," she finally replied. "We tried to have another child, but I couldn't conceive. The doctors don't know why. There doesn't seem to be a valid reason for it. John tested fine, so it's me."

"I'm sorry," Shelly said.

"It's okay. I'm happy I was able to have Sam. Are you worried? Most women are fine, you know."

"I know. Do you think I'd make a good mom?"

"Of course." She smiled at Shelly. "Steve will make a great dad, too."

Shelly smiled back. "Yeah, he'll spoil the kid rotten."

Carolyn laughed. "Yes, he will. Go ahead and take the drinks upstairs. Don't worry. I won't give away your little secret, but you have to promise to let me know when you start trying."

"Of course." Shelly grabbed the box with the drinks and left the room.

Carolyn poured the chips into a bowl while the knot of worry in her gut became more pronounced. Ignoring it, she pulled out a large tray, loaded snacks, napkins, and plates on it, and left the kitchen. She climbed the stairs, keeping a firm grip on the tray.

Their voices reached her when she approached the den. Arnie was talking, which wasn't unusual. She smiled affectionately at his enthusiasm.

"It's so much better with the upgraded scope. That's right above us. We don't need it to be dark, but it has night vision. It picks up things at a greater distance than the other one I had."

She paused at the screen door. "Could someone get the door for me, please?"

John, closest, opened it for her, and she stepped outside. She glanced around to make sure no equipment blocked her and wove through the chairs and potted plants scattered around the balcony. She set the tray down on the table. She noted the citronella candles scattered around the balcony, grateful that John had remembered to put them out.

The others already had open drinks on the tables. John opened a cooler and handed it to Carolyn.

"Thanks." She looked at the television they'd set up. "Is it recording?"

"Everything on the screen is being recorded. The picture is so clear you can zoom in on anything that passes overhead," Arnie replied.

Steve said, "I love that you don't have to tilt your head up and get a sore neck."

Everyone was watching her, waiting for her approval. She released her fears.

"It looks amazing."

The others visibly relaxed, and Carolyn silently connected to her angels and guides: *Archangel Michael, Guardian Angels, Spirit Guides, I ask you to surround us with your protection.*

The knot in her stomach dissolved. She trusted her angels were there to help her and took a deep breath, sucking in the warm night air. A slight breeze took the edge off the stifling heat. She wasn't uncomfortable herself, but she knew the others were suffering from it.

John's T-shirt was wet with perspiration. So was Steve's. Even Arnie looked wilted. Shelly seemed comfortable enough in her shorts and T-shirt. She'd tied her coppery hair back in a ponytail, and Carolyn decided the effect was cute.

Arnie fiddled with his camera, positioning it on the tripod.

"That'll let me pan it across the sky with one hand." He let go of the camera. "Whatever footage we get tonight, I'll post on the website. You can all access it from there."

The website was Arnie's baby. He and Ralph had started it three years before, mostly to have an online repository of videos and stories about UFOs. Every sky watch they'd ever had was documented on their website.

A small but involved community of users visited regularly and compared notes on UFO experiences and conspiracy theories. Carolyn was surprised that after coding all day, Arnie would want to do more work on the website, but he insisted it was what he loved to do.

"I don't think you should do that," she said. The knot was back in her stomach.

"Don't start that again. We've got tons of footage up there, and no one cares." Arnie scowled.

She fell silent, gazing back at him. Nothing she said made a difference. An image of a runaway train hitting a brick wall came into her head. She picked up her drink and took a sip. She looked out over the balcony railing into the forest beyond and shivered despite the heat. She felt exposed, watched.

Everything was silent. For a moment, it was as if the forest held its breath. Then she heard the frogs and crickets again, and the moment passed. She turned away from the forest, back to the gentle light of the citronella candles on the balcony.

Her thoughts went to a time when she was in elementary school, grade two it was, and the class was on a field trip to the museum in Toronto. The kids were lined up in twos, holding hands, and waiting to get onto the school bus to return to school. Carolyn was lost within herself, staring into space. Her stomach tingled, and in her mind, Stuart Gibbs stumbled out onto the road, a taxi careening into, and then over, him.

The image snapped her out of her reverie. She must tell Miss Doolittle, the teacher, something bad was going to happen to Stuart Gibbs. She dropped her partner's hand and moved toward the teacher.

Mrs. Garvey, the parent volunteer in charge of Carolyn's group, immediately stopped her. "Sweetie, we stay in our groups. Come back and hold Monica's hand."

Carolyn met the woman's gaze and said, "But I have to tell Miss Doolittle that Stuart is going to get hurt."

Mrs. Garvey looked over at the boy in question, who was quietly sucking on a rainbow lollipop he'd bought at the museum gift shop.

"Stuart's fine," she said. "Please get in line."

Carolyn hesitated, reluctant to do what Mrs. Garvey asked. She wanted to prevent a serious accident. Trembling, Carolyn crossed her arms over her chest.

"It's okay. Everything is fine. We'll ask him." Mrs. Garvey called out in a tone that, to Carolyn's ears, sounded patronizing. "Stuart, dear, are you enjoying that lollipop?"

He looked up, puzzled. "Sure."

Mrs. Garvey smiled. "See, dear? No trouble at all."

Carolyn frowned, returned to her place in line, and took Monica's hand. Then everything seemed to slow down.

Frankie Darwin snickered, and in a whiny voice, he mimicked Mrs. Garvey while he grabbed at Stuart's sucker. "Stuart, dear, are you enjoying that lollipop?"

Stuart smacked Frankie's hand away, which started a shoving match between the pair. Mrs. Garvey, seeing the commotion, approached the two boys.

Carolyn's eyes went wide, and she screamed, "Stop! Stop him."

At that moment, Frankie gave Stuart a shove that sent him stumbling backward. She glimpsed Stuart's startled, scared eyes as he flapped his arms, trying to keep his balance, and then spiralled off the curb.

Her vision turned into reality when a taxi barrelled into Stuart, knocked him forward, and thudded over him. Horns blared and fell silent. The car skidded to a stop and everything grew deathly quiet.

Tears cascading down her face, Carolyn fell to her knees, muttering, "I said stop him. I said stop him."

The other kids backed away from her.

After that, the kids at school treated her with a mixture of fear and awe. Most of them were afraid to come near her, but they didn't make fun of her, either. Since then, Carolyn lived in constant fear and guilt herself: fear of something like that happening again, and guilt that knowing what would happen didn't let her change the outcome. She often wondered if Stuart would still be alive if she hadn't said anything.

What if this is the same thing? What if by trying to prevent something from happening, she was actually orchestrating its inevitability? *Enough already. I give up. Whatever happens, happens.* That didn't make her feel better, but at least it was a decision.

All was silent, except for the forest sounds beyond the balcony. The temperature dropped as the night deepened. Carolyn stood up to go in the house and get a sweater, but stopped when Steve said, "What's that?"

He pointed to the TV screen. "A light. Arnie, go up a little."

Arnie grabbed the handle on the camera and manoeuvred it around, searching. He quickly found the light and tracked it using the attached scope.

"Satellite?" asked Carolyn.

"So far it could be. It's moving steadily. It's not a shooting star, that's for sure," Arnie said. "Too high up to be a plane. Plus, no flashing lights. It's a steady light. Man-made, no doubt."

She looked up and watched the light track a path across the sky.

"Ralph insists we can't see satellites from earth, especially not with the naked eye. He says they don't reflect anything and have no lights on them."

"He's wrong. When something is low enough and large enough, you can see it with the naked eye. You can see the Space Station for sure. It even has solar panels that provide reflection," Arnie replied.

The last time she'd seen Ralph Drummond he was convinced the government was after him. He'd talked about men in black and being run off the road after a sky watch. His intensity had been unnerving, and she'd been relieved when he told them he wasn't going to attend any more sky watches. Two weeks later, he was in a psychiatric hospital in Toronto.

Carolyn had asked his wife, Beth, about what had happened and when he was coming home, but all Beth had told her was, "He's not stable,

Carr. He thinks he's being stalked by lizard men and by government agents. The doctor thought it would be best if he received full-time care. He was becoming violent."

Then Beth told her never to call again.

Carolyn wanted to respect their privacy. If Ralph wanted her to know what was going on, he'd call her. They'd been friends for years, and he'd confided in her numerous times. Yet when she thought about him, she felt as if she'd deserted him.

The sense of danger returned.

Maybe some of Ralph's paranoia is rubbing off on me. The uneasiness grew stronger; perhaps Ralph wasn't so crazy after all.

"There's something," Steve said.

A white ball made its way slowly across the screen. Arnie tracked it. It stopped. Then the white light intensified. The ball moved down. Arnie followed it.

"What the hell is that?" asked John. "Arnie, have you seen anything behave like that before?"

"Yeah, a helicopter."

The light became brighter, then sped up, moving erratically across the screen and shooting up. Two smaller lights moved toward it, imitating the pattern of the larger light.

Carolyn looked up at the sky but saw nothing. "How high up is that?"

"High," Arnie said. He pulled out a laser pen and shone it up into the sky, angled away from the lights.

The lights moved in the direction of the beam, which was invisible to the group. Arnie clicked it off.

"They're following the laser. Definitely not space junk, and not a station or a satellite. It's got to be a craft of some kind, but that's no helicopter."

They all stared, hypnotized, while the lights moved around on the screen, first separating, then converging, and then moving in formation. The larger ball of light got brighter and larger.

They're coming. Dread filled the pit of Carolyn's stomach.

"Let's go inside. Now," she said. "Something is coming, and it knows we're here."

They all turned and looked at her.

"Now. Please." She walked to the door, but when no one moved to follow, she stopped.

The ball of light on the screen grew, blotting out the stars and filling the screen. Abruptly, it winked out. The stars returned.

"Wild," Arnie said.

She exhaled and giggled, self-conscious. The others talked at once.

Steve was saying, "Man, did you see that? What was that? That had to be alien. Nothing on earth moves like that."

Arnie was saying, "That was incredible."

John was saying, "Could the military have craft that does that?"

"Not the Canadian military," Shelly interjected. "Maybe U.S.?"

A creeping brightness grew around them.

Carolyn caught movement out on the grass at the back of the yard and glanced again at the screen but saw only stars and sky.

Arnie and John were high-fiving, but they moved slowly. Then they dropped their arms and stood motionless. Arnie started to rise. His eyes widened and his mouth opened, but he didn't cry out. He rose above her.

She tried to tilt her head up, but couldn't. Her legs felt like lead.

There was a sound like the clicking of insects and like the hissing of gas leaking from a ruptured tank. Her chest felt as if a weight were crushing it. She tried to speak, but her lips wouldn't move. Her eyelids were heavy, but she forced them to stay open.

Carolyn realized she was rising and looked down. She was at least five metres above the others and continued to rise, shouts accompanying her ascent. Terror built, but then it drained out of her. Her muscles relaxed, and her head fell forward. Everything faded away.

***

Michael saw the bright light overhead and pulled out his binoculars, aiming them above the house. The huge craft floated down toward the roof of the building, hovering over the house and the yard. All the windows in the house went dark. Power outage.

He thought he could hear shouts coming from the yard, but when he focused on it, he heard only silence. He glanced in the road's direction, where he'd left his car.

Nothing moved.

He gazed back up at the spacecraft in time to see a body, probably Arnie—it looked like one of the men—rise toward the craft. The light enveloped Arnie's prone body. He floated, a corpse-like shadow. Shortly after that, a female body drifted up the same way.

Carolyn.

Michael checked his watch. It was 12:33 AM. They'd be gone two hours. He pulled out his thermos of coffee and poured himself a cup. He settled in to await their return.

It took over two hours.

Michael was pouring his third cup of coffee and wondering if he should have another sandwich when a flood of light engulfed the Fairchild home. He set aside his thermos and snatched up the binoculars. A spacecraft hovered over the house. A vertical cylinder of light shone from it, connecting the house and the craft like an umbilical cord.

Carolyn returned first. Her body floated to the house, and Michael almost dropped the binoculars when she somehow went through the solid roof as if it wasn't there. A few minutes later, Arnie performed the same impossible feat.

Michael wondered what it looked like from inside the house and made a mental note to review the surveillance footage. Motion-activated cameras should have triggered when Carolyn and Arnie were inside. He'd review them in the morning.

When both abductees had disappeared, the light cut off. By the time Michael's eyes adjusted to the darkness, the craft was gone. Light shone in the windows again.

Listening for any sound of activity from the house, he stood and made his way to the backyard but didn't want to get too close. He used the binoculars to scan the back balcony. No one was there.

A light was on in the kitchen. His heart lurched when he saw movement in the dining-room window, then relaxed as he recognized the cat.

He was jumping at shadows. Time to call it a night.

Michael returned to the spot where he'd set up his surveillance and packed up his things. He headed to his car and checked the time. Three twenty-five. He hoped Jess was asleep when he got home.

CHAPTER 9

Fox, Carolyn's cat, sat on her chest and pawed at her face as he did every morning. Carolyn opened her eyes. Beside her, John slept.

For a moment, everything felt normal. The alarm clock on the night table said 6:43 AM. She pushed the cat off her chest and rolled over. Then she realized she didn't remember going to bed and sat up in a panic.

"John. Wake up." She shook him.

He opened his eyes. "What?"

"Last night. I remember nothing after we saw that light."

John stayed silent for a moment. "Me neither."

Fear in her voice, she said, "You're still in your clothes." She looked down at herself. "So am I."

She climbed out of bed and went to their en suite bathroom. When she checked herself in the mirror, she thought she appeared tired but otherwise okay. She twisted her long hair up and ran her fingers along her neck and behind her ears. Nothing unusual. She relaxed a little and used the toilet.

As she pulled up her shorts, she noticed a bruise on her upper right thigh. It was about five centimetres in diameter, an ugly red and bluish-purple mixture of colours. She pressed on it with her index finger—a little sore, but okay.

She washed her hands and put some toothpaste on her toothbrush. Leaning over the sink made her queasy, but she managed to brush her teeth.

I'll feel better if I wash up.

She tied her hair back and splashed some water on her face. Her nose ran and she sniffled. A drop of blood splashed into the sink. She tensed and yanked a tissue from the box on the vanity.

With shaky fingers, she pinched her nose. The tissue saturated, and she grabbed another one, switching them out and throwing the used one into the garbage. She grabbed a towel and blotted her face.

In the bedroom, John still lay in bed. He sat up when he saw her. "Nosebleed?"

She nodded and told him about the bruise. "Check yourself out."

John went pale but said nothing. He got out of bed and went to the bathroom.

Carolyn ran to the den and scanned the room. Everything seemed normal, except Arnie was asleep on the couch. She woke him up, told him to check himself over, and went to find Steve and Shelly.

They were in the living room on the sofa. Steve lay on the longer piece of the sectional; Shelly lay curled up on the shorter section. She stirred, loose hair spilling over her face and into her eyes.

Carolyn knelt beside her friend. "Are you okay?"

Shelly opened her eyes. "Yes. What happened last night?"

"I don't know, but we're all present and accounted for."

Steve mumbled something and sat up.

Carolyn rose and went into the kitchen, Steve and Shelly behind her.

"You look rough," Carolyn said to Steve. Did he always have so much grey in his hair? She lifted the bottom of her shorts a little, uncovering the bruise on her right thigh. The sunlight coming in from the kitchen window deepened the colours, making the bruise a stark contrast to her pale skin.

"Shit. You okay?" Steve asked. He glanced at Shelly.

"I think so," Carolyn replied. "I think my nose has stopped bleeding." She took the tissue away from her face, holding it close in case it dripped again. Nothing happened.

In childhood, she'd suffered from recurring nosebleeds. The doctor could find no cause for it. When she joined the UFO group to feed her interest in the paranormal, she learned that nosebleeds with no physical cause were a sign of alien abduction. She hadn't had one of her nosebleeds since moving to Newmarket five years earlier.

Arnie walked into the room. "I found a bruise on my hip. My shorts cover it."

Steve and Shelly exchanged glances and left the room.

Carolyn faced Arnie. "Doesn't that freak you out?"

He shook his head. "I'm used to it."

She ground beans for coffee but found it difficult to focus on what she was doing. She turned on the coffeemaker as John walked into the room.

"No marks on me," John said.

Steve and Shelly walked into the kitchen as John finished speaking.

Steve said, "Just Carolyn and Arnie, then. That makes sense, doesn't it? You two are the ones with a history."

"Arnie is," Carolyn replied.

"You know you are too," Arnie said.

"I've seen one. I have no recollection of being abducted." Carolyn went to the fridge to get the things they'd need for breakfast, and for a while, everything felt normal as they prepared eggs, toast, and sausages. While they ate, they chatted about the previous night, Arnie exuberant about what they might have caught on film.

Carolyn's appetite diminished when she thought about the possibility of alien abduction. Shoving congealing eggs around on her plate, she nibbled at a piece of toast. She looked across the table at John, who was busy eating and didn't notice her staring.

His hair is getting a little long. I should remind him to make a haircut appointment.

She dropped her fork and stood, picking up her plate and reaching for Shelly's.

"Are you done?" she asked.

"Yes," Shelly replied, her voice a whisper. "Thanks."

Carolyn stacked some dishes and took them to the kitchen. The others stirred and left the table. Shelly strolled over, carrying a stack of dishes, and set them in the sink. The pair worked in silence, Carolyn gazing out into the backyard while she rinsed.

The plants in her garden drooped toward the ground. Patches of yellow dotted the lawn. No rain in the forecast and the town bylaw demanded she only water her plants on even days. She sighed. At least she'd do the flowers before they died.

Something in the grass caught her eye. At first, she thought it was a small, brown animal lying there.

"Shelly, look over there."

"Where?"

Carolyn waved her hand at the back of the yard. "There. Three indents in the grass."

Shelly peered out the window, craning her neck and squinting her eyes.

"I see them," she said. She turned away from the window and hurried to the living room.

Carolyn added the last few dishes to the dishwasher and followed Shelly. The guys were setting up the camera as Shelly told them about the marks in the grass.

"Can you get your camera, John?" Carolyn said. "It's better than mine."

He nodded and headed for the stairs.

Arnie paused long enough to get his Geiger counter and tape measure from his equipment bag. Grabbing a pen and paper from the kitchen counter, Carolyn went outside and walked in her bare feet across the dew-damp grass. Shelly, Steve, and Arnie followed. They stopped when they reached the first depression.

The three round holes in front of them reminded Carolyn of photos of UFO evidence she'd seen from Rendlesham Forest in England. The encounter involved military personnel and was nicknamed "the UK's Roswell."

UFOlogists insisted it was a legitimate, verifiable sighting, while debunkers claimed it was an optical illusion from a lighthouse and the depressions in the ground were nothing more than rabbit scrapes.

"We should get some plaster casts before they're destroyed and people try to tell us they're rabbit holes. If we can prove once and for all aliens are visiting our planet, we can stop focusing on finding proof and deal with the implications of extraterrestrial contact, like we should already be doing," Arnie said.

He bent down to one circle and measured it. "It's twenty-five point four centimetres in diameter."

Carolyn recorded it.

Arnie went to the next hole and measured it, then the last one. All the holes were twenty-five point four centimetres. Arnie and Steve measured the distance between the holes. Each length was three metres.

Arnie snapped the tape measure closed and grabbed his Geiger counter.

"Let's see if it's giving off any radiation."

At the mention of radiation, everyone took a step back. The Geiger counter sputtered at them in response.

Arnie checked the reading. "It's not lethal, but it's higher than normal."

The back screen door banged open.

John stepped outside and walked over to them, holding his video camera and snapping pictures as he approached. He moved next to Arnie, who bent down and stretched the tape measure over the hole at their feet so John could photograph it.

While John continued to snap pictures, Carolyn walked closer to the trees. Two trees at the edge of the yard showed evidence of damage. She strode to the nearest one.

The forest covering the back acre of their property consisted of mostly maples, beech trees, some birch trees, and a variety of evergreen trees. She found scorch marks on two birch trees.

"John," she called out, "come here and look at this."

He moved to her side and examined the trees.

"It's like they've been burned," he said and snapped a few pictures.

"Do you have enough photos?" she asked.

"I think so."

"Let's go see what's on Arnie's camera," Carolyn said, raising her voice so everyone in the group could hear her.

Nodding acknowledgement, Shelly turned and headed toward the house.

Steve, crouched in front of one of the holes in the dirt, stood and followed his wife. Arnie caught up to Steve.

When John started after them, Carolyn grabbed his arm.

"Wait."

He stared at her, puzzled. "What?"

"If there's footage of an alien craft, we have to be careful who we share it with. Help me convince Arnie not to splatter it all over the Internet. He'll cause trouble for all of us, especially for himself, if he's not careful. Okay? Promise me?"

"Let's see what's on there first before we get hysterical about it."

When she opened her mouth to protest, he held up his hand, forestalling her. "I'm not saying you're wrong. Let's just see what's on it."

She frowned. "Maybe there's nothing but static anyway," she said without conviction.

Together they walked into the house.

CHAPTER 10

In the living room, Arnie fiddled with the camera. Carolyn's stomach twisted into an anxious knot. In all the years spent hunting UFOs, they'd never found anything concrete. Arnie had stories, but he'd only recovered memories after working with a hypnotist. The hypnotist himself had explained that forensic hypnosis was unreliable at best, and verifying if memories were false, imagined, or real was impossible. To Arnie, they were real, but no proof existed.

Six summers before, Carolyn, too, had spotted a craft while taking an after-dinner walk near an elementary school. The evening was warm, and she walked for about an hour before turning around and heading home down a street that ended at the schoolyard. When she approached the deserted school, an enormous, metallic craft appeared and hovered over the soccer field. Windows covered the outer rim. She continued to approach, expecting it to disappear like a mirage. She looked around for other witnesses and found none.

Not one single soul walked down the street, drove on the road, or stood out in the yards of the surrounding homes. On a beautiful summer evening, the neighbourhood resembled a ghost town. She considered knocking on doors to get someone to come out and verify it for her, but feared they wouldn't see it, and she'd only get confirmation she was losing her mind. Then she thought of her cell phone. At least she could take a picture.

She reached down to her hip but remembered she'd left it at home. She considered walking underneath the craft, but all the science fiction movies and television shows she'd ever seen ran through her head, and she changed her mind. Better to run home and get her camera. If it was still there when she returned, she'd get pictures, which would prove to everyone, including herself, it was real. If not, she wouldn't have proof, but she'd survive to talk about it.

After that, her recollection grew hazy. She recalled running down the street, but not walking into the house. Her next memory was of folding laundry in the laundry room. She could never explain why she hadn't returned and couldn't remember what she'd done or thought when she arrived home. When she'd told the story to Arnie, he asked her about missing time, a common occurrence with UFO abductions.

Carolyn couldn't tell him. She hadn't checked the time and had noticed no anomalies. She couldn't even tell him if the sun had set by the time she arrived home. Though he bugged her to undergo hypnosis, she refused. She'd feared the memories would be terrifying. Arnie's retrieved memories included an invasive physical examination by alien beings that made him feel angry and violated. Carolyn recoiled at the prospect of exploring that possibility.

Noise from the television dragged Carolyn back to the present. Arnie started the video. The frame wobbled. That must've been when Arnie adjusted the tripod. The sound cleared and they heard Arnie giving his tech talk, explaining how the camera and scope worked, and what they were looking at. Carolyn's voice chimed in, asking someone to open the patio door. For a time, the sky was light, though the powerful scope was able to pick up stars far up in the sky and display them on the screen.

Carolyn realized she was standing and sat beside Shelly. She kicked off her slippers and pulled her knees up under her chin. She shivered. On the screen, a satellite moved steadily while Arnie tracked it. Carolyn cringed inwardly at the sound of her voice.

She checked the clock, trying to remember how long it would be until the strange lights appeared on the screen. She shivered again, stood up, and went to get her shawl.

When she returned, she found the others staring open-mouthed at the screen, where a white ball made its way slowly across the picture. Carolyn stood behind John and put her hands on his shoulders.

"Your hands are freezing," he said.

"Sorry," she whispered and removed them. She watched, barely breathing, while she relived what she remembered from the night before: the appearance of the white ball, Arnie using his laser pointer to attract it, her fear when she realized they were coming for her, and the refusal of the others to go inside. When the light disappeared, she'd hoped they'd left, but she'd been wrong.

Shelly's voice piped up on the video. "What's that? Look over there."

Arnie's voice answered her. "I see it. Over by the trees."

Carolyn's voice: "The power is out. What's that vibration? Do you feel it?" She sounded like she was shouting. She couldn't recall experiencing any of it.

The picture grew fuzzy, but the voices continued. John's voice said,

"I can't move. I feel so heavy."

Shelly's voice came next, fearful, trembling: "It's above us."

The image showed nothing, just bright light getting brighter, and a grainy picture. The audio crackled. Then, something dark moved across the frame, something unrecognizable, because it was so close to the camera lens. Darkness filled the screen, blotting out the light. The dark blob morphed into the shadow of a man's body as the distance between the camera and the body increased. Arnie's silhouette.

Carolyn's mouth went dry. She tried to swallow but found it difficult. Her gut knotted up again. She had a memory flash of lifting, floating up.

"It's got Arnie." Shelly screamed, a despairing cry. "I can't move."

Then Steve shouted, "Carolyn."

Carolyn watched in horrified fascination when another dark blob on the screen morphed into her own silhouette. The voices stopped as if cut off. A white flare filled the screen and then burst apart. The sky returned. Stars sparkled overhead. Everything fell silent except for the crickets.

Then, Steve's voice: "I'm going to lie down."

"Good idea." Shelly. "I'll go with you."

John, calm, casual: "We have to go to bed. They'll be here when we wake up."

The patio door gave a whispered swoosh as it opened, followed by the sound of footsteps walking near the camera. Then another swoosh and a click indicated the patio door was closed.

The group in the room watched in silence, and the video quietly played on.

"I don't know what to think," Steve said. "Does anyone remember any of that? It didn't jog my memory at all."

"At least the camera kept rolling," Arnie said. "Even batteries have been known to go dead at times like this. I wonder why they didn't."

"Maybe the craft wasn't close enough," John speculated.

"You guys didn't seem too perturbed we were gone," Arnie said.

"Nothing personal," John replied.

"Smartass."

Steve said, "If I could remember anything, I'd be able to explain that. One minute, it sounds like we're freaking out, and the next, we're calmly going off to bed. I'd say there was some kind of influence there."

"Perhaps the camera caught something when Arnie and I came back," Carolyn suggested.

They continued to watch, but the scene didn't change.

"Arnie," Carolyn said, a realization dawning, "you agreed not to use the laser pointer, and yet you did."

"I'm sorry. I did it without thinking. When those lights appeared, I wanted to see if they'd be attracted to it. No planes were around. I had no issue with using the pointer."

"I know, but you broke the only concession you'd been willing to make," Carolyn insisted. "I'm glad nothing happened, but we know the problem wasn't with the pointer. It's with the video. Now we need to decide what to do with it."

"I want to post it to the group," Arnie said.

"I knew you'd say that." Carolyn immediately jumped on it. "That's a bad idea."

She was so tired of arguing with Arnie. Why was it always her against him? He'd do something reckless, she'd try to stop him, and he'd go ahead anyway, even if it caused problems for all of them. Yet no one else got into the argument. She supposed they didn't want to take sides, but she wished that, just once, one of them would.

"Do me a favour," she said. "Don't post it until we all agree to it. I know it's your video and your UFO group, but it's our lives."

"We don't have to say who's on the video or where we filmed it. People need to know the truth," Arnie said.

"What about what Ralph says about government threats?" Carolyn was determined to hold firm.

"You don't believe Ralph. You never have. Why are you using him as an excuse now? Because it's convenient?" Arnie asked. "That's how you justify suppressing it? The government doesn't care what we do. Most home videos on the Internet get ignored, but it should be shared. People want to see this."

"I don't mind showing it to legitimate UFO investigators. That doesn't mean you should post it online. Keep it under wraps for now. Please? Until we figure out what to do." Surely, he'd be reasonable now.

"I'll consider it." Arnie frowned.

"How long has the video been running?" Steve interrupted.

Arnie checked the camera. "Over an hour. It recorded seven hours total. We should see Brent and get him to hypnotize us."

An expert hypnotherapist, Brent Morgan worked with several UFO experiencers. Arnie and Carolyn consulted him frequently, and both trusted him. Carolyn had known him for a few years now, the expert she turned to whenever she had questions about hypnosis. She also referred clients to him when she thought they'd benefit from his services. She liked his professional attitude and kind nature.

"I'll agree to that," said Carolyn. "We need to go soon."

Arnie took out his phone and went into the other room. Carolyn heard him talk, but not what he said. She gazed back at the television screen though there was nothing to see but stars. Occasionally, a plane flew across the frame or a bird passed overhead. They saw a shooting star and two small lights most people would call satellites, but Ralph would insist were alien spacecraft.

Carolyn felt trickling in her nose and sniffled. She put her hand to her face, and blood seeped through her fingers. She jumped up, grabbed a tissue, and went into the kitchen just as Arnie hung up the phone.

"What did Brent say?" Carolyn asked, her voice nasally. She went to the sink and washed her hands, one at a time, while she squeezed her nose shut using the tissue. Some blood trickled down her throat, making her nauseated.

"He'll see us this afternoon," Arnie replied. He stared at her but didn't comment on the nosebleed. "I'm surprised you're agreeing to this. I thought you were against regression hypnosis."

"It has its place."

"Come see this," Steve shouted.

They hurried back into the living room.

On the screen, a greenish glow infused the entire frame. The stars had vanished. A background hum vibrated from the speakers. This lasted for ten minutes. Then, as if a switch had flipped, the light winked out, the noise disappeared, and the stars and sky returned. All was quiet, except for the natural sounds from the yard.

"That was probably us returning," Carolyn said. "What time was that?"

Arnie checked the camera. "2:53 AM."

"Look," Steve said.

Three red dots appeared. They converged, forming a triangle. Five other red lights appeared, encircling the three. Then the five lights shot away in different directions. The three remaining lights hovered in triangular formation. Then, one by one, they disappeared. They didn't fly away, but simply vanished from sight.

"Hours of footage remain, but I suspect we've seen everything. Carolyn and I should leave to see Brent soon. Are you coming, John?" Arnie said.

"Yes," John replied. "What about you two?" John looked over at Steve and Shelly.

"We have to go home. I'm dying for a shower," said Shelly. "We'll catch up to you later."

Steve and Shelly stood up to leave.

"Well, thanks for an interesting evening. I don't think I'll ever remember it," said Shelly.

When the couple was gone, Carolyn turned to John and Arnie. "Okay with you guys if I use the shower first?"

When both men agreed, Carolyn headed up the stairs. She hoped a shower would calm her nerves. The prospect of what the hypnosis session would pull from her unconscious mind terrified her.

CHAPTER 11

Michael left the house before Jess woke up and arrived at the office by eight. He'd spared himself the guilt of having her watch him dress and leave on a Saturday morning, but he hadn't spared himself the guilt of leaving.

So far, the morning had been fruitful. He'd trolled through the video and audio files from the Fairchild residence. Most of the group's conversations were banal chitchat though he found Carolyn's premonition interesting. And he'd been taken aback when she said she'd been unable to conceive since her daughter's birth. It'd given him another stab of conscience, and he'd chalked that up to guilt by association. Either the Agency or the aliens were responsible.

He finally located the recording he'd come to the office to see: Carolyn and Arnie returning to the house after their abduction. It was a short clip, but mind bending. When Carolyn, the first to return, floated into her bedroom, the camera activated, and he watched while she drifted into her bed.

At that point, he made a mental note to check his bedroom for surveillance cameras. Though the purpose of the cameras in the Fairchild home was to pick up footage such as the one he currently viewed, footage in the archives would also show Carolyn and John having sex. Nothing was sacred to the Agency, and considering how things had been going, it wouldn't surprise Michael to learn they were watching him just as closely.

He moved on to the next file and watched Arnie drift to the couch in the den. Neither clip caught the abductee coming through the ceiling. That would've been an amazing sight, but the cameras weren't angled to capture anything on the ceiling.

Both clips ended when the abductee set down. When motion ceased, the recording played for thirty seconds more, and then the camera

48

stopped filming.

Michael turned his attention back to the files he'd stolen from the evidence room. He'd saved them to a memory stick so he could carry them with him. He didn't want to leave them in his desk in case Torque snooped around.

Indicators he'd set would tell Michael if anyone had rummaged through it. So far, nothing suggested anyone had violated his privacy. He also regularly checked to see if any suspicious processes were running on his computer. Again, things seemed to be okay. No one monitored what he did there either.

He'd taken similar precautions at his home office. He felt some empathy for Ralph Drummond. Paranoia was time-consuming.

Currently, he focused on trying to learn why the Rudolphs and Fairchilds were on the list of those who must be silenced. Neither couple was especially vocal or public about their UFO activities. In Carolyn's case, she actively discouraged it. Why would the Agency want to kidnap someone who sought to keep what little she knew under wraps? It made no sense.

He dug into his briefcase and removed the folders he'd scooped from the evidence room. Whoever had stolen this for Ralph knew exactly what to take. He leafed through it, pausing to read anything that related to himself, Torque, or Cornell. To his relief, he found only minimal information about himself—not much more than a vague description and a reference to his former position when he'd lived in Nevada.

Michael opened the next folder. This looked as if it might have something. Reports, describing in detail the results of tests performed on the abductees by the Agency. He scanned for anything on Carolyn, Ralph, and Arnie. Most of the reports centred on Carolyn.

He read with some horror about the tests they'd performed when she was both conscious and unconscious. After each session, they erased her memories. The tests concentrated on her psychic abilities. Each round assessed a different function.

They seemed particularly interested in her ability to remote view. She could not only accurately view things in a specified location within the same building, but also anywhere on earth, provided she had something on which to focus. Her accuracy was astounding. The two most involved in leading the experiments were Cornell and Torque.

This explained why they wanted her. It also explained why they'd want John out of the way. Michael blanched and went cold. How could he go along with this? It wasn't only that the aliens wanted to experiment on these people. The Agency did too, and from the look of it, they wanted to use the people with the greatest abilities as weapons.

It reminded him of the MKUltra experiments the U.S. government had conducted on unsuspecting people from the 1950s to the 1970s. They'd experimented with mind control, using drugs, torture, and other means to manipulate their subjects. It also brought to mind the experiments in remote viewing done by the Stanford Research Institute and the CIA's Stargate Project in the 1970s.

Where would he be himself if the Agency had never approached him? Would he have believed the conspiracy theories, ending up on the receiving end of a death ray?

What if, like Ralph, he'd found out the Agency was accelerating the destruction of life on earth? Would he have acted to intervene? Should he intervene now, or just continue to save himself and his wife and count himself lucky to be among the chosen ones?

They had told him when he first joined the Agency that it existed to ensure American interests were protected in any dealings with extraterrestrials. The first offer they'd made him was for a job at Area 51 in Nevada at Groom Lake.

When he accepted, they told him about the existing treaty between extraterrestrials and the United States government, though they didn't tell him the details of the treaty. The Eisenhower Administration had made the original agreement. Every administration since then had upheld it, and other countries, including Canada, had jumped in.

The president himself was kept completely ignorant of it through each administrative change. Conspiracy theorists were fed enough disinformation to make them believe something was being kept from them while at the same time making them appear crazy for having that belief.

Michael placed the folders back in his briefcase and closed the files on his computer. After placing the memory stick back in his pocket, he checked the time. Eleven o'clock. If he hurried, he could go home before Jess got too mad at him. He shut down his computer. When he stood to leave, the door opened.

Torque stepped into the room. "What are you doing, Mick?"

Michael stopped himself from glancing at his briefcase. He kept his eyes focused on Torque's and his expression neutral.

Torque closed the door behind him. "You might as well tell me. I know what you were up to last night."

CHAPTER 12

"I came in to review the surveillance footage from the Fairchild house. Is that a problem?" Michael sat down, leaned back in his chair, and draped an arm over each armrest.

Torque moved to the chair in front of Michael's desk and sat, fingers interlaced, elbows on the armrests, his ankles crossed.

Playing it cool, Michael supposed. He waited for his partner to break the silence.

"It depends. You shouldn't have been there in the first place. What happened that made you want to snoop around in here on a Saturday morning when your wife is already pissed at you? What's so important that it couldn't wait until Monday?"

"I needed the peace and quiet."

"I've never known you to complain about Jess being too loud. What are you doing here? The truth."

"You want to know? I can't face Jess. Something's up with her and it's making things at home unbearable." He exaggerated the situation, but not by much. Things were tense between them. He'd play that up, and hopefully, Torque would believe he was hiding from his domestic problems at the office.

"You're lucky it's me Cornell has monitoring you. I'm willing to cut you some slack because I know you've been distracted by whatever's going on between you and Jess, but don't you think you ought to man up and talk to her about it? Get a fucking hobby if you want to be away from home. Don't throw yourself into stuff that's not your concern."

Michael rose. "Sure. I was just going to leave when you walked in. I found nothing in the surveillance footage anyway. Carolyn and Arnie were abducted, as scheduled, and returned, as scheduled. Nothing unusual happened, which makes me wonder why they suddenly need to be silenced. There's nothing new here. Nothing suspicious."

Torque stood and walked around Michael's desk. The computer had already powered down. He stared at Michael, suspicion in his eyes, but some relief too.

Michael met his gaze. "I told you," he said, "I was just leaving."

Torque stepped aside.

Michael grabbed his briefcase and walked to the door. He turned back to face his partner.

"Root around my office all you want. I've got nothing to hide."

Torque's face remained neutral though his eyes might have flickered.

Michael left without a backward glance. He wasn't worried. Everything he had to hide was on him.

***

Just before one-thirty, Michael arrived home. He went into the house and called to Jessica. Silence greeted him. He checked the kitchen. Empty. Her car was in the driveway so she couldn't be far.

"Jess?"

He moved on to the living room when he continued to receive no response. Fear streaked through him. He reached under his jacket, pulled out his gun, and cocked it. He made his way up the stairs, gaze darting around, watching for an ambush. At the top of the stairs, he stopped and listened. He thought he heard a sound from the bedroom.

The bedroom door yawned open. Michael crept up to it and listened. It sounded like someone was retching in the en suite bathroom.

She's sick. That's all it is.

He exhaled loudly, relieved. Still, he scanned the room before entering and continued to hold his gun up and ready. After verifying the room was empty, he made his way to the bathroom.

She was there, hunched over the toilet, wiping her lips with a tissue. He slipped his gun back into its holster as she turned to face him. She spoke before he could say anything.

"Where have you been?"

"I had to go to the office." The old standby, which always came out sounding like "I needed to get the fuck away from you."

Her eyes betrayed her disappointment.

"I'm back now." It was such a useless thing to say. He hated himself for saying it. What he wanted to do was hug her, but he feared she'd push him away.

"I'm sorry you're not feeling well." That was better.

She acknowledged it with a nod.

He considered what he needed to do.

"Why don't I help you set up outside on the lounge chair? You can relax, read a book. I'll bring you whatever you need."

She continued to stare at him, wary.

Michael kept talking, distracting her. He put his arm around her and guided her out of the bedroom.

"Don't worry about anything. I'll take care of lunch. You relax. I've got some work to do, but I can do it here."

He had to get her out of the house, and he had to make it look natural.

"The sunshine and fresh air will be good for you." He wondered then why she remained silent. "Jess? Are you okay?"

To his horror, she burst into tears.

"No. I'm not okay."

"What's wrong?" He couldn't get into it. Not now. He needed to get her out of the house. He wanted to check the place for bugs, for cameras, but he couldn't let her see him do it.

"You're what's wrong." There was pain in her eyes, and he knew the same pain was reflected in his own. It hurt because it was true.

"Come outside. Get some air." He doubted there'd be listening devices out there.

Get out of the house, damn it. It was all he could do not to give her a shove. He took a breath. She wasn't feeling well. He had to calm down.

They made their way down the stairs and to the back of the house on the main floor, then out to the patio. He closed the sliding doors behind them, knowing it would shut off anything in the house that was motion activated.

He walked her to the lounge chair under the gazebo next to the pool. The filter was running, the sound reassuring. It would help to mask what they said even if there was a bug out here.

"Sit, Jess. I'll get you some water."

"Michael." There was a sound of desperation in her voice.

He did hug her then, and her body felt good against his. He stroked her hair.

"I just have some things I need to do inside, and then we'll talk. It'll be okay." He tried to believe it so that she'd believe it.

She relaxed against him and sighed. It sounded like relief.

He kissed the top of her head.

She looked up at him.

He brushed the tears from her face.

"Come on. Sit."

She looked a little green, as if she might throw up again. He hoped it wasn't food poisoning. She let him seat her on the lounge chair.

When she was settled, he went back into the house and got her some water and the book she'd been reading. She didn't protest when he suggested he make her tea and put food together for her. He went inside,

53

closed the doors, and shut the drapes.

Michael began in their bedroom, the memory of Carolyn floating into her bed motivating him. It took him two hours to go through the whole place while at the same time making Jess tea and something to eat so she wouldn't be compelled to come inside. He found nothing.

Done, he went into his closet and pulled out their bug-out bags—bags he'd prepared for them when they first moved to Canada. These packs would allow them to leave at a moment's notice, and they could survive anywhere, provided the environment wasn't toxic.

He hid the files and the memory stick in a safe in the bedroom closet. The map to the alien base in Algonquin Park he put into his bag.

Satisfied that the house wasn't under surveillance and that his secrets were safe, he went outside again to face Jess. It was time to have that talk he'd been putting off.

She was asleep, the book lying open on her lap.

He set the book on the table next to her, gently kissed her lips, and returned to the house.

CHAPTER 13

Carolyn tried to relax. She'd never been hypnotized before and feared nothing would happen. She sat in a reclining leather chair, a shawl over her shoulders to ward off the chill of the air conditioner. John sat on a couch opposite her, while Arnie waited in the room outside so he wouldn't be influenced by anything Carolyn said. Brent Morgan, the hypnotherapist, perched on a stool next to her. A digital recorder and box of tissues sat on the table beside him.

Does he expect me to cry?

Brent had a way of disarming and charming people, making them comfortable and secure. If anyone could make her unselfconscious enough to cry, he could. He was easy on the eyes, too, dark and handsome, but without Arnie's in-your-face sexuality.

What she liked most about him, however, was his integrity and compassion. She'd seen him a few times when she'd had difficulty coping and confided intimate details to him she hadn't even told her husband in over eighteen years of marriage.

Brent smiled. "Do you have any questions before we begin?"

Carolyn considered and then shook her head.

"All right. Let's begin. Keep your eyes open and get comfortable."

She gazed ahead and tried to relax.

"Take a deep breath. Breathe slow and deep ..." He led her through the induction.

Her eyes drifted shut. She eased into the chair, comfortable and warm. There was a whir when the air conditioner kicked in and cool air wafted through the room. The shawl around her shoulders was a warm hug.

" ... Now, we're going to go back in time, to your last birthday. Can you recall your last birthday?"

"Yes."

"How old are you?"

"Thirty-nine."

Brent asked her some more questions about her day and then asked her to talk about what happened after her workday was done. Carolyn described her happiness at going out for a birthday dinner with John. She smiled, reliving it.

"Okay, good. Now, I'd like to move forward in time a little. We're going to go to last night. It's around six o'clock. Tell me where you are."

"I'm in the kitchen, standing in front of the oven."

"What are you doing?"

She told him about making pizza, Arnie's arrival, and how that triggered a vision that made her fearful of setting up the camera for the sky watch. Her voice rose in pitch, and her stomach churned. Her hands curled into fists, swatted the air in front of her, and then wrapped around her elbows. She hugged herself, and her body shook.

"You're okay. Just observe. Do you set up the equipment?"

"Yes. I don't like it, but they all want to, so I stop arguing. I don't know what the bad thing will be, so I can't argue. They won't listen. They never listen."

"Okay. We'll leave that for now. Let's skip ahead, to later in the evening. It's around midnight. Where are you?"

"Sitting outside. We're on the balcony."

She recounted seeing the lights, her fear that something was coming, and her nervous relief when the lights disappeared. She giggled, reliving the moment, then frowned.

"What happens next?" Brent prodded.

"There's something at the back of the yard. Right there." Her arm rose, her index finger pointing at an object only she could see. "I can't make it out." She dropped her arm.

"How do you feel?" Brent asked.

"Scared. I can't move." She was frozen in place and watching Arnie float away. She clenched her jaw, gritting her teeth. Her hands fisted, nails digging into her palms.

"Go on."

"Arnie disappeared, and I'm lifting off the ground." Her voice softened, and she gave a slight sigh. Her hands unclenched to rest open on her thighs. It was okay.

Nothing to worry about.

"How are you feeling?" Brent asked.

"Peaceful. I get the message I'll be okay. I don't want to fight."

Over on the couch, John stirred.

"What do you see?"

"A bright light. I'm floating in it. I see darkness in the centre of the light, and I'm moving toward it."

"What happens when you get to the top?"

"I'm moving into a tunnel. I pass out. When I wake up, I'm lying naked on a table. I turn my head and see Arnie unconscious on another table. There's a tube sticking out of his head." Carolyn's hands covered her eyes. She wanted to hide. Her mind rebelled at the sight of the beings standing around the table on which she lay exposed and defenceless.

"I'm scared. Creatures are doing something to Arnie. They've attached something to his leg. Some machine thing presses against my leg." She screamed when a leathery hand touched her bare flesh. "No, get away. Get the fuck away from me." Her eyes squeezed shut, and tears rolled down her cheeks.

From a distance, Brent's voice broke through the terror, calm, assuring. "It's okay. You're safe. It's as if you're watching a movie of what happened. Take a deep breath, Carolyn. You're going to relax and observe. Tell me what you see."

She stopped crying and relaxed. She lowered her hands to her thighs again. It was okay. She could just watch.

"I can't move, and they're doing something inside my nose. It hurts." She grimaced. Her hands twitched, clenched, and unclenched.

"What's happening?" Brent asked.

"I can't lift my arms to stop them. I can only lie here, and they do what they want."

"You're okay. Just relax and observe. Can you tell me what they look like?"

They surrounded her. "Yes."

"Describe them to me."

"Small, grey. Large heads. They look like the aliens on the covers of books and in movies. There's another one, bigger. The doctor. He gives the orders. They don't speak aloud. I see people. They look human. They have blond hair and they're wearing blue uniforms."

"What happens next?"

She sighed and her arms relaxed at her side. "One of them points at me, like he sees that I see them, and suddenly I'm calm, tired. I try not to sleep, but I think I fall asleep. The next thing I know, I'm waking up in bed."

"Okay," Brent said. "I'm going to bring you back now." He paused and continued. "You're relaxed. When you come back, you'll be refreshed, alert—like you've had a lovely nap, and tonight, you'll sleep deeply and well."

He counted her awake. "How do you feel?"

"Good."

"Do you remember everything?" Brent asked.

"Yes," she said. "It all came back to me. I remember how I got the bruise on my thigh, and they stuck something in my nose. Arnie was there, and they did things to him."

"Okay. How do you feel about that?"

"Angry. They have no right to do that."

"We can do more sessions if you like, and see if you can remember other incidents. It'll be easier for you to recall now."

"I'll have to think about it. Is it okay if I stay in here while you talk to Arnie?"

"It's up to him," Brent replied.

He went to the waiting room and ushered Arnie into the room.

"How'd it go?" Arnie asked.

"Good," she said. "Would you be okay with me and John staying and observing your session?"

"Sure. We're all friends here."

She relinquished the chair and went to the couch. She sat close to John and took his hand.

He released her hand and put his arm around her. "Are you sure you want to stay? We can listen to the recording later."

"I'd like to be here for Arnie. It was helpful to have you here," Carolyn said. She studied Arnie. He seemed relaxed, unconcerned even. She found it hard to believe he wasn't afraid of what was coming.

She recalled the creatures she'd seen and shuddered. In the past, she'd thought she'd be curious or amazed or awed by meeting alien beings, perhaps even humbled by their presence. She hadn't expected the overwhelming surge of rage and hate. Probably she'd doubted they'd victimize her the way they'd done last night.

Brent led Arnie into the hypnosis. He reclined comfortably. His eyes drifted closed, and his hands rested loosely on his thighs. After asking some basic questions about the past, Brent directed his attention to the events of the previous night.

Carolyn's stomach did a back flip while she listened to Arnie describe setting up the camera on the balcony and turning it on. A rush of heat spread through her body, and her underarms and the back of her neck became moist though the office was cold.

Arnie's description of the beings and the tables was identical to Carolyn's. He described the pressure on his head, verifying her story that a tube protruded from it. Everything he said echoed her version of events. John's arm around her tightened. She leaned her head onto his shoulder and put an arm across his chest, hugging him.

An urge to leave the room overwhelmed her, but she forced herself, for Arnie's sake, to stay and listen. Finally, it was over, and Arnie described waking up on the couch in John and Carolyn's den. Brent's low, quiet voice started the process of bringing Arnie out of the hypnosis.

John's expression was grim. Carolyn couldn't tell if he was more shocked, scared, or worried. Silently, she asked her angels and guides for help.

In front of her, Brent sat back in his chair and shut off the digital recorder. Arnie stretched, now completely awake and alert.

"Thanks, Brent," he said.

"You're welcome. What do you feel about what you remembered?"

"Nothing."

"You were taken aboard a spacecraft against your will. Your friend was forced aboard also, and she suffered trauma. You must have a reaction. What are you experiencing?"

"I used to hate them. I used to want to fight them, to take back my power. Now? I live with it. What matters to me is the government's role in this. They know about alien abductions and do nothing to stop them. In fact, they encourage it."

His voice rose, and he leaned forward, hunching up his shoulders. "They pretend they're oblivious because they're a part of it. They're benefiting from it. I don't know how, but they are. We need to expose what's going on. It's not fair that many of us can't sleep in our own beds without thinking we're going to wake up on an alien's operating table, experimented on like some lab animal."

Brent sat back in his chair and crossed his legs. He fiddled with the wedding band on his finger, a habit that triggered when he was trying not to state the obvious.

"What are you feeling?"

Arnie smiled and his shoulders relaxed. "Okay. I'm angry and frustrated at the apathy of other people. I'm a monkey in a cage, and no one cares. Well, my friends care, and my family would care if they knew, but I don't want to worry my mother with this."

"Is it possible your mother's also an abductee?"

Arnie started. His expression revealed he'd never considered that possibility, even though he knew abductions ran in families.

"No," he said, softly. "She can't be. I'd have known."

"Perhaps that's something you might want to broach with her," Brent said. "Or maybe she can tell you if your father had any strange experiences he never shared with you."

"What's the point of that?"

"It'll help you understand what's happening with your family and to investigate whether they've discovered ways to cope you can use. Mostly, it's because you need to get support from others who've experienced this. Now you and Carolyn share this experience, perhaps you can support each other through the times when this happens."

Arnie considered. "What about getting this out there? Carolyn doesn't want me to post the video. I think we should. The more people know about what's happening, the better." He turned to her. "It's when victims remain silent that abusers get away with what they do."

She considered. "But it's dangerous."

"We have to stick our necks out for something. This is important. We can't just meekly submit. I don't know how else to lodge a protest than to get the proof and put it out there for everyone to see. We have the tools to do it now. People had to suffer in silence before, but not anymore. We can help ourselves by finding others in our situation and getting them on our side."

She had that sensation again of speeding at a brick wall on a train.

"Arnie, it'll be bad."

"We'll deal with it together. They can't silence all of us."

"But you don't have any kids to worry about. I do. I don't want that out there. Let's report it to MUFON and then forget about it."

"You should do this to help Sam. What if she's an abductee too?"

"She's not."

"Until yesterday, you insisted you weren't. Sam may have kept it a secret, or she may not remember."

"You mean like your parents? A minute ago, you didn't want to go there. Now you're telling me I should?"

"If my parents were abductees, I'd want to help them by going public and encouraging people to do something about this." He turned to John. "What do you think? Sam is your daughter too."

They all stared at John. He looked only at Carolyn.

"Carr, I think Arnie's right. You don't understand what it's like to be forced to witness this and not be able to do anything about it. The more people we can make aware of this, the more power we have against it."

"Ralph says we're being watched, and they'll come after us if we're not careful."

"Maybe we can get enough people together on this that we can help each other. If many of us say the same thing, they can't continue denying it, and they can't silence all of us. We must create a tipping point."

"Why does it have to be us?"

"It has to start somewhere; why not with us? I can't continue to live like this. Can you? They'll come for you again. Do you want that?"

That stopped her. She thought about going through it again. And again. Would it last a lifetime or did they stop after a while? What if something they did to her had caused her to be infertile? What if they were coming for Sam too? Would Sam be unable to have children too? Somehow, she found herself agreeing. "Okay."

CHAPTER 14

Monday morning, Michael sat down at his desk and booted up his computer. He picked up the report the receptionist, Helen, had left for him. He skimmed it, barely registering the information—something on the world situation, collated from the other agencies. It looked bad.

He opened his web browser and Drummond's blog loaded. A new posting from Arnie included a video.

Nice going, Arnie. You're going to raise a shitstorm over this, my friend.

Surprised Cornell hadn't called yet, Michael glanced at the phone as if thinking about it would make it ring. He ran the video and watched it in its entirety. It had been condensed down to thirty minutes of footage, showing the lights overhead, the bodies of Arnie and Carolyn sailing up, and the lights returning. What was happening was obvious to anyone familiar with the UFO abduction scenario.

Even more troubling was the transcript from the hypnosis session. Images of physical evidence from the backyard supported their claims. The call to arms to end alien abductions and expose the government's involvement with UFOs ensured Arnie would find himself in the trunk of Torque's car in the next few days.

Michael considered Arnie's position. His life was pretty much over, and he didn't know it. Everyone was expendable, and the closer it got to doomsday, the less concern the Agency bosses had over wiping out or disappearing the troublemakers sooner rather than later. They were all sitting on a powder keg and those asshat UFO nuts were striking matches.

On that cue, Torque tapped on the open door and stepped in, closing it behind him.

"Cornell wants us to make a couple of house calls. Pay a visit to

Arnie and escort him to his new accommodations at the home for wayward UFO experiencers. Also, he wants John silenced. We'll use the TR and make it look like a heart attack."

Michael nodded. The "TR" was the Tesla Ray they'd used on Patty Richards. Physicist Nikola Tesla had created the plans for a death ray, which the FBI confiscated at his death. The American government subsequently developed it into doomsday machines.

The Aurora Project created high-frequency radio transmission dishes around the world, which could affect the weather and otherwise inflict damage and destruction on a large scale, and the Sleep Project developed pocket-sized death rays that could make it appear a person had died of a heart attack or stroke.

Torque continued, "We have to make it look like Arnie committed suicide."

Michael nodded and didn't speak. He wasn't going to argue. He'd expected Arnie to pay large for going public.

"Where is he right now?" Michael asked.

"At his condo. His mother is there though. We'll have to watch for him to come out."

"What about getting him during the night? We could give his mother a bit of something to keep her asleep and take him out," Michael suggested.

"That might be an option. Or we might take care of John first. That'd flush out Arnie. He'd want to see Carolyn," Torque replied.

"A small group of people having accidents, incarcerations, heart attacks, and committing suicide looks suspicious, but it'll all be written off as a huge coincidence. It's unbelievable when you consider it," Michael said.

"Let's execute this in an hour." Torque grinned and turned away. "I'll be in my office. I've got some things I need to do before we go out."

Michael returned to his computer, but couldn't focus on anything. He glanced at the clock. Almost fifty minutes. He opened up one of Drummond's files. This one had some interesting notes in it. Drummond's contact had given him information about the alien base in Algonquin.

According to the source, who went by the code name "Dragonfly," a group of aliens opposed to experimenting on humans had set up a base where they helped people avoid further abductions.

How was that possible, considering the Agency also kept tabs on abductees?

Michael also found evidence that showed Drummond and his family were planning to head to the base. It was too bad for them that Michael and Torque had gotten to Ralph before they could get away. Michael clicked on another file, opened it, and started reading.

When he glanced at the clock again, it was time to head out. He shut down his computer. He removed his gun, a 9mm Glock, from his desk and slid it into his shoulder holster. He'd sign out the death ray as they were leaving.

He considered changing but decided the business attire would be appropriate if they were spotted. They'd be sitting in Torque's car in the plaza next to John's workplace. The building in that plaza contained professional offices; jeans and T-shirts would make them conspicuous.

Michael made his way to Torque's office.

Torque sat at his desk, leaning over his computer, chin on his hand, staring at the screen. He sat up when Michael stepped into the office.

"Ready to go?"

"Be right there."

Michael closed the door. "I was thinking about some of the things in those blogs. Maybe silencing these people would martyr them and escalate their cause."

"Did you see the comments after the video went up? And since then, activity on the MUFON site has gone crazy. I swear Griffen has lost his mind. Did he think he could spout off about this stuff without repercussions?"

"Now that you ask, yes, he did. As far as he's concerned, it's a free country."

"Perhaps, but if it continues to escalate, they're going to encourage someone to come to them and give them more information than is good for us."

"You mean Drummond's source?"

Torque stared at him. "Why'd you say that?"

Michael swallowed, realizing he'd let slip something he should have kept to himself. It was hard to think of Torque as someone he couldn't trust. He tried to recover.

"I'm assuming Drummond had some inside information. I read his blog. He talked like he knew things that come close to hitting ETAP."

"Where exactly in his blog did he mention anything about ETAP?"

Michael deflected. "Read between the lines. He alludes to things close to the truth. I'm wondering what else he says that might be correct."

"Where are you going with this, Mick?"

"Do you think there's any truth to what he says about how much of this crisis the government has deliberately created?"

"Of course not, and you'd better be careful who you talk to about this stuff. If Cornell heard you talking like that, you'd find yourself in the cell next to Arnie."

"We've been partners a long time, right?"

"Yeah."

"I trust you."

"Glad to hear it. I trust you too, partner."

"So if you knew the truth you'd tell me?"

Torque didn't hesitate. "Sure, Mick. Of course."

Michael nodded, but looked away, certain Torque was lying. His stomach felt queasy when he realized Torque had threatened him with a cell next to Arnie rather than with termination—a fate reserved for abductees.

CHAPTER 15

Michael and Torque sat in the parking lot of the office building next to John's workplace in Aurora. John spent a lot of his time in and around the loading dock area at the back of the building. Michael waited and watched. He wanted to time it so John would be lifting something heavy when hit with the death ray.

"What do you want to do for lunch?" Torque asked.

"Chinese food?" Michael suggested.

"We just had that on Friday. How about Thai?"

"I'm not in the mood. How about Italian? That Italian place here in town serves the best veal sandwiches."

"I could do that. How's it looking? Any activity?"

"It's busy. I want to make sure there aren't too many others around. Wouldn't want to make a mistake," Michael said. "Gotta hit the target."

Torque nodded. "That'd be a major screwup, my friend. Take your time."

Michael settled back in his seat. The day was sweltering again, and he was glad they could keep the windows rolled up and the air conditioning on. They'd have to be careful though. The town had a law against idling, and if they were tagged for it, they'd have to call off the hit and think of another plan. Torque monitored the surrounding area in case a police cruiser came into view.

John stepped out of the open loading bay doors and glanced toward the road, probably looking for an overdue truck.

Michael's hand twitched. He waited. If a truck were about to pull in, then perhaps there'd be an opportunity. Most unloading would be done with fork trucks, but if he were lucky, John would have to do some heavy lifting.

Michael took a deep breath and ran his hand through his hair.

This time, Torque wasn't oblivious. He grinned. "It's a wonder you're not bald."

"Very funny, wise guy. It's a habit."

Torque snickered.

They continued to wait.

Minutes later, a transport truck pulled into the loading dock. John waved the driver into the berth.

Michael continued to watch and wait.

How would Carolyn handle the death of her husband? Best not to think about that. Michael was in no position to second-guess orders right now. However, it bothered him that he'd found nothing to justify eliminating John other than to clear the way for kidnapping his wife.

Michael reminded himself that the ones who died before the shitstorm hit were the lucky ones. It wouldn't be long before those in on it headed to the underground facilities the government had been working on for the last few decades. Most of those left topside would perish.

He was relieved to be one of the chosen few but didn't have any illusions about why that was so. He was a scientist, survivalist, and, most of all, a trained killer. His skills would be in great demand when the world turned upside down.

John, his back to them, bent down to lift a box sitting at his feet.

Michael aimed the ray, removed the catch, and waited. The TR suddenly weighed heavy in his hand. John's only crime was that he'd married a super psychic the Agency wanted to get their hands on.

"What are you waiting for?" Torque said. "You'll never have a better shot."

"What did he do?"

"What do you mean?"

"I mean, what did he do that makes it necessary to kill him?"

"I don't know. I don't need to know. Cornell said to do it, so we're doing it. You're going to lose your chance. He's getting up. Press the fucking button."

John stood, the box in his arms.

Michael continued to stare at the target, vacillating.

Torque cursed. His hands covered Michael's, forced his finger down, and triggered the ray.

Four seconds later, John collapsed. The box pitched forward to the ground while John went down in a heap behind it.

Torque dropped his hands.

Michael released and locked the button and lowered the TR. He turned to his partner and waited for him to say something.

Torque's face was red fury. He popped open the glove box.

"Put it in there."

Michael did as ordered, and Torque locked it up. He shoved the car into drive and pulled away. They drove in silence from the parking lot.

When they were clear of the area, Torque said, "You fucked up. What the hell was that?"

Michael steadied himself. He had to speak convincingly—make Torque believe he was okay with what happened.

"I wanted to know why we had to eliminate him because it made no sense. I was going to do it, but I just wanted a reason."

"When the fuck did you turn into Mother Teresa? Listen to me carefully, amigo. I won't tell Cornell how badly you just screwed up. Any more hesitating, though, and you're done. I won't cover for you again. I've never seen you like this before. What happened back there?"

"We're neutralizing a lot of people. Don't you think I'm entitled to know why?"

"No, you're not. You know you're not. You've been fucking *programmed* not to question orders."

Michael didn't reply, and they drove in silence to the restaurant.

CHAPTER 16

Two veal sandwiches plus an hour-and-a-half later, they were back in Toronto. Torque pulled up in front of their office building.

"I've got an appointment, so I'm dropping you here. You go ahead and report to Cornell. Tell him everything went as planned, and I'll back you up. This time. Tell him I'll catch up to him later. I shouldn't be too long."

"Where are you going?"

"I'm following up on a suspect."

As Torque expected, Michael didn't ask for details, but stepped from the car and slammed the door. He started to walk away but turned back.

Torque lowered the window.

"The TR is in the glove box."

"No problem. I'll sign it in when I get back."

Michael waved acknowledgement and headed into the building.

Torque pulled into traffic, drove down the street a few blocks, and then turned the corner to pull up to a doughnut shop at street level in an office building. He found a parking spot not too far from his destination and went inside.

She was already there, sipping a tea and trying to read a book. She looked lovely. Sometimes Torque envied Michael Valiant his wife, and as he approached Jess, he drank in her loveliness—long brown hair, deep blue eyes, though she hid those behind glasses. Some would've called her plain because she dressed in drab colours, but Torque had always appreciated the beauty of her face, especially her eyes and the shape of her lips. He thought there was nothing plain about her face.

When he stepped in the door, she waved to him, confirming she hadn't been concentrating on the book.

Torque waved back. As he reached her table, he said, "Thanks for meeting me."

"I was surprised to hear from you, Gerry. In all the time you've been Michael's partner, you've never asked to talk to me. I hope it's nothing serious. Grab yourself a coffee and tell me what's going on."

"I don't want to worry you, but I do want to talk to you a little and see how you two are doing. Putting my nose in your business a bit, but he's my partner. Want anything while I'm up there?"

"No, thanks. I'm still enjoying my tea. I sat down about a minute before you got here, so I'm okay."

He gave her a nod and walked to the counter. It was busy, and he found himself standing in line behind five other people. While he waited, he glanced back at Jess, who had returned to staring at her book. He hoped what he found out from her today would help him draw Michael back into the fold.

Torque feared they were losing him. After what had happened earlier, he was glad he'd set up this meeting. Perhaps after talking to Jess, he could figure out a way to regain his partner's trust and return things to the way they were.

The red-faced, muddy-haired boy-man behind the counter brought Torque out of his head.

"Can I help you, sir?"

He stepped forward and asked for a black coffee. When the kid handed it over, Torque carried it to the table.

"How's the book?" he asked, sitting down across from her.

"It's okay. Let's get to the point. What's wrong?"

"Okay. I'm worried about Michael. He seems distracted lately, unfocused. Please don't mention to him I met with you. It would probably upset him, but I'm concerned he's losing his motivation. I want to see him get ahead, and if there's anything I can do to help him excel, I'll do it. I hate to see him lose it now when he's so close to success. Have you noticed any changes in his behaviour lately?"

Jess studied him for a moment without answering.

Was she contemplating lying to him or was she reflecting on Michael's behaviour?

Finally, she spoke. "I guess his behaviour is different at home. We've been disconnected lately. He acts as if he's under stress, but he refuses to discuss it. He avoids me and spends most of his time at the office. Even when he's home, he locks himself in his office and spends hours there, working, even weekends. He stays up late into the night, and that's if he doesn't go back out. I'd suspect him of having an affair if I didn't know him better. He's always got his briefcase and his netbook with him, and he takes his field kit along all the time."

"How are things between the two of you?"

"Like I said, distant. I'm worried about him, but I think things might be looking up. At least, I hope he'll be happy with what I have to tell him."

"What's that?"

"Well, I'd prefer to tell Michael first, but maybe he won't mind if I confide in you. You're his best friend, and it's sweet you're so concerned. A few weeks ago, I suspected I might be pregnant."

Torque's mouth went dry. He waited for her to continue.

"Remember when Michael and I went away for that three-day visit to my sister's cottage? He was upset because I forced it on him, but he needed to get away. It went well. He was more relaxed than I've seen him in years. We were like newlyweds. Last week, I got confirmation from the doctor that I'm pregnant."

"Congratulations." He pasted a smile on his face. "That's great news."

This was *not* good news. The last thing he wanted was for Michael to have a family to protect. If anything, this would push him further away from the Agency.

"You haven't told him yet?"

"No. He's been so distant and absent that the time never seemed right. I want to surprise him with a nice dinner and a happy announcement. I wanted to give him some time, but I'll have to tell him now that you know."

"Perhaps you should give him the rest of the week. He'll have completed a couple of major assignments by then. That should ease things for him. Plan that special dinner for Friday. I'll make sure he's there for it."

"Thank you so much. That's so sweet. I'll wait. I'm sure it'll make things better for us to be planning our baby's arrival. No doubt that's all he'll need to snap him out of this melancholy. It's been so hard to keep quiet, but he was so moody I was afraid he'd be angry about it. He always said he didn't want children. He said his work didn't leave room for them, but my work does. I don't mind raising them with little help. I know how hard he works, and I think he'll be happy we did this. Don't you think?"

"I'm sure he'll be happy. How could he not like kids, especially his own? It'll be fine. I'll prime the pump for you a little, feel him out, and encourage him. I bet when he knows there'll be a little Michael Junior around, he'll be over the moon."

That was the problem. Michael *would* be happy. When he got used to the idea, he'd want that child, and that would be bad.

Torque hadn't been delighted when the couple announced their engagement. He'd even tried to talk Michael out of marrying Jess. People in their line of work shouldn't try to settle down and have families, but

Michael was in love and refused to let anything stop him.

They married, and, Torque thought, the relationship had slid into a downward spiral ever since. At one point, it had been on the verge of complete disintegration when Michael came close to having an affair with Althaea Dayton, a colleague. Torque had done his best to push Michael into the woman's arms, even orchestrating a brief period where the two were partnered on assignments.

The chick transferred to one of the alien bases, and Michael had snapped out of it, much to Torque's dismay. This child would solidify Michael's marriage and force him to consider everything from the perspective of a new father. It would turn him from the Agency, and Torque would be forced to have him neutralized.

This child couldn't be born, and Torque accepted that as a solution. He needed to make sure it happened before Michael even knew Jess was pregnant. Releasing him from his troubled marriage at the same time, killing two birds with one death ray, so to speak, was, Torque decided, the most pragmatic way to go.

He smiled at Jess and patted her hand. "Don't worry. I'll take care of everything."

CHAPTER 17

Carolyn ushered her client to the door. Alis had just received her third Reiki session and seemed much more relaxed and peaceful now. She described herself as chronically tense, a "Type A" personality. Carolyn worked on assisting her client to relax enough to at least stop clenching her teeth through a session.

Alis, a cupcake of a woman, hugged Carolyn at the door. "Thanks so much. I think I was able to relax this time. I feel good."

"That's wonderful." She smiled. "I think you're making real progress. By next visit, you'll be sleeping like a baby. Maybe you'll turn into one of those people who fall asleep on the Reiki table."

Alis laughed. "I'd love that. See you next month."

Carolyn stepped outside.

Alis walked to her car, a Civic, parked in front of the garage. The Civic crawled backward toward the road, and Alis gave a final wave before she disappeared from view.

Carolyn stood for a moment, breathing in the fresh air. It was hot out, but she found it comforting to stand there in her sundress and soak in the sun.

The moment passed. It was as if a dark cloud had obscured the sun though the brightness of the day itself didn't change. She tensed and held her breath. Something was wrong. She scanned the property to see if anything was amiss.

Plants in the garden below swayed subtly in the slight breeze. A squirrel darted across the grass. Almost lazily, a robin flew by and landed in a tree. She continued to wait, the uneasiness growing, then turned and walked back into the house.

The phone rang. A chill ran through her. She snatched it up, knowing it was bad news involving John.

"Hello?" She held her breath and waited.

"Is this Carolyn Fairchild?" The voice on the other end was male.

"Speaking."

"This is Paul Reid. I work with John."

"I remember you, Paul. What's wrong?"

"I'm so sorry. John might have suffered a heart attack. He collapsed on the loading dock a short while ago. They took him to the hospital in Aurora."

"Is he ... is he okay?"

"I don't know anything. Are you okay to get there yourself? Do you want me to have someone drive you over?"

"I'll drive myself."

"Please call me if there's anything I can do for you."

"Thank you." She ended the call and looked around the room, trying to orient herself.

Arnie. She dialled, praying Arnie would pick up.

"Carolyn?"

Thank God for call display. "Something's happened to John." She explained the situation and asked him to meet her at the hospital.

After she hung up the phone, she hurried upstairs to get her keys and purse. Afraid to feel, afraid she'd find out before she got there that it was already too late, she made herself go numb. She grabbed her purse and fumbled for her car keys, feeling as if she were moving in slow motion.

When she reached the door, she threw it open and slammed it shut behind her. She stopped when she was halfway down the stairs and ran back to lock the door. When that was done, she realized she'd forgotten to open the garage and had to unlock the door to press the button on the garage door opener. Then she slammed the door again, locked it, again, and headed back down the stairs.

She stepped into her car and started it up. Time was racing. She glanced at the clock on the dashboard. Too much time had passed. She had to get to John. Car in reverse, she looked behind her, making sure the driveway was clear. She backed out of the garage, trying to control the trembling in her hands.

She eased the car down the driveway and had to force herself to stop when she reached the bottom, reminding herself to check for oncoming traffic. She took a deep breath. It wouldn't help John if she got into a car accident trying to get to him. She said a prayer to her angels, asking them to help John and to protect her. Then she pulled onto the road and headed into town.

Twenty minutes later, she was walking through the doors into the hospital's emergency department. A triage nurse greeted her and directed her to get in line.

Carolyn shook her head. "No, please. My husband. He's here. They said he had a heart attack."

The nurse took her details and directed her to Laura, one of the volunteers, a grey-haired woman in a blue uniform, peering out a window embedded in a set of double doors. Carolyn followed Laura, who said the doctor would see her in the Family Room.

Perhaps Arnie had arrived already. Carolyn searched the Emergency area for him but didn't see him.

Everything was a haze. It occurred to her she should have sent John some Reiki. Never mind. She'd give him Reiki when she found him. She needed to find him and verify he was okay. Why did she have to go to this Family Room? Why couldn't she just see John? Was he in the Family Room?

They arrived at their destination, and the volunteer ushered her in. Chairs lined the perimeter, and a coffee table, covered in magazines, sat in the centre. A television, bolted to the wall, silently ran a newsreel. A crate of toys and children's books sat under the television. There was no hospital bed. No John.

Laura was saying something, but Carolyn couldn't hear her. A buzzing noise drowned out whatever the woman said. Carolyn tried to focus when Laura repeated herself and realized the volunteer was asking her if she'd like a coffee or something to drink. Carolyn shook her head.

Numbness spread through her. A roaring sound in her ears shut out everything else. She watched the volunteer's lips move some more but none of the words registered.

When would things become normal again? There had to be a mistake. She only had to wait, and John would come out and explain. Someone called her name, a man's voice.

John? Thank God. She turned to face him.

Arnie had arrived and stood by her side. How had he found her? It didn't matter. Why was it taking her so long to find John when Arnie found her so easily?

He took Carolyn by the elbow and said something to Laura, who nodded and touched his shoulder.

A man appeared. Nurse? Doctor? Yes, it was a doctor. He gave his name, but the buzzing drowned it out. The doctor's mouth moved. She thought he was saying sorry. Why was he apologizing?

Arnie hugged her, and she put her arms around him. The doctor was saying John didn't make it.

Carolyn frowned, confused. "He didn't make it? You mean he's not in the hospital?"

"Mrs. Fairchild, I'm sorry. I mean he died. We did everything we could to resuscitate him, but he passed away."

"No. I'd know. I want to see him. Where is he?" Her voice was getting shrill. She couldn't help it.

"He's in a room down the hall. Laura will take you to him, and you can have some time alone."

She wished the buzzing would stop so she could hear what people said. She put her hands to her ears. The fog was everywhere. Pain raced through her body. The smells from the hospital overwhelmed her.

Floral scents, sweet, pungent, cloying; disinfectant, bleach, soap, medicine, sweat, and grease, mingled, everything at once. The buzzing vanished. Something dripped somewhere, voices mumbled, carts crashed along the hall on rickety wheels, rattling, shaking, and noise from everywhere at once.

A spirit stood in the doorway of the Emergency room. He was confused, just starting to recognize he'd passed. His spirit-wife was trying to get his attention. In another room, a young man wearing a soldier's uniform, also in spirit, waited for his cancer-riddled mother to leave her body. Carolyn knew he had a couple of days waiting ahead of him, but his mother sensed he was there, and it comforted her.

Each life's thread passed into Carolyn's awareness and then out again, to be replaced by the cacophony of visions, smells, and sounds that drowned each other out and made everything a blur of confusion.

She hadn't put up any protection. As if struggling to climb out of a deep well, she silently called on Archangel Michael to come and clear her body and aura. She visualized a mirror ball of light growing out of and around her.

At once, the racket stopped and the pressure in her brain eased. The present, immediate noise and bustle of the hallway outside the room came to her ears. A muted odour of disinfectant replaced the other smells. Fog no longer obscured the doctor, and his voice came to her clear and final.

"If you like, we can call a priest or someone for you. Would you like the hospital chaplain to come over, or do you have a parish priest you'd like to contact?"

She shook her head. "I want to see my husband."

Arnie kept his arm around her, and they followed Laura through the corridors into a room where a single bed stood, machines hovering near the head of the bed. Someone moved out of her way when she walked into the room, and she only noted that a person had crossed her path. A haze in front of her eyes parted when she blinked, and she realized it was tears. She reached the bed and looked down at John.

His eyes were closed. His hair, the hair she'd thought needed cutting on Saturday morning, framed his face in a sticky mass. A blue blanket covered him up to his chin. He was white and pale, but he still looked like he might open his eyes and speak to her.

Carolyn went to him and stood next to his beautiful face. She put her hand on his cheek. She could feel his absence. It was too late to give him Reiki. There was no longer anyone there to send it to.

She looked over to the other side of the bed. That's where he was. He'd waited for her after all. He'd watched while they worked on him. She saw the whole thing as if through his eyes. His grandmother stood next to him. She'd come through and would help him cross. Thank God she'd come right away. He loved his grandmother and it would be comforting to him to have her take him home.

"Please, John. Why? Not yet. Not now." She didn't want him to go. She didn't want to make him stay. "It's okay," she told the space on the other side of the bed. "I want you to be okay."

The emptiness across the bed struck her, and she hung her head and sobbed.

Beside her, Arnie's body shook. He cried too, but quietly.

She turned and hugged him.

"He's gone," she said.

CHAPTER 18

After saying goodbye to Jess, Torque rushed out to his car before she could get up to leave. He opened the glove box. The TR was there, where Michael had set it after their last job. Should he do this now or wait another day or so?

If he waited, he risked Jess revealing the pregnancy to Michael. If he did it now, there'd be no taking it back. Soonest would be better though. Even if Michael somehow found out she carried a baby, it was better than having him get used to the idea of fatherhood and worrying about his kid's future.

From where Torque sat, he had an unobstructed view of the entrance to the doughnut shop. Jess wouldn't stay in there long. She had to get back to work too. For a moment, he considered that Michael might close himself off even more if his wife died, but then Torque dismissed that. He'd make sure Michael knew his best friend was there for him. Then it would be like it had been before the couple married, when Michael could come and go as he pleased and they worried only about themselves.

It was a time of freedom Torque wanted back. Michael should never have tied himself down to a committed relationship. Torque had never gotten involved seriously with any woman. In that regard, he completely understood Arnold Griffen.

Griffen's mistake was getting involved with married women or women who had boyfriends. It wasn't so much the morality of it Torque objected to as it was the personal repercussions. He wouldn't want to risk attracting attention from an angry boyfriend or spouse.

He checked his watch. He'd spent almost an hour with Jess. Surely, she'd leave the doughnut shop to head back to work soon. She worked nearby, so she'd be walking, and her route would take her past his car, though on the other side of the street.

There she was now.

How lovely she is. Too bad she has to be put down. If only she hadn't married Mick. Torque's gaze followed her as she walked to the intersection and pressed the button to cross on her side.

He held the TR up and aimed it at her head. The intersection was busy, but it wasn't anything he couldn't get around. He unlocked the TR.

She stepped onto the road.

He panned along with her while she crossed the street.

She neared the road's centre.

He flicked the button to turn on the weapon. For a second, she looked up and over. Their eyes met, and she smiled when she recognized his face.

Then the second passed, and she staggered, careening into the traffic going the other way. A car cutting into another lane struck her and flung her across the hood.

Opening the glove box, he dropped the TR into it and pulled away from the curb. He turned down a side street, away from the commotion at the intersection. He had to hurry back to the office to be there when his partner received the news about Jess. Michael would definitely need his best friend at his side for what was coming.

***

Michael sat on the couch in the living room of his home. He and Torque had returned from the hospital, where Michael had identified Jessica's body. He tried to grasp that it was really Jess lying there cold on the hospital bed, dead before he even arrived. Relieved that Torque had been there to drive him, Michael felt as if he'd been cut adrift.

He glanced at the DVD player to check the time. It read 4:43 PM.

On a normal day, he'd still be at the office, and Jess would arrive home at six o'clock. She'd make some dinner for them and wait for him to come home. When he didn't show, she'd eat alone. Then she'd wait for him to come home some more, and when he didn't show, she'd go to bed alone.

What had become the norm for Jess wasn't a happy life, and it was his fault. He never should have married her. Torque had warned him not to tie her to him, but Michael had believed—they'd both believed—that all they needed was to be together. For weeks now, he'd told himself each day that he'd come home and at least have dinner with her. Yet each day, when the time came, he'd remained at the office.

Half the time, it wasn't because he was too busy to come home. He'd been too nervous to face her. He was afraid she was ready to call it quits, and when it came to it, he didn't want her to leave him. But how do you tell someone you love her when you've been showing her day after day that you don't?

"Mick? Can I get you anything?"

Michael shook his head. "It's so empty here. I planned to make things up to her, you know."

"Yeah. It's rotten luck. She knew you loved her."

"I keep expecting her to call me to ask when I'm leaving work. She'd call me around this time every day. I always told her 'soon,' and I never meant it. She deserved better than that."

"It's not your fault. It's this business we're in. I don't know anyone who made it work whose spouse wasn't in the business too. You want me to stay here tonight and keep you company?"

Michael shrugged. "I'll be okay, but thanks."

"Listen, if during the night you can't cope, you call me. Jess meant a lot to me, too. She was a lovely person. I'm sorry she's gone. Perhaps we should consider, though, that she won't have to go through what's coming. She's safe now, from everything."

"Yeah. I guess that's one good thing, but I'd rather have her with me."

"Of course, but she's been spared a lot, and that's a consolation."

Michael said nothing. He stood up and went to the kitchen.

A glass sat on the counter where Jess had left it. She liked to reuse the same drinking glass during the day and would leave it on the counter in the morning when she went to work. Then she'd use it again when she came home, putting it into the dishwasher before going to bed.

He picked it up and studied it.

When he saw the faint smudge of her lip print on the edge, the thought he'd have to live without her now surged rage and fear through him. Tears threatened, and before they could flow, he wind-milled his arm over his head and smashed the glass to the floor.

Torque rushed into the room. "You okay? What happened?"

"I can't do it. I had no idea how much I depended on her to just be here. She can't be gone. I thought the worst thing in the world would be for her to leave me, to divorce me. But this? I never knew what the worst thing was until this."

"You don't think so right now, and I don't blame you, but it'll be okay. You need some time."

"This is what we're putting Carolyn Fairchild through."

"Don't go there. We can't do anything about that. She'll have to get through it too. They all will. They brought it on themselves. This wouldn't be happening to them if they weren't traitors to their country."

"How are they traitors? I see a bunch of UFO nuts who want the government to acknowledge what's happening to them. How does that make them traitors?" Michael's voice had risen and held a hysterical edge.

"You don't have the whole story. They're interfering with the Project. If they destroy what we're doing, then no one will survive what's coming. They'll ruin everything."

"What will they ruin? They won't be protected. They'll have nowhere to hide. How does it help them to protect the Project when the Project isn't in place to protect them?"

"No, it's in place to allow humanity to survive. Mick, there are limited spaces. We're protecting those we can."

"How the hell are these people traitors? You still haven't explained that to me. What have they done? What are the Fairchilds doing?"

"That's classified. You have to trust me. We don't randomly exterminate innocent people. Why are you questioning this?"

"I need to know we're doing the right thing. I joined the Agency because I wanted to serve my country. I left my country to join the Project up here because I wanted to serve the world. This was supposed to be for the good of all mankind. It smells like world domination."

"You're wrong. I'll see you through this and help with the arrangements for Jess. We'll take a couple of days and forget about what else we have to do. Jim understands.

"The targets are occupied with John's funeral. We'll get past the next couple of days and then go back to it. We'll get Arnie and Carolyn locked up at the Agency by the end of next week. If that doesn't scare Shelly and Steve into silence, then we'll take care of them, too, but only if it's necessary. Right?"

Michael nodded but couldn't think straight. He let Torque guide him back to the living room and onto the couch.

"I'll clean up the glass. You sit. Do you feel like eating something? I can order a pizza," Torque said.

The thought of food sickened Michael. He shook his head.

Torque went back to the kitchen, and Michael heard his partner open the closet door beside the stove and take out the broom and dustpan. Michael picked up the remote and turned on the television. He flipped through the channels without registering what was on the screen. It wasn't until the screen blurred that he realized he was crying.

The phone rang.

***

When the phone rang, Torque paused in his sweeping. "Want me to get that?"

"No, I got it." Michael shuffled over to the phone, picked it up, and said, "Hello."

Torque tried to listen as he swept glass into the dustpan, but Michael's voice was muffled. When Torque dumped the last of the debris from the dustpan into the garbage can, he heard Michael hang up the phone. Torque put the broom and dustpan away and hurried into the living room.

Michael stood by the phone, staring at it. His face contorted in an expression of grief worse than any Torque had seen on him yet today. The sight of it chilled him.

"Who was that? What happened?"

"She was pregnant." Agony dripped from every word.

Torque's bowels tightened. "Who told you that?"

"The doctor—from the hospital. He called to tell me what they believe happened. He said the heat and her pregnancy affected her. She became disoriented and stepped into traffic. When the car hit her, it shocked her system into heart failure. She was fucking pregnant. They said she was almost five weeks along. She never told me."

Torque went to Michael, took him by the arm, and walked him over to the couch.

"I'm so sorry. She should have told you. Maybe she was waiting for the right time."

"Yeah, and you know why she never found the right time? Because I wasn't here. She had something on her mind, and I thought it was that she wanted to leave me. She just wanted to tell me she was pregnant, and she was afraid to because she knew I didn't want to have a baby. I'm a cold son of a bitch, Torque. She didn't deserve to be treated like that. I didn't deserve her."

"We have someone you can talk to. Do you want me to ask Helen to set that up?"

"I don't need grief counselling. I appreciate everything you're doing, but I'd like to be alone now. I have to go to the funeral home tomorrow and make arrangements. Her family will be flying in from California. I can't wait to deal with her mother. She'll find a way to blame it all on me no matter what happened to Jess."

"I'll leave, but if you feel the need to talk or you want anything, call me. It doesn't matter what time it is."

"Okay. Thanks."

***

After Torque left, Michael wandered around the house, trying to figure out what to do. Jess had spent many hours alone in the house. He wondered how she could stand it. Now he was here by himself, all he could do was imagine her wandering around, waiting for him, but knowing he probably wouldn't show up until long after she'd gone to bed.

He went into his office and powered on the laptop, but as it booted up, he decided he didn't want to dig anymore. Torque was right. His obsession with the UFO group members was a waste of time. It was an excuse to stay away from home and Jess, and he didn't need that excuse anymore. He'd focus on quietly burying his beautiful Jessie, and the baby he'd never know, and then put all his energy into his work.

Arnold Griffen would soon find himself at the Agency.

CHAPTER 19

They were at Carolyn and John's—now just Carolyn's. The group alternated between hovering over her and keeping their distance. A pallid shock suffused them. Carolyn sat curled up in the corner of the big couch in her living room.

Flowers had already arrived. An enormous bouquet from John's workplace sat in the middle of the dining room table. Whenever she got an urge to vomit, she'd focus on the white lilies, roses, and carnations, and the purple delphiniums and irises, and the feeling would go away.

So far, she'd managed not to throw up, though once, she'd run into the bathroom, gagging. She didn't want to picture night after night without the man she'd loved for more than half her lifetime. Carolyn tried to push it from her mind because if she didn't, she'd go mad. How much time would it take to heal this wound? An eternity wouldn't be long enough.

"He wasn't old enough to have a heart attack," she said.

The others stared at her, brows wrinkled with concern. Had they also been thinking that, or was this news to them?

He was too young. He was barely forty.

The uneasiness from earlier returned. Something nagged at the back of her mind. Something was wrong that she couldn't identify. It wasn't just that her husband had suddenly dropped dead.

Arnie cleared his throat, and, his voice even and soft, said, "What happened, then?"

"I don't know," she admitted. "He had a physical recently and checked out fine. His cholesterol levels were okay, his blood pressure was okay ..."

"Sometimes people check out fine and then this happens. It's not fair, but it has happened before," Steve said. "But I'm not sure if that's true in John's case. He wasn't the most physically active guy, but he wasn't out

83

of shape either."

"Heart attacks don't run in his family," Carolyn said.

"So what happened? You don't think someone at work did something, do you?" Steve asked.

"No. The people at work respected him. No one there would've wanted to hurt him. I find it a little suspicious, though, that he dropped dead shortly after we posted that video and wrote those blog posts," said Carolyn. "If you remember, I was opposed to using the video camera Friday night." *I told you so.*

"Do you think someone killed him? There were people all around him. How can you orchestrate something like that? Do you think something was done to him on Friday night during the abduction?" Shelly asked.

"I don't know, but I asked them to do an autopsy. They resisted, but I pressed them to do it. I don't know how to prove this wasn't just a heart attack. Maybe Ralph's right and the government is after us," Carolyn said.

"Ralph is saying some weird shit though. He's talking reptilians. I've never seen lizard men anywhere, not any of the times I've been abducted, and not anywhere that wasn't on video. The videos on the Internet could be fakes," Arnie said.

"The reptilian theory might be too out there, but what if there's truth to some of the other stuff? Perhaps we should take a look at what he's said." She shuddered and wrapped her arms around herself.

"What do you propose to do?" asked Shelly.

"I want to talk to Ralph, but I won't try to go through Beth. I'll go to the hospital and get his doctor to let me see him."

"Want us to go along?" The kindness in Shelly's voice touched Carolyn.

"No. The doctor might let one or two of us in, but not all four. Arnie can come with me." She looked at Arnie.

"Of course I will, Carrie," he said.

She nodded, grateful. A lump grew in her throat and she bit her lip to stop the tears. He hadn't called her "Carrie" in years. She'd outgrown the name. Coming from Arnie now, it seemed more poignant than anything else they'd said to comfort her.

"Okay. Thank you. We'll go tomorrow." She fell silent, her thoughts returning to John. She hadn't felt John's presence since the hospital but might sense him when alone. "You guys don't have to hang around here. I'll be fine."

"I should go spend some time with my mother," Arnie said. "If you need me at all during the night, call me. I don't care what time it is."

"I promise." She gave the flowers another glance for reassurance.

Arnie stood up to leave and she hugged him, his cheek pressed against hers. Pulling herself away, she smiled at him, comforted.

He returned the smile and walked away. At the door, he waved to them and checked for the cat before he stepped outside.

She followed to watch him leave.

Arnie hurried down the stairs to his car. While he was getting in, Shelly and Steve stepped out onto the porch. Arnie waved to them one last time and backed out of the driveway.

**

At Arnie's appearance on the front porch, Michael called Torque. When Carolyn, Shelly, and Steve also stepped outside, Michael remained crouched behind the trees and spoke softly into the phone. "Don't move. He's not alone. Steve and Shelly are coming out behind him. We'll have to wait for a better opportunity."

"Okay," Torque answered. "He's planning to come back in the morning. We can probably get to him after he drops her off."

Shelly and Steve got in their car and reversed down the drive. Arnie was already gone. They pulled onto the road and drove away. Carolyn remained on the porch for a moment, then went inside and shut the door.

Michael watched the house, imagining Carolyn inside by herself. He wondered if she'd be able to sleep. Michael hadn't slept at all last night. He hadn't eaten much since Jess's death either.

He shook his head and remembered where he was. Torque would be wondering why he wasn't back at the car. He needed to focus on what they had to do. If he could get Arnie and Carolyn to the Agency cells, then he would take some time off. It was Tuesday now. Jessie's funeral was scheduled for Friday. All he needed to do was keep busy until then.

Cornell had suggested they let someone else handle Arnie and Carolyn, but Michael had a compulsive need to do it himself. Besides, if he were left alone at home he might go insane.

At least Carolyn has her daughter.

Michael rose from his hiding place and returned to the car.

CHAPTER 20

Shelly and Steve arrived at their apartment after a mostly silent drive. Steve sat on the couch in front of the television. Shelly suspected he wasn't seeing what was there since he kept randomly flicking from one channel to another. She'd parked herself on the edge of the loveseat diagonally across from the couch.

Should she continue to sit or get up and do something? Restlessness made her want to move, but instead, she sat and stared at her husband.

She tried not to think about what would happen now John was gone. His loss was like a hole in her heart, but she also felt twinges of jealousy. She couldn't get the idea out of her head that something would develop between Carolyn and Arnie. Carolyn was now free and single, and if she wanted to turn to Arnie for comfort, it shouldn't bother Shelly, but it did.

It irritated her that she couldn't stop thinking about him. She'd been planning to break it off with him anyway. This should make it easier for her. It's not as if he'd been faithful to her. She hadn't been faithful to him—she was married for God's sake.

When Arnie and Carolyn had hugged, Shelly's stomach had dropped a metre and then bounced up into her heart. She tried to shake it off. Carolyn was her friend. Arnie was, well, Arnie. He owed her nothing, certainly not fidelity.

No doubt, she was just projecting. Carolyn and Arnie had been friends for years, and nothing physical had ever developed between them.

Steve set down the remote. "We shouldn't go to any more sky watches for a while."

Taken aback, Shelly said, "Are you afraid?" It was the only explanation for Steve's pronouncement.

"It would be safer for us to lie low for a while. I don't care what Arnie wants to do. It's his crusade, not ours. We need to look out for ourselves."

"Okay." She wasn't opposed to keeping her distance for a while. "Do you want some tea?"

"Sure."

She sauntered into the kitchen and filled and plugged in the kettle. She set the teapot on the table, opened the fridge, and saw there wasn't any milk.

"I'm stepping out to the store. I can't have my tea without milk."

"All right."

She picked up her purse and took twenty dollars out, which she stuffed into the front pocket of her shorts. She'd walk. The sun was down, the heavy heat from the day easing up. She wouldn't be gone long. The store was nearby.

"I'll be back in a moment," she called out. "I'm not taking my keys." She verified her cell phone was hooked to her waist and headed for the door.

"Isn't it a little late for you to be going out by yourself?" Steve asked.

"What are you, my mother?" she said. "I'm just going down the street. I'll be back in twenty minutes."

"Okay. But you'd better hurry. Don't make me come after you."

She stepped into the hall and closed the door, her thoughts on Arnie again. How fun it was to spend time with him. He was a nice guy, attentive, a bit wild. If he were a one-woman man, he'd be perfect. She wondered how many other women had suffered over him, wanting him, but unable to have him. He was like a drug.

The elevator door opened when she reached it. She stepped in and pressed the 'G' button. She watched the floor numbers count down while the elevator descended. Her thoughts returned to Arnie.

She'd phone him tonight when Steve was asleep. Maybe he'd meet with her tomorrow afternoon, when Steve was at work and before she started her shift as a personal support worker at the old folks home.

The elevator reached the third floor and pinged open. A man stepped in, reached out to push a button, saw the glowing 'G,' and dropped his hand. Shelly didn't recognize him. Probably a visitor.

He looked young, twenty or so, but she couldn't be sure. The hood of his sweatshirt covered his hair and shaded his face.

Sweat pants and a sweatshirt? In this weather? He must be roasting.

At first, it confused rather than frightened her when he reached out and pressed the "Stop" button, causing the elevator to halt. Puzzlement turned to fear when he pulled out a knife. He shoved her against the back of the elevator and pressed the knife to her throat. The point stuck into her neck but didn't break the skin. She heard a whimpering sound and realized it came from her.

"Give me your money, bitch." He grunted.

She looked into his eyes. They were intense, frenetic.

"What are you staring at?"

"N-n-n-nothing." She tried to look away, but her gaze was frozen onto his.

"Give me your fucking money."

"Okay, okay. Please, don't hurt me. I'll give you everything I have." She stuck a hand into her pocket for the twenty dollars.

"Here." Her voice trembled. Her mouth was dry. The breath caught in her throat.

The man snatched the money out of her shaking hand. He leaned forward and kissed her on the mouth, forcing his tongue inside.

She wanted to resist, but feared what he'd do, so she kept her mouth still while he rolled his tongue around inside it.

He squeezed her breast, kneaded it.

She gagged, and he dropped his hand.

He glanced down at the bill she'd given him.

"That's not enough." He sliced the knife across her throat.

She gurgled and slid to the floor when her legs gave out. The pain took over. Her head dipped down, her chin dropping to her chest. A moan tried to escape her lips and failed.

The man started the elevator again.

By the time the doors opened, Shelly had stopped twitching, and the blood soaked her top and shorts. Everything faded to black.

CHAPTER 21

*T*he room reminds Michael of a hospital room—a private one from the look of it since there's only one bed. He ignores Jessica holding the baby in her arms and zeros in on the absence of a television.

"There's no TV."

She smiles. "I'll manage."

He scans his surroundings.

Three men in brown robes stand in the corner. They remind him of monks. Were they always there? They say nothing. They observe.

"How'd you get here?" he asks.

"I escaped."

"Is that our baby?"

"Yes. Don't worry. She won't be gone for long. You'll see her again."

"She? A girl?" He doesn't know what to make of that. His thoughts, ever since he'd found out about the baby, were of a little boy. Mike Jr., perhaps. Seems so silly now.

"Yes. She wants you to call her Christina. Tina."

He doesn't question the logic of that. "Of course. Are you okay? Why are you in the hospital?"

She flashes her beautiful smile, the one he fell in love with. He tries to savour the moment, but she speaks and the smile is interrupted.

"They said I need to rest. I wanted to tell you I was okay so they let me see you."

He searches for a place to sit. He wants to spend some time with her. There's no chair, so he stands in the doorway.

She came back, *his mind screams. Then it goes blank. He should ask the important questions but he can't remember what those might be.*

"You have to go. They won't let you stay here," she says.

"No. Jess. Please. I just got here. Please. Stay with me." He realizes

she's dead. She's here, but she's dead, and now she says she has to go. No. She said he *has to go. He won't. He'll stay. They can't make him leave. He just realized he was with her. He doesn't want to let her go again.*

"*No, Jess, please ...*"

Michael awoke, his face moist from sweat and tears, and he regretted he hadn't run to her and held her. Why had he just stood there? It was only a dream, but he ached for her. He'd felt her with him. He rolled over and tried to go back to sleep. If he dreamed it again, he'd put his arms around her and squeeze her tight. The thought that he'd missed an opportunity made him want to scream or punch something.

He lay in bed, but after fifteen minutes of rolling around, he admitted he couldn't sleep. The clock read 1:43 AM. A whole two hours of sleep tonight—a record these days. He sat up and turned on the light, automatically looking over to Jessie's side of the bed.

Still empty.

***

Carolyn awoke in the middle of the night to the ringing of the telephone. *Arnie.* She answered it, but he gave her no chance to speak.

"Something's happened to Shelly."

"What? Is she okay?" But she knew the answer before he said another word.

"She's dead."

"No, no, no, no." It spilled out of her in a screaming flood.

Over the phone, Arnie shouted her name.

The thought came to her that she should tell him to stop before he woke his mother. Through choked sobs, she said, "What happened?"

"I spoke to Steve's brother. Shelly was found stabbed to death in the elevator in their building. It looks like a mugging."

"A mugging? Their building has security. How'd a mugger get in?"

"They think he buzzed apartments until someone let him in. Or he was a guest. It was a crime of opportunity. He took her money. Steve's brother said she didn't have any money when they found her. Maybe she resisted."

Carolyn knew. "She didn't resist. She gave him money. It wasn't enough."

Arnie didn't comment on that. "There's something more." He paused.

"What?" She held her breath.

"Steve said he doesn't want us contacting him again. He's afraid it's because of the UFO group that Shelly was killed. He doesn't believe it was a mugging."

90

"That's ridiculous. We should go to him."

Arnie sighed. "When I talked to Steve's brother, he told me Steve's a basket case. He can't handle this, especially after what happened to John. We haven't even had John's funeral yet, and this happened to Shelly. Ralph was institutionalized. It's got to be more than a coincidence. Do you want me to come over and stay the rest of the night with you?"

"No, thank you. I'll manage. I don't want to make you leave your mom," Carolyn said, though she wished she could ask him to come.

"Are you sure? The nurse will return first thing in the morning. I can leave a note for her," Arnie replied.

"I'm sure. Come over when the nurse arrives. We'll have breakfast together; though, I don't know how much I'll feel like eating. Get some sleep."

"Okay. I'll call you when I'm on my way."

She hung up the phone, dazed.

Shelly was gone. It couldn't be true. How could this have happened? Friday they were all together, enjoying each other's company and looking forward to an evening of watching the stars.

Then it all fell apart.

Knowing she wouldn't be able to sleep, Carolyn got out of bed and went to sit on the back balcony. Everything was quiet, no traffic noises, just crickets.

A deer cried, off in the woods. It sounded like a baby. Tired, but alert, she pulled her feet up onto the chair and hugged her knees to her chest. The air was warm, moist, and fragrant. It felt nice to be outside in only her sleep shirt and panties.

She wished she could go to Steve. Her heart ached for Shelly and John. Shelly was so cute, like a pixie. How could anyone hurt her?

Shelly, where are you? Can you hear me? Are you out there somewhere? She was able to connect to departed loved ones—it's what she did as a medium. For some reason, though, she found it harder to connect to people she loved than to connect to strangers.

Carolyn realized she was crying again and swiped the tears off her face. The prospect of morning and what it would bring scared her. She'd have to deal with the funeral parlour and try to talk to Steve to tell him it wasn't their fault. She'd have to visit Ralph.

It wasn't their fault. John's death was, but not Shelly's. However, she had no proof. The autopsy would be performed on John the following day, but she was sure they wouldn't find anything. The doctors expected he died of a heart attack, and they'd see only evidence of a heart attack.

She sensed a presence.

CHAPTER 22

The balcony was empty though Carolyn felt she wasn't alone. She peered inside through the sliding screen door. Nothing moved. She forced herself to relax, trying to get a feel for who it might be. A figure stood to her left, barely there. She could see one of the chairs through it.

A tall male, hands at his sides, stared at her. *John?*

Before the opportunity slid away, she said, "I love you, John."

A wash of warmth, flowing from the figure, spread love over and through her. Her heart ached to touch him, but just seeing him reassured her.

"What can I do to help you?" she asked, but the figure disappeared. If he wanted to tell her anything about how he died, it wouldn't be tonight. Perhaps he'd return. She wished Shelly would also come to her.

Shelly is with Steve tonight. Yes, of course.

Did Steve know Shelly was still with him? Perhaps he sensed it, but he wasn't a believer. He might brush off any intuitive feelings and write them off as manifestations of his grief.

She stood. Her heart was lighter now than at any time since she'd received the news of John's death. What a relief to know he wasn't completely gone. There'd be many days when she'd question whether she'd seen him tonight, but right now, she knew she had.

Carolyn returned to her bedroom. She could probably sleep now. In bed, she closed her eyes and put her hands on her thighs, palms down. Reiki flowed into her body. After a while, she drifted off to sleep.

***

Michael woke to the insistent beeping of his cell phone. He must have slept through the initial call, probably because by the time he'd fallen asleep, it was around 4:00 AM. His alarm clock said 6:11 AM. He checked to see who'd called. *Torque*. At 5:06 AM. He called his partner back without listening to the message.

"What's up?" Michael said when Torque answered. "You called at the crack of dawn. No wonder I slept through it."

"Shelly Rudolph is dead."

"What do you mean? Did you do something?"

"Of course not. She was stabbed to death during a mugging, but her friends are speculating that it was wet work by the government. Cornell was furious. He'd jumped to that conclusion too and thought we'd gone ahead without taking care of Griffen and Carolyn Fairchild first."

"So it's a coincidence?" Michael asked. He tried to process Torque's news. "What does it mean? I just woke up, so bear with me."

"It means we leave Griffen alone today. We'll see what this does to their little group." After a pause he said, "Then there were three."

"Did Cornell suggest we stay away from Griffen?" Michael asked.

"We both agreed it would be for the best—at least until the dust settles from this Shelly thing."

"Okay. I'll be at the office in an hour." Michael set the phone down on his night table and got out of bed. It was going to be a long day.

* * *

By 6:30 AM, Arnie was knocking on Carolyn's door. She greeted him wearing a short, light housecoat over what could be a nightshirt. Even under the circumstances, he appreciated the sight of her legs.

"I'm so glad you're here," she said when she opened the door. She threw her arms around his neck and hugged him.

He hugged her tightly and kissed her cheek. "Are you okay?"

"Yes." She released him, and he stepped inside. She closed the door. "I managed to get a little sleep. I've put coffee on. Are you hungry? I can make some toast or eggs for you. I'll have a protein shake, if you'd like that instead."

"Shake's good. I don't have much of an appetite this morning. That will at least keep me going. Gonna be a long day," Arnie said.

He felt it weighing on him, making him tired and heavy. Perhaps it was the lack of appetite. He hadn't wanted to eat much lately. His mother nagged him about it, which made him more frustrated and further curbed his appetite. He'd been glad to get away to Carolyn's this morning, and his mother cheered up when he told her he was going for breakfast at a friend's place.

"Yeah, I'm dreading it. Making the arrangements will be difficult," Carolyn said.

They went into the kitchen, and she pulled out her bullet blender. "Chocolate, berry, or vanilla?"

"Chocolate," he said.

She prepared the shakes and then he followed her into the living room. They sat at opposite ends of the sofa.

"What time is your daughter arriving from school?" he asked.

"I'm not sure. She's coming with a friend. I suggested to her that she stay at her friend's place while she's here. Sam shouldn't be around here while we're afraid our UFO activities are causing harm to people. I told her I'd be occupied. Are you okay to hang out while I shower?"

"Yeah, no problem. I'll do some work on my laptop," he said.

She fell silent and then said, "Thanks for being here."

"It's no problem. John was my friend—one of the few I hadn't pissed off."

There was a moment of discomfort while they both considered why Arnie didn't have many male friends. Carolyn smiled at him, dispelling the awkwardness.

"You've got a good heart, Arnie." She turned and headed to the shower.

He carried their blender cups to the kitchen and rinsed them. He'd have at least an hour before she was ready. He went out front to the patio and looked around. It was another hot day though better than yesterday. Perhaps the heat wave would ease up. Some rain might be nice.

He went to his vehicle, an emerald green sports car. He was proud of it and loved how it impressed people, men and women. It was amusing to drive his little old mother around in it. She didn't like getting in and out of it, and she chastised him about how frivolous it was, but she seemed pleased he could afford luxuries.

Arnie removed his laptop from the trunk at the front of the car and returned to the house. He booted the laptop up on the dining room table. He'd established a connection to the home's WIFI years ago and connected automatically to the Internet.

Forty minutes later, he posted a blog in honour of John and Shelly. He accused the government of silencing them for wanting to get acknowledgment and help for abductees and for having too much knowledge about covert government dealings with UFOs. He also stated he was afraid for his own safety and the safety of the other members of his UFO group, though he didn't mention any names.

The sound of a car pulling up the driveway made him get up and look out the living room window. He didn't recognize it. It parked and the occupants stepped out. The driver, an olive-complexioned young man in his early twenties, paused to admire Arnie's car. A young blonde woman appeared next to the young man, and she smiled when she recognized the vehicle. She was the spitting image of her mother though she was a much flashier dresser. Samantha Fairchild was home.

Sam bounded up the stairs to Arnie when he stepped outside to meet her. "Oh, Arnie." She threw herself into his arms.

"I'm so sorry, Sam."

She sobbed against his chest, and he held her for a moment longer. He glanced at the young man and eased Sam away. Arnie held her by the shoulders and looked into her eyes.

"I thought you were going to meet us later? How did you get here so fast?"

"We left before dawn. I couldn't sleep and wanted to be with my mom. I can't believe this happened. Dad was fine when I saw him at Easter."

"I know. It shocked us all. How are you holding up? I'm glad you have a friend with you."

Sam smiled. "Arnie, this is Jack. We're in the same program at school. He's been great since I found out about my dad. At least school is finished for the summer. I only had to take time off work to come here."

The two men shook hands, and then Arnie turned back to Sam. "Your mom will be happy to see you."

He opened the door and ushered them into the house, Sam swishing in behind him, rattling bracelets and beads as she walked. Jack stepped in last and closed the door.

"Your mom's getting dressed," Arnie said. "The funeral will be on Saturday. We're waiting for some of your dad's family to arrive. They'll be staying with your mom's folks in Toronto."

Sam walked into the living room, waving Jack in after her. "Why did she sound as if she didn't want me to come to the house?" she asked, dropping onto the couch.

"She wanted to make sure you had a friend to lean on in case she was distracted with all the stuff she has to get done."

"She sounded afraid. Is it true her friend Shelly is dead too?"

"Yes. They say it was a mugging. We're not so sure."

"What else would it be?"

"It's complicated. Have you been reading my blog?"

"The UFO thing? Yes. I think you're being a little paranoid. Dad died of a heart attack. He didn't look like he had heart problems, but that's why they call it the silent killer. Shelly's mugging was a coincidence. Mom told me she was taking the elevator down by herself at night."

"They live in a security building in a good part of town."

"It can still happen. Wouldn't the security cameras have picked up something?"

"I'm assuming they did, but I don't know what's happening with the investigation. Steve cut us off. He's afraid it's connected to our UFO experience the other night and I agree."

"Is my mom in danger?" Sam's voice dropped to a whisper.

"I don't know. We might all be in danger."

"That's crazy," Jack said. "What would the government want to go killing people for? It doesn't make sense. They wouldn't be able to get away with that."

"You're wrong," Arnie said. "They do it and they get away with it."

"Arnie!" Carolyn walked into the room. "Shelly died in a random mugging. She was in the wrong place at the wrong time. I know it. Please don't scare the kids. They have enough to deal with right now."

"I'm sorry, but I don't agree, and they should know what's going on."

"You've told them. Now let's talk about something else. Please. Sam, honey, I'm so happy to see you." She went to Sam, who rose to let her mother hug her.

"I'm glad to be home. Are you okay?"

"I'm fine. I'm glad you're here."

"I dropped off my things at Vanna's. She asked me to spend the night. Jack can drive me over after we go to the funeral home. Will you be okay here? Do you want me to stay with you instead? I figured I'd come back tomorrow."

"Don't worry about me. I can call Arnie if I need anything."

"Maybe you shouldn't be alone tonight, Carr. Why don't you have Sam and her friends stay here?" Arnie said.

A flash of fear crossed Carolyn's face. "No. I'll be fine." Her tone was abrupt. Then her face softened, and she said, "I'll be getting ready for the funeral all day. Everyone will be coming back here afterward, so I have cleaning and shopping to do, too. It'll keep me busy."

"I can keep you company if you want," said Arnie.

She hesitated and said, "I don't mind being alone. I feel more connected to John when I'm alone." She met Arnie's gaze. "Did you get any work done?"

"Yes. Which reminds me, I'd better pack it up." He went to the dining room table and began to power down his laptop.

***

In Toronto, Jim Cornell finished reading Arnie's blog post ten minutes after it went live. Cornell's ulcer gnawed and burned his stomach. He reached for his phone and dialled Torque.

"Muniz here."

"It's time for you to move on Griffen. Enough is enough. If Valiant isn't up to it, grab Carlyle and take him with you. I want this guy gone."

CHAPTER 23

Carolyn waited for Arnie to park the car in front of her garage door before she spoke. She'd stewed in silence ever since they'd left the funeral parlour. He'd either assumed she wanted to be left alone or didn't realize she was stewing about him.

"Thanks for everything, Arnie."

"You're welcome. Do you want me to come in?"

She paused, considering how to say what she had to say. "I saw what you posted this morning. While we were at the funeral home, I received an email message on my phone from one of my clients who follows your blog. You should've told me you were going to post about John and Shelly."

She decided to be upfront about it. He meant no harm, and he'd shown kindness to her and supported her ever since John died, but his actions continued to put them at risk, and he had to stop.

"I only spoke the truth."

"Shelly was mugged. What you did puts the rest of us in more danger."

"No, it doesn't. The more we publicize it, the safer we'll be."

"I don't agree, and you should've at least warned me you were going to do that. It involves John and me. I should have a say in what goes up on the Internet about us."

"Don't tell a journalist what to print."

"You're not a journalist. You're running a blog site, and I'm your friend. That post shouldn't have gone public. Take it down. Hopefully, it's not too late. You could cause a lot of trouble for us. Can't we at least get through John's funeral?"

"I love you, Carr. You're one of my best friends. You're my only female friend. I'd do anything for you, but I'm not going to let them get away with this. They have to be stopped."

"What you're doing is making them want to stop us, not the other way around. Take it down. Please."

Arnie changed his strategy. "Shelly didn't deserve to die the way she did."

"No, she didn't. What does that have to do with you putting up the blog?"

"People need to know her death wasn't random. She was executed."

"She wasn't executed—not the way you mean it." Carolyn wanted to shake him.

"It's an awfully big coincidence that she was killed right after John died, right after our UFO incident."

"That you went public with even though I warned you not to."

"Are you saying it's my fault John and Shelly are dead? You agreed to let me post it. Or are you forgetting our conversation at Brent's office?"

"No, it's my fault too. I let you and John talk me into it against my better judgement, and you contributed to getting us all on their radar. They didn't execute Shelly though."

"John and Shelly are martyrs. They were murdered for what they believe and for going public about it." Arnie scowled, and his voice rose.

"John and Shelly didn't go public. You did. If it's a government conspiracy, why haven't they silenced you?"

"They silenced Ralph. If I don't shine a spotlight on myself so the world sees what happens to me, then if I'm next, no one will notice."

"That's an interesting perspective, but it'll make them work harder to silence all of us. Do you think they care if it looks suspicious? Many suspicious deaths have been attributed to the government. No one has ever proven anything." Carolyn continued, matching him shout for shout. "You're painting a target on our backs. I can't let anything happen to me. Sam is down to one parent."

"It'll be fine. I didn't mention you. What happened to John and Shelly shouldn't be allowed to happen to anyone else. Ralph, too. He didn't go into that hospital on his own."

She jumped on that. "You're not going to write about Ralph now, are you?"

"I might."

She sighed, and when she spoke again, fatigue filled her voice. "Please. Leave them alone. Take down this morning's post. I wish I'd seen it earlier. There's no telling who has read it by now. What will Steve say? He's already mad at us. This'll make things so much worse between us, especially between you and Steve."

Arnie didn't reply. When she opened her mouth to speak again, he quietly said, "I'll consider taking down the post. I'm not promising anything. It needs to be said, but there's something else I need to tell you. I don't want to cause Steve any more pain, but I was having an affair with Shelly."

Carolyn recoiled. "How could you? Steve is your friend."

"I know how it sounds, how it looks. She came to me. That time we all went camping, and I forgot the power inverter? Did you notice she'd been flirting with me? When everyone went to bed, she came to me. Before I knew what was happening, we were making out. I never meant for anything to happen with her. We were friends for years, and I stayed away the whole time. But *she* came to *me*."

"And you couldn't say 'no'?" Then the timing of it dawned on her. "You've been having an affair for almost two years?"

"I'm sorry. I always end up hurting the people I care about. I don't know why I do this. I try, but I can't stop myself," Arnie said. "I didn't want to tell you about Shelly and me, but now she's gone, what should I do? Steve won't talk to us. Ralph won't talk to us. That hurts. Especially after losing two of my close friends in a couple of days. And I'm sure it wasn't a coincidence. If you turn your back on me now, I don't know what I'll do."

Carolyn sighed. "I'm upset with you, I'm angry with you—and with Shelly, too, to be honest. It was her responsibility too. She betrayed her husband." Then it occurred to her that Steve was oblivious. "Steve doesn't know, does he?"

"No," Arnie said. "He has no idea."

"Keep it that way. It'll hurt Steve if you decide to clear your conscience. Let him keep the good memories of his marriage."

He nodded. "Are you and me okay?" He gazed at her, his eyes pleading.

Her heart skipped a beat.

"I won't abandon you. It's not as if I don't know who you are. You should talk to a professional, though, since you're willing to admit this behaviour causes problems in your life. What do you think John would've done if Shelly had thrown herself at him? Don't you think he would've turned her down and suggested she work on her marriage? Somehow, you always manage to find a way to justify infidelity."

Arnie shrugged. "If it makes you happy, I'll do whatever you want."

Carolyn sighed again. "Don't do it to make me happy. Do it to make your life better. Do it for you."

He stared at her, a woebegone expression on his face.

You'd think I'd just asked him to moon the Pope. "It's okay. I'll help you through it. You need to get counselling. See Brent."

He nodded but didn't speak.

She wasn't sure if his silence meant agreement or disagreement, so she hugged him and said, "I have to go now and call people about the funeral."

"Okay. Can I visit you later?" he asked.

"Of course. Give me a call to make sure I'm here. I'm free for the next few days. I've rescheduled my clients for after the funeral. Most of them plan to come to the visitation, the funeral, or both, anyway."

She leaned over and kissed him on the cheek.

He smiled and took her hand. "I'll come back later, and we'll figure out what to do."

She got out of the car and walked toward her front porch. Something made her turn back and watch as his car backed out of the driveway. She had an urge to run after him and stop him. She tried to shake it off, and when the feeling of fear intensified, she took a few steps after him and called out his name.

Arnie, his head turned away from her, didn't notice. His car backed into the street, and he pulled away without looking at her.

She considered calling him and telling him to come back. She took out her cell phone and stared at it, trying to both talk herself into calling him and into not calling him.

He had to get home to spend time with his mother. He'd probably say she was being hysterical. She might be worrying for no reason. But he might really be in danger. She dialled his number.

His voicemail kicked in. When the beep sounded, she said, "It's Carolyn. Be careful. Don't trust anyone. Call me when you get home."

Feeling better, she turned off her phone and went inside. The cat trotted up and meowed at her. She followed him into the kitchen and dropped some cat treats into his bowl.

"I'm glad you're here, Fox. This place is so empty. Not even a spirit around to keep me company right now." She smiled at the cat, then stood up and went into the living room. She picked up the phone and dialled Steve's number.

"Hello?" It was Ryan, Steve's brother.

"Hi, Ryan. It's Carolyn. I'm so sorry about what happened to Shelly. How are you holding up?"

"I'm managing, but Steve isn't. Did Arnie tell you he doesn't want contact with any of you?"

"He did, but I was hoping that was just the grief talking. We're his friends. I want to talk to him. Shelly was one of my best friends. We need each other right now."

"That's not how Steve feels about it. I'll ask him for you, but don't be offended if he won't talk to you. He's a wreck. Wait a moment, okay?"

"Thanks."

She could hear Ryan speaking to Steve. The conversation was

muffled, but she could tell Steve was arguing with Ryan. Soon, he came back on the line.

"Carolyn?"

"I'm here."

"I'm sorry. He blames the group for her death. It sounds crazy to me. I doubt the government would do something like that, but Steve is sure none of this would've happened if you guys hadn't publicized the footage from Friday's sky watch. Give him some time. Please respect his wishes and don't come to the funeral. He won't be attending John's either, though he says to tell you he's sorry for your loss."

"Ryan, please. He's wrong. It was a mugging. It had nothing to do with the UFO group. Tell him."

"I'm sure you're right, but Steve believes otherwise, and the police haven't arrested anyone. Right now, what he believes is what matters. Please respect that and don't call him anymore. I'm sorry about John. We all hope you're able to heal from it. Goodbye."

The line went dead before she could respond.

Carolyn stood in the living room, tears falling. She dialled Arnie again to tell him about it. There was no answer. She hung up without leaving another message.

CHAPTER 24

Michael and Torque sat in Torque's car, watching Arnie's empty parking spot in the underground garage of his condo building. Torque chewed on a chocolate bar and sipped on a takeout coffee. Michael had brought his thermos of coffee and was working his way through it.

"You know, if he doesn't hurry up, I'm going to have to take a piss," Torque commented.

"Maybe he's gone back to Carolyn's. We should've watched for him there," Michael said.

"He'll be back. They only went to the funeral parlour, and he'll have to check on his mother at some point."

"I think it's a bad idea to snatch him. Did Cornell discuss it with you?" Michael asked. "He didn't explain anything to me."

"No. No doubt it'll scare the shit out of the other two, but we gotta do what we gotta do," Torque replied.

"Sometimes it would be nice to know why we have to do what we do."

"No one is indispensable. You know that. Do your job, keep your head down, and survive. That's it."

"Interesting. What if I want to thrive and not just survive?" Michael insisted.

"You are thriving, smartass. You get paid very well."

"Maybe money's not everything."

"Be grateful the Agency values you enough to make sure you survive what's coming. If it can't be prevented, and it's impossible for everyone to live through it, I'd think you'd be happy you're one of the animals making it onto the Ark."

Frowning, Michael turned his face away from his partner and stared at the empty parking space. Arnie had a good job, made a decent living, and

102

was making a crusade out of exposing the UFO conspiracy, probably in the name of justice, perhaps to give meaning to what he experienced.

Michael had always thought that his job at least had a valuable purpose, something that made the body count justifiable. He was starting to see the mould growing on his slice of cheese. Torque was right: Michael needed to ally himself with those in power if he wanted to survive the coming cataclysm, but was it worth the price of his soul?

Daylight splashed in when the garage door opened. Both men stared at the entrance. Arnie's car crept in, gingerly stepping over the speed bumps.

"Ready?" Torque asked.

Michael slipped on a pair of gloves and loosened the revolver in his holster. He patted his jacket pocket, verifying the kit with the hypodermic was there. He nodded.

Arnie pulled his vehicle into its parking spot. Before he finished putting it into park, the two agents were walking toward him. The engine shut down, and he picked up his cell phone. He fiddled with it and stuck it to his ear, probably picking up his voice mail messages. After listening for a moment, he turned off his phone and opened his car door.

Torque gripped Arnie's arm and hauled him from the car.

"Don't move, asshole," Torque said. He shoved a gun into the software developer's ribs.

Reflexively, Arnie cried out and said, "What the fuck?"

Michael snatched the car keys from Arnie's hand and glanced around to make sure they were still alone. No one was in view.

"Keep to the left and walk to that car over there," Michael said, indicating Torque's car with a head tilt. If they hugged the wall, they'd avoid appearing on the surveillance cameras. He handcuffed Arnie's hands behind his back, and when they reached the car, Torque opened the trunk.

"Get in."

"Are you serious?" Arnie scanned the area, perhaps seeking help, perhaps looking for someone he knew to jump out and tell him it was all a joke.

"We're the guys you keep warning people about," Michael said. "Congratulations. You were right. Now get in the trunk. We don't have to kill you, but we can if you don't cooperate." He was lying. They were not allowed to kill him no matter what, but Arnie didn't need to know that.

Michael removed Arnie's cell phone from the clip at his side and shoved it into the pocket of his own pants.

"Get in the trunk. Now."

Arnie's gaze darted around again, but he climbed into the trunk and

Torque shoved him down. Michael pulled the kit out of his pocket, opened it, and injected Arnie with the hypodermic needle. His eyes closed, and he sagged into the trunk.

Torque closed the lid with a gentle slam, then went to the driver's side of the car and opened it. Before climbing in, he said, "Follow me. Make sure you keep to the speed limit. Enjoy driving that car."

Michael returned to Arnie's car, got in, and adjusted the driver's seat and mirror. He waited for his partner to pull out ahead of him and then shifted into reverse to inch out of the parking spot.

Arnie's phone vibrated against his thigh, and he took it out to see who was calling. *Carolyn.* Michael shut off the phone, turned on the radio, and flipped through the channels until he found the rock station. He settled in for a long drive.

Two hours later, both cars drove down a dirt road on the outskirts of Peterborough. Torque pulled into a wooded area, skirting "Road Closed" and "Detour" signs. They followed the road for a few kilometres to where it dead-ended at a deserted gas station. Construction equipment lay abandoned along the road, indicating recent activity. The gas pumps were off, the buildings dark and lonely.

Torque pulled his car to the side of the road and stepped out. Michael parked next to the pumps. He stepped from the car, giving it a wistful glance. It was a shame to have to destroy such a high-end vehicle. He strolled over to his partner, who was putting on a pair of gloves.

"Sure we can't keep Arnie's car and torch yours?"

"Very funny," Torque said. "Stay here. I'll be right back." He ran to the lone building, used a key to open the padlock hanging on the door, and stepped inside. A few minutes later, he returned, a full body bag slung over one shoulder. He motioned Michael to open the sports car's door. Michael obeyed and stood aside.

Torque set the body down next to the car and unzipped the body bag. He beckoned Michael to give him a hand, and together they removed the body, which felt like ice from the storage freezer. The dead man was close in height and weight to Arnie though he looked nothing like him. That wouldn't matter when they were finished.

After about twenty minutes of fiddling, they'd set the stage. The body sat in the driver's side of the car, and they'd drenched the body and the interior of the car with gasoline. It would appear as if Arnie had committed suicide by setting himself on fire and driving his car into the gas pumps.

Dental imprints taken from Arnie would go to the coroner to use in his report to positively identify the body. Since the coroner worked for the Agency, he'd list it as a suicide.

Michael stepped away from the car. The smell of gas overpowered every other scent.

"Back your car away, and get your netbook connected to the network so we can crack into the car's computer system," he said to Torque. "Get ready to peel out when it hits the pump."

With a nod, Torque returned to his car. He fiddled with the netbook, and when it was ready, he waved Michael over and handed it to him.

In less than ten minutes, Michael had control of Arnie's vehicle. He opened the driver's door, holding his breath against the assault from the fumes that wafted out. He put the car in gear, lit a match, and tossed it in. It ignited with a woof, and he slammed the door shut. He ran to Torque's vehicle and jumped in.

Flames licked the interior of the sports car.

"Back off. We're still too close," Michael said.

Torque reversed another fifteen metres while Michael used the netbook to hurtle Arnie's car backward.

The crash mangled the back end and shoved the gas pump off its island. The ground shook when the car exploded. Torque drove to the road, and they watched the flames flare upward, black smoke pluming into the sky.

"Okay, let's go," Michael said. "It won't take long for this to attract attention." He ripped off his gloves and threw them in the back seat.

"Yup," Torque agreed and spun the car around. "Arnold Griffen has ceased to exist."

He drove along the dirt road toward the highway at an easy pace. Behind them, they heard an explosion and more black smoke poured into the sky.

"That was a good one," Torque commented, glancing into the rear-view mirror. "Want to hit a fast-food joint after we drop Griffen off at the Agency? I'm hungry."

"Sure."

Torque met Michael's gaze and grinned. "And then there were two."

CHAPTER 25

*Y*ou've reached Arnie Griffen. I'm unable to take your call ...

Carolyn hung up before the beep. She'd called so many times already that leaving a message was pointless. Why wasn't he picking up? Why didn't he call her back?

He might have fallen asleep or put it on silent so he could get some work done, but they'd planned to try to see Ralph, and she still wanted to do that. Now more than ever she needed to talk to their institutionalized friend and learn what had happened to him.

She sat on the couch in her living room, staring at the phone and willing it to ring, to be Arnie on the other end, to have something turn out all right. Unease slicked her skin with sweat that trickled down the small of her back. The phone rang, startling her. She checked the call display. Arnie's home number flashed on the screen. *Thank God.*

She grabbed the phone, pressed the "Talk" button. "Arnie?"

"No," a female voice replied. "It's Beverly—his mom's nurse. I can't reach him. Can you tell me where he is?"

"I'm sorry. I thought he was heading home when he left here earlier. That was hours ago. Has he contacted you at all since this morning?" Carolyn asked.

"No, and I'd like to go home. This isn't like him, and, to be honest, I'm worried. He checks in with me regularly to make sure his mother is okay and to let me know his ETA. When he left this morning, he said he'd be gone most of the day, but it's getting on night now, and he should've called."

"Let's give him a little more time," Carolyn said. "It's seven o'clock. If he's not back by nine o'clock, we'll call the police."

"Have you tried calling his office?"

"Yes. A couple of times, but I don't want to panic and call the cops if he's out with one of his women."

106

"If it were that, he'd at least pick up his messages and call back."

"I doubt he's with a woman, anyway. I'll tell him to contact you if I hear from him."

"Thanks."

They ended the call.

Where was he? She could try remote viewing. She went up the stairs to the den and lay down on the couch. A short while ago, Arnie had lain there, after the extraterrestrials had returned him to the house. She still felt his energy.

Carolyn closed her eyes and tried to focus on him, to sense his vibration, to receive information about where he was. She saw only darkness and felt nothing. The harder she tried, the less likely she'd be to get anything, so she forced herself to relax. She deepened her breathing, let thoughts come in, acknowledged them, and let them go.

I should call Sammie ... Ralph, does Ralph know what's been happening? ... Call Beth ... Arnie, focus on Arnie ... tell me about Arnie ...

The darkness, everything was darkness. She breathed deeply and let calm spread from the top of her head down to her toes. When her body released all her tension, she drifted off to sleep.

Carolyn stokes a woodstove's fire in a three-room log home. She wears a long dress and an apron. Someone knocks on the door.

She heads toward it, but before she can reach it, the door flies open. The little girl from next door bursts into the room, bonnet hanging down her back, dark braids coming apart, and dress dirty and torn. Tears carve a grimy streak down her pale face.

"What is it?" Fear wells up inside Carolyn.

"They took my mama," the little girl says. "They said she's a witch. Please, help me."

Carolyn runs outside. A trail winds away from her house, and she looks across the cornfield to the road. Men in a horse and buggy are heading to her house. They're coming for her.

"Into the house, quickly," she tells the girl, Jamie. "They want us, too."

She closes the door, desperately looking for a place to hide. She opens a closet door. Piles of clothes and blankets sit, neatly folded, on the floor. She pushes them aside. "Get in here. Stay very still and don't make a sound. Maybe they won't find you."

Jamie whimpers, but she does as she's told. Carolyn throws blankets over her and closes the door. The girl will be frightened of the dark, but it's the only option. They're already at the door, and she has no time to hide. They burst into the room.

The first man through the door approaches her. He looms over her.

She stares at him, trying to figure out who he is, why he seems so familiar. He has black hair, an aquiline nose, and full lips.

It isn't until the second man steps through the door that the terror surges through her. This man reeks of hatred and the pleasure he derives from torturing and killing. The first man grabs her and holds her in a bear hug.

She struggles and screams.

He clamps a hand over her mouth. "Silence, witch. You have no power anymore. Time for you to burn."

He drags her to the horse and buggy, which turns out to be a horse pulling a rickety cage on wheels. Arnie is in there. Carolyn knows the prisoners are all similar to her. They all can sense things, but some of them don't know that yet. The men want them for their powers.

Arnie lies naked on the bottom of the cage. He's so still that, for an instant, she fears he's dead. Then she spots the slow rise and fall of his chest. His skin looks raw and red, as if burned. A thin, gritty coating of something she can't recognize covers his body.

"Bring that one here," the other man shouts, pointing at a young woman huddled in the corner of the cage.

Carolyn recognizes Liza, Jamie's mother. Liza screams, and then she's outside of the wagon, the man holding her down. He pulls out a jar of what looks like sand and starts rubbing it onto her bare skin. She's completely naked now, and where the sand touches her, it burns her flesh. Her shrieks meld together, as if she's no longer taking breaths between the screams. Then there's an unearthly silence. Liza has fainted.

The man turns to Carolyn, points at her. "She's next."

She struggles, but she's naked now, and he's approaching, the jar of sand in his fist.

"You're to be marked, witch." He tells her this without emotion, without remorse, without regret, or sympathy. It's just something that has to be done. The first man is holding her tight.

She begs. "Please, no. This is wrong."

His arms pinion her to his chest and she's weak, weaker than she'd have thought. Her arms feel like lead weights, and they drop to her sides.

The man holding the sand rubs it into the skin on her arms, covering her in flaming agony. She opens her mouth to scream ...

Carolyn awoke, drenched in sweat, her mouth open, but the scream stifled. It was dark in the den. She sat up. The dream faded, but the sensation it left behind was still raw and fresh. She marvelled that a simple dream could affect her physically. The ghost of the burning grit prickled on her arms. She glanced at the clock. It was after 9:00 PM. No call had come from Beverly saying she'd heard from Arnie.

We have to notify the police.

CHAPTER 26

Carolyn lay awake the entire night, rising at 5:00 AM when she had enough of tossing around in bed. Being up was nominally better, but no matter what she did, the knot in her stomach persisted.

It was worse every time the phone rang. Carolyn jumped on it, hoping it was Arnie. So far, every call, and there were many, had been someone offering condolences about John, or asking if she needed anything or wanted company. She was grateful, but it made her heart leap into her throat every time the phone rang, and her nerves were frayed.

By now, she was sure something had happened to him. The previous night, the last time she'd talked by phone to Beverley, they'd decided the nurse should call the police. She texted shortly after, saying she'd filled out a missing person report.

Carolyn tried to sense him in the spirit world and found some consolation in being unable to locate him there. What worried her was the darkness she felt whenever she tried to connect to him. It meant he was still alive, but she couldn't get a reading from him. She repeatedly called his cell and only stopped when the voice mail registered full.

Aimlessly, she wandered around the house with a dust rag and a can of furniture polish. When the whole house was dust free, she pulled out the vacuum. She went over the carpets in the entire house, washed the floors in the bathrooms and kitchens, cleaned the tubs, and still received no word. She booted up her computer and checked his blog. The posting they'd argued over was still live. There were no additional posts.

Frustrated, she called Sam.

"Hello?"

"Hi, sweetie, it's me. How'd you sleep?"

"Not good, but I did get some sleep. How are you?"

"I'm having trouble sleeping too. Arnie hasn't answered his phone since he left here yesterday, and the nurse who works for him didn't hear from him either. Would you mind coming home? For a little while? I'm afraid something's happened to Arnie, too."

"I'm sure he's fine, but I'll ask Vanna to give me a lift over. I'll be there in about twenty minutes, okay?"

"Thank you. Be careful."

"Okay. Don't worry, Mom."

Carolyn disconnected.

What should she do now? She had to keep herself busy. She opened Arnie's blog again and read posts from the archives, starting with the ones Ralph had written before he went to the hospital. One post in particular caught her attention. Ralph had written about a woman, Patty Richards, who was doing the talk circuit of UFO conventions.

Ralph seemed to hold her in high esteem and worked closely with her, but Carolyn had never seen her before at any of the sky watches. She did a quick search on Patty to see who she was and if she belonged to other UFO groups. The first link that popped up in the search led to Patty's obituary.

A chill ran through Carolyn when she read Patty had died suddenly of what appeared to be a heart attack. This had happened at the end of April, only a short time before their last sky watch and after Ralph had gone into the hospital. The phone rang, and she snatched it up.

"Hello?"

Sobbing greeted her on the other end. She waited, breath held, her body tensing. At last, a voice she recognized as Beverly's said, "They found him. He's dead. The police were just here." She started sobbing again.

Carolyn went numb. "What happened?" It was the only thing she could manage to say.

"They said he committed suicide. They found his body in his burned-out car. He loved that car. He wouldn't have done that."

"What makes them think he killed himself?"

"They said he set a fire in his car deliberately and then drove it into a gas pump. He's burned up, but they got his dental records. His cell phone was in the car too. He left no note, but they said it was obviously suicide."

It wasn't suicide. "I don't believe it."

"It's what the police told me. I'm sorry. I have to go. His mother is torn up. I had to give her a sedative."

"Okay. I'm so sorry. Tell his mom I'll come and see her when she's feeling up to it."

They hung up. Carolyn glanced up at the sound of the door opening. Sam stepped into the house. At the sight of her mother's face, she froze.

"Did you hear from Arnie?"

Carolyn rushed over to Sam and threw her arms around her. "Oh, God. They found his body. They said he killed himself."

Sam burst into tears, clinging to Carolyn. After a moment, she pulled away from her daughter and closed the door.

"It can't be right. I didn't sense him in spirit," Carolyn said.

"Maybe you can't know all the time."

"He's one of my best friends. He'd come to me, or I'd at least know he'd passed."

"Do you think they made a mistake?"

"I don't know what to think. I want to talk to Ralph. He might have been right all along. Will you come with me?"

"Of course."

"Let me shut down." Carolyn went to her computer.

Patty's face stared out at her from the screen. Carolyn tried to connect to Patty. She didn't get a response but located the woman in spirit. She tried Arnie again, but she sensed only darkness.

She shut down the laptop and went to get her car keys.

CHAPTER 27

It took some doing, and Carolyn was sure the doctor would call security and have them escorted out. In the end, she convinced him they'd come out of concern for Ralph and wouldn't say anything to cause him distress. In other words, she lied. Not about being concerned for Ralph—that part was true—but she was sure what they had to say would cause him a great deal of distress.

So, here they sat, in his room. The door was propped open, allowing staff to peek in on them. Ralph perched on the edge of his bed while Sam and Carolyn occupied the only two chairs in the room. A table stood between the two women with Ralph's laptop resting on top of it. They'd already dispensed with the small talk, and Carolyn steeled herself for the conversation to come.

"They said you didn't want to see us. Is that true?"

"Yes." Then he qualified it. "But only for your sake."

"What do you mean?"

Ralph glanced at Sam, uncertain.

"It's okay," Carolyn said. "Sam knows I suspect you were forced in here."

"Let's go for a walk," he suggested.

"Are you allowed to leave your room?"

"Yes. Let's go into the yard where we can get some air."

She nodded, and they all stood.

He ushered the women from the room and led them down the corridor to an exit.

White French doors opened onto a white stone porch. A set of stairs descended to a concrete path. On either side of the path stretched lawns, bordered by flowers and trees, abutting barbed wire-topped fences. Carolyn couldn't see a gate.

No one else was outside. She wondered at that. It was hot for May, but she expected that on such a bright sunny day someone would've been out here getting some sun and air.

"We can talk more freely here," Ralph said. "I don't trust my room isn't bugged."

"Really?" She didn't wait for him to answer. "How have you been? Did you really ask them to put you in here?"

"I'm feeling okay, but I'd rather be at home. I'm here to keep my family safe. It's safer for all of you, too, if you stay away from me."

"Did you hear what's been happening?"

"I heard Arnie posted a video of an abduction. I talk to Beth once a week. They screen what I can access on my computer, so I can't read the blog. Beth said Arnie has called her several times and no one else has tried to contact her."

"We're respecting your wishes. I did try once to talk to her, but she made it clear she didn't want me to contact her. Your doctor doesn't want me to talk about anyone or anything relating to the group, but I think you have a right to know what's happened."

"What?"

"Okay … John died at work of a heart attack on Monday. Then Shelly was stabbed to death in a mugging at her apartment. Now, Arnie was found dead, and they say it was suicide. I doubt Arnie would kill himself. Sorry to lay it on you all at once, but I'm worried about Sam and me. I was hoping you could tell me what to do."

Ralph didn't speak. His face went white, and his hands crept over his stomach in a protective gesture. "Jesus, Carr. John is dead? Shelly? Arnie?"

She nodded as he listed each name.

"I have to sit down." He walked to one of the Adirondack chairs scattered around the lawn and sank into it.

She gave him a moment to process it. She noticed the grey in his blond hair, the dark circles under his eyes, and the stoop to his shoulders. His round, usually cheerful face was now gaunt and lined and sorrowful. His eyes seemed to sink into his face, making them appear small and squinty.

She reached out and touched his cheek. "I'm sorry."

Ralph gazed up at her. "I'm sorry too—for you, too, Sam. I can't imagine what it must be like for you."

Sam nodded her head and then lowered her eyes.

Carolyn continued. "Steve has refused to talk to us since Shelly died because he blames the group. It hurts he won't talk to us, and it hurts you wouldn't talk to us. I'm running out of people I trust or who understand what's going on. I can't tell my family." She tried to keep the despair and bitterness out of her voice and wasn't sure she succeeded.

He rose and hugged her. Some of the tension eased out of her. He held her head to his chest and she let her mind clear. Then he dropped his arms, and she stepped away.

"Thank you for seeing us. I don't know what I'd have done if you'd refused." Her voice broke.

"I've missed you, all of you. I don't refuse to see you by choice. They threatened my family. I shouldn't see you again, but I wanted to see you one last time."

"What can we do now?"

"Go away. There's a place in Algonquin Park—a base. The aliens there are helping abductees. I heard about it from someone who has been there. I have a map to it at my house. It's in a safe hidden in my basement. Tell Beth I said you could have it. Go to that base and ask them to help you."

"Aliens? A base?" Carolyn was confused. Did he expect her to go to the very beings who kidnapped and experimented on her?

"They're different. They don't abduct people. They're against it. They help you to avoid getting taken again."

"How?"

"My friend says they do something that makes you untraceable to the others. I don't know how it works. I ended up here before I could verify it."

"Then how do you know this person told you the truth?"

"It was someone with inside information. I can't elaborate."

"Why didn't you mention this before—especially to Arnie? He was your best friend."

"I wanted to investigate it and then tell you. It's important to keep it from the government. They'll destroy it. Something like this goes against what they're trying to do. They're using their own citizens as bargaining chips with the hostiles. Anyone who interferes will be eliminated."

"What makes you think they don't already know about it?"

"I don't. They didn't know about it when I came to the hospital; I believe that much."

"Is it possible your house was searched?"

"It was. They made me commit myself. Then they went through my things and took all my files. Beth had to let them go through everything in my office, but the map isn't in my office."

"What about me?" Sam asked.

"Right now, you're not on their radar. You'll be safer at school."

"I don't want to leave you, Mom."

Carolyn placed a hand on her daughter's arm. "It'll be okay. I want to make sure you're safe, and I'll take care of this for good."

"What if something happens to you? I can't let you go by yourself."

114

Sam's tone held a touch of panic.

"She's right," Ralph said.

Carolyn stood her ground. "She can't come. Sam must go back to work and school and carry on as if everything is normal. If we both disappear, it'll look suspicious."

"So how are you planning to disappear?"

"I'll tell people I'm going camping. I'll leave after the funeral, after you go back to your apartment in Cambridge. The neighbours can check the house for me each day and feed the cat. I wish Arnie were here. I'd have him come along."

Carolyn stopped talking when a white-coated staff member approached them.

"Mr. Drummond, Dr. Randal wants you to come in for your group therapy session."

"Okay, thanks. I'll be right there," Ralph said and then turned to Carolyn and Sam. "I have to go. I'm surprised he gave us this long. Follow me. You have to go through the building to get back to the main entrance."

He spun around and headed back into the hospital, the two women hurrying in his wake.

CHAPTER 28

Less than an hour later, Carolyn pulled into the Drummond driveway and parked the car. Sam remained behind while Carolyn walked up to the house alone.

Over the years, Beth had spent a lot of money on landscaping, perfecting the outside. Carolyn noted the overgrowth of weeds, the uncut grass, and the shades pulled down over the windows. She wanted to cry.

A moment after she reached the porch and rang the doorbell, footsteps approached and the door opened.

Beth supported herself with one hand on the door. Her once dark hair, now turning grey, was pulled back into a ponytail, a few errant strands plastered against her sweaty face. Her tired eyes were rimmed with red. The T-shirt and cut-off shorts she wore were faded, and the nail polish on her fingers and toes was chipped. She frowned, making a sound like a wounded raccoon, and took a step backward when she recognized Carolyn.

Carolyn tried to speak first, "Beth, I—"

Beth over-rode her, her voice shrill. "What are you doing here? You're not supposed to come here."

"Please, let me explain. I visited Ralph. He told me to come see you."

Beth's eyes narrowed. "He wouldn't do that. We're not supposed to have contact with any of you." She stepped outside and closed the door. "Let's move off the porch."

She's worried about bugs too. Carolyn walked down the steps to the grass. "Have you heard what happened?"

"Whatever it is, keep it to yourself and leave. Please."

"Ralph suggested I get something from you. If you give me what I want, I'll leave and never return. Please. Will you do that?"

Beth hesitated, frowned. "What, exactly?"

"A map. Ralph says it's in a safe in the basement. Please, get it for me?"

"No, I'm sorry."

"Why? We've been friends for years. If you give it to me, I'll leave you alone. I swear."

"It's not that I don't want to help you, Carolyn. I can't give it to you because I gave it to the agents who were here."

"Oh my God. Why?"

"To save my family. They said if I gave them everything, my family would be safe. I gave it to them. My family comes first."

Carolyn wanted to scream, to lash out with her fists in frustration. She hugged herself, trying to stop the trembling. Tears threatened, and her voice broke when she spoke. "Do you know what you've done?"

"I had to."

"But they never would've known if you'd kept it."

"They know everything. I couldn't take the chance."

"They'll destroy that base."

"I can't help that. Maybe there are others?"

"How likely is that? If the army, or whoever is behind what's going on, descends on that base, they'll destroy it. That base was our one hope to escape from this. Ralph is an abductee. Surely, they could've helped him too. Why would you take that away from him?"

"He's locked up. There's no help for him." Beth sounded bitter.

"What about your boys? These abductions run in families. Your boys may already be victims."

Beth shrugged. "Ralph sometimes gave Brent copies of things he had. Go ask him for the map. I didn't tell the agents about that. I only did what I had to do to keep my family safe."

"Thank you. I'm sorry for everything you're going through. I hope things get better for all of you." Without waiting for a response, Carolyn returned to the car.

"She won't give it to you, will she?" Sam asked.

Carolyn shook her head, feeling unsafe talking in the car or using her cell. Was her home bugged? She backed onto the road and headed toward the nearest coffee shop with a pay phone.

Sam frowned but said nothing. When Carolyn parked the car and got out, her daughter followed.

The two women walked to the pay phone, and Carolyn dialled Brent but got his voice mail.

"Hi, it's Carolyn. I'd like to stop by your office tomorrow morning. Please text my cell with a time." She hung up and they went to the car. Before they got in, she said, "You'll stay at Vanna's tonight."

When Sam started to protest, Carolyn held up her hand to stop her. "It's okay. Don't worry about me. I'll ask Erika or another neighbour if I can stay the night there. Erika offered to keep me company, and I'll take her up on that."

Sam's face brightened. "Okay. I'm glad you'll be with someone tonight. If you need me for anything, call."

"I will. Everything will be fine. You'll see."

They got in the car and left the parking lot.

***

Torque and Michael gave Carolyn a head start before pulling out after her.

"Drummond has her jumping at shadows now. She's acting like she thinks her phone is bugged and she's being followed," Torque said.

"Her phone *is* bugged, and she is being followed," Michael replied. "It's not jumping at shadows if it's true."

"Fair enough. It'll be more difficult for us if she makes calls using pay phones unless she's calling someone whose phone we've tapped."

Michael nodded and picked up his cell phone to call the office. If she'd called Steve, Brent, or any of Sam's close friends, they'd have the identity of the person she'd called and what she'd said. He pitied Carolyn. She didn't stand a chance against the Agency.

CHAPTER 29

When Carolyn pulled into her driveway, the uneasiness started. She'd felt fine when she'd dropped Sam off at Vanna's. The girls had promised they would stay in all evening, and Vanna's parents were home. Carolyn had kissed Sam goodbye and driven away, confident that her daughter would be safe.

Brent still hadn't texted. However, that wasn't the source of Carolyn's uneasiness. When Arnie hadn't contacted her, she'd immediately sensed he was in danger. Her intuition told her Brent was too busy to respond.

She unlocked her door, anxiety escalating. She had to get out of here. Inside, she picked up her phone and called Erika. Voicemail. When the beep sounded, she left a message and hung up.

She peered out the living room window. Nothing moved, but she felt watched. Even though the sun would still be up for another hour, she closed the curtains.

Carolyn hurried upstairs to her room and dug around in the clutter of her closet for a duffel bag. She dragged it out and threw some clothes and toiletries into it. She checked her phone again, hoping there had been some response from Erika, even though she'd have heard any incoming texts or calls.

Her bag packed, she considered what to do next. What if Erika was out for the night? Perhaps she should try another neighbour.

I have to get out of here. She told herself it was all in her head, that she was making it up, but that only increased her angst. Ginger, another neighbour who lived up the street, might welcome an overnight guest.

Carolyn hurried into the den to get the landline, keeping the cell phone free in case someone tried to call. When she reached out to pick up the phone, she thought she heard a noise from downstairs. Her breath caught in her throat. She listened, hoping it was just the cat, but sensing there was someone in the house.

She jumped when the cat brushed against her leg, proof it wasn't Fox moving around below. A floorboard creaked, and she was certain an intruder prowled the main floor. She picked up the phone to call the police.

No dial tone.

She snatched up her cell phone, but her hands shook, and she almost dropped it. She pressed 9-1-1. Phone to her ear, she made her way to the patio doors. If she could get outside, she could get down to the ground and run into the forest.

The distance to the doors seemed to increase with each terrified step she took. When she reached the door, she clicked the lock open, cringing at the sound it made, loud as a backfiring car to her ears. Slowly she eased the inner door open, trying to be silent, but her terror rose at the soft tap of footsteps on the stairs.

She slid the screen door open with less caution, and it made a slight whoosh as it slid.

The footsteps sped up.

She clicked open the lock on the outer door, sliding it open fast, no longer caring about the noise. When she stepped through the door onto the balcony, a man appeared in the den and spotted her.

There was no sound from her phone. Why hadn't anyone picked up? She glanced at the screen. Call failed. She whimpered and hit "Retry." There was no time to stop to close the doors. No time to open the gate to get down the stairs.

Her first thought was to jump over the side of the balcony, but the drop was over six metres. She couldn't land without injury.

The man stepped outside.

She backed against the railing.

He pointed a gun at her. "Don't move." He inched toward her.

She focused on the gun, unable to take her eyes off it. She forced her gaze away and looked over the side of the railing. It was a long way down, and below her sat a woodpile. She wouldn't be going that way.

The intruder snatched the phone from her hand and glanced at it. He put it to his ear. Satisfied she hadn't been able to place a call, he turned off the phone and threw it over the balcony.

Fear overwhelmed her, and she thought she would be sick. She swallowed, but her throat was dry. Taking a deep breath, she tried to clear her head. To survive she needed to think.

Get him talking. "Who are you?" She squinted, trying to see his face in the darkness. If she managed to escape, she'd need a description.

He towered over her—at least by four inches, which would make him about six feet tall. He wore jeans and a plain, white T-shirt under a grey suit jacket that, when buttoned, concealed his shoulder holster. His black, slightly wavy hair and tan complexion enhanced the aura of darkness around him. Bangs drooped over his forehead, almost hanging into his brown eyes. His full lips pressed together, and tension oozed from him. He was one of the witch hunters in her dream.

"Who are you?" she demanded.

He didn't reply, but grabbed her by the arm and yanked her back toward the house. She resisted and tried to pull free.

"Stop struggling. I'll only tell you once. Then I'll slug you."

She ceased fighting and walked, trying to think of something to say that would make him let her go. He pushed her inside.

Carolyn called on her guardian angels and spirit guides. *Angels, guides, and departed loved ones, I call upon you now. Please help me. Guide me through this. Help me connect to this man's guides so I can reason with him.*

She tried to get a sense of the man's energy. Pain, anger, and cold flowed into her.

Ask him about Jessica. "Who is Jessica?"

The grip on her arm tightened, and he audibly sucked in a breath.

"You're hurting me," she said.

The man scanned the room, and then pulled her outside again, closing the patio doors behind them.

"How do you know about Jessica?"

"I just know. My house is bugged, isn't it?"

"I'll ask the questions. Why did you ask about her? Is this some kind of trick?"

"No. I was guided to ask," she replied.

"What do you mean 'guided'? Guided by what?"

"If you've been spying on us, then you know the answer. She means something to you. I can tell by your reaction. She's ..." *Wife.* "She's your wife," Carolyn said.

The man pulled her close to him so her ear was next to his mouth. "How do you know about my wife?" His voice was a low growl.

"The information is coming from my guides. Don't you think you have more explaining to do than I do?"

He forced her inside again and dragged her to the door of the den. At that moment, the sound of a key turning in the front door's lock reached her ears. The stranger halted and yanked her back into the den. The front door opened, and footsteps filled the entryway.

Her heart in her mouth, Carolyn froze. The man pinioned her to his chest, his arms around her, keeping her still. He pressed the gun to her temple and whispered, "Quiet."

From below, her daughter's voice called out, "Mom? Are you here? Hello?"

CHAPTER 30

At the sound of Sam's voice, Carolyn choked down a moan. *Oh, God, no. Angels, please, tell her to leave. Don't let her come up here.*

"Sounds like no one's home. Mom must be at the neighbour's," Sam told whoever was with her. "I'll grab my stuff from my room. Check the kitchen cupboard for munchies. My mom won't mind." The footsteps faded in the kitchen's direction.

"Please, don't hurt them," Carolyn whispered. "It's my daughter and her friend. I'll do whatever you want, just please, leave them alone."

"If they don't bother us, I won't bother them," the stranger murmured in her ear, his breath blowing on her hair.

She froze.

An eternity of seconds ticked away. Sam and her friend walked around on the main floor. Then they were rooting around in the cupboards. Was this the last moment she'd ever have with her daughter? A sob caught in Carolyn's throat, and the man tightened his arms around her.

"Shut up. You bring them up here, and I'll shoot them both."

Her eyes welled. She closed them, and the tears streamed down her face. There was more movement from the main floor, and the footsteps approached the entryway.

"Ready?" The voice was male. Where was Vanna? This sounded like Roger. What happened to Sam's promise to stay at Vanna's and watch videos? *Not important. Oh, God, Sam, please leave.*

"Yeah. Just had to leave a note for my mom," Sam said.

The front door opened, closed, and then the key turned in the lock. The kids were gone. Carolyn let herself breathe again.

The man released his grip on her. "Let's go."

Out of habit, she locked the patio doors, recognizing the irony as she

122

did so. She turned to walk to her room with a vague notion she should get her purse.

The man grabbed her arm and yanked her back to the stairs. "What do you think you're doing?"

"Getting my purse," she replied, feeling foolish.

He looked at her like she'd lost her mind.

"I've never been kidnapped before," she said, knowing how ludicrous that sounded. At least if she left her purse behind, people would suspect something was wrong.

The stranger guided her down the stairs. When they reached the bottom, she turned to walk through the living room and into the kitchen.

He pulled her backward. "Not that way." Irritation laced his voice.

"I'm going to read my daughter's note," Carolyn said. "If you try to stop me, we'll have a fight."

He stared at her for a moment, perhaps debating whether to force her out the door, shrugged, and followed her into the kitchen.

She retrieved the note from the counter: *Mom, gone to Nichole's with Roger. Vanna and Jack are already there. Grabbed some snacks. See you tomorrow. Love you, Sam.* Tears running down her face, Carolyn folded the note and put it into her pocket.

The man, his voice strained, said, "Go. Now." He held her upper arm and led her back to the front door. He unlocked the door and opened it.

Carolyn gazed down at her bare feet. "My shoes are upstairs."

"Then you're going barefoot."

They stepped outside. He closed the door behind them, and she said, "My keys. They're inside."

"Leave them," he said. "Walk. I've had enough of this."

She moved down the stairs, gaze darting from side to side. Maybe she could run into the forest when they reached the bottom. She could try to outrun him even though she was barefoot. Once he had her in the car, escape would be unlikely.

As if reading her mind, he said, "Don't try anything. You'll be dead before you reach the trees."

She nodded to indicate she'd heard him. The gun pressed into the small of her back, and his grip never left her arm. Together they shuffled down the steps. Silently, she asked her guides for help.

She sensed a presence. A spirit. The night was hot, but cold air pressed against her left side, and her left arm tingled. A female presence. She knew who it was.

"Jessica?" she said.

The man halted. They were halfway down the stairs.

"What are you doing?" His tone was angry.

"She's here," Carolyn said. "Michael. Your name is Michael."

He spun her around until they locked gazes.

"What the fuck?" He holstered his gun and gripped her arms. Face thrust into hers and enunciating each word, he said, "How do you know that?"

The pain of his grip made her eyes water. She'd have bruises on her arms where he held her.

"You're hurting me."

"Not as much as I'll hurt you if you don't tell me what the fuck you're doing. Are you screwing with me? Where'd you get that information?" He kept his voice low, but it sounded loud in her ears. His anger and panic flowed into her. The harsh, vulgar words were like a slap.

"Please. Don't. I'll tell you, but you'll have to have an open mind. Your wife is telling me. Jessie's here," Carolyn said.

"Impossible. She's dead."

"Stop for a second and pay attention. Let me speak. She wants to communicate or she wouldn't be here."

"Sit."

Carolyn crumpled to the steps.

Michael planted himself in front of her. He held the railing on either side in a tight grip. She wouldn't get past him.

"Okay. Explain."

"I'm a psychic and a medium. That means I can communicate with spirits. You must be aware of that. Right?"

"I know what you claim to do."

"It's fine if you're a skeptic, but right now, your wife is trying to communicate with you. I can prove it. I'll ask her to tell me more things I wouldn't know, though I've already told you a lot." She opened herself up to receive messages.

Jessica, my name is Carolyn, and I'd like to talk to you. If you have a message for Michael, I can tell him.

Dizziness overcame her, and her whole body hurt. Pain seared her head. A car hurtled at her.

"She was hit by a car," Carolyn said.

Michael's face went white. "Go on."

She waited, then looked down and to the right—her typical stance when receiving messages.

Pregnant. She saw in her mind an impression of a woman, long brown hair, walking across a busy street. The woman stumbles and staggers into traffic. There's a squeal of brakes, a shriek of tires.

Carolyn looked up, away from the sight.

"I'm so sorry," she said. "She was pregnant. That must have been horrible for you."

His eyes filled with pain, and his breath caught in his throat.

The ray. "What's 'the ray'?" Carolyn asked. "I just got 'the ray.' I don't understand what it means."

Gerry. The ray. "I got 'Gerry' and 'the ray' and they were repeated. Usually that means it's significant."

Michael gripped her arms again and pulled her to her feet. "What are you saying?" He again enunciated each word precisely.

"I'm telling you what I'm getting. Who's Gerry?" she asked. "He's your partner?" she said, answering her own question.

"Yes. What's she saying?" He shook her while he asked this.

"Please, stop hurting me. Give me a minute." She listened. "He was there." Suddenly, she knew. "He met with her, and then he killed her."

Michael said, his voice a whisper, "Why? That makes no sense. What are you trying to do?" He frowned. "You're trying to turn me against my partner. Forget it. Let's go."

"I don't know you or your partner. I'm only telling you the messages I'm receiving as I get them," Carolyn said. "Your wife is trying to help you learn the truth."

"We have to go. He's waiting, and he'll get suspicious if we don't come down to the car. Move." He pulled her arm, and she stumbled down another two steps.

"You call him Torque? Jess is the one who calls him Gerry, isn't that right?"

He glanced at her, opened his mouth as if to reply, nodded his head, and said, "Walk." He held her arm, escorting her down one step at a time. The sound of the gun sliding from its holster reached her ears, and he shoved it into the small of her back.

"Must you do that?"

He didn't reply, and the gun stayed put.

Carolyn picked her way down, watching where she stepped. Would pushing him down the stairs allow her time to get away or just make him angrier? Again, she received sudden knowledge, and her own thought echoed the knowledge.

"They'll get you too," she said. "She's telling me they'll lock you up."

He halted again. "Who will?"

She listened. "A man named Cornell. He no longer trusts you."

Don't get in the car.

"She says we shouldn't get in the car."

By this time, they'd reached the driveway. Michael gripped her arm, leading her to the road. The gun was in his right hand. He continued to point it at her.

"We can't get into the car. Please. Jessica says not to," Carolyn insisted.

"What do you expect me to do? Believe you're talking to my dead wife?"

"I *am* talking to your dead wife." She tried to stop walking, but he tugged on her arm, making her stumble. "Stop. Just listen. Please. Jessica, please tell me what you want Michael to know. Tell me something to help him know it's you."

A woman's voice spoke into her left ear. *Gerry didn't want me to have the baby.*

"She says Gerry killed her because he found out she was pregnant."

Michael froze. "Gerry knew about the baby?"

The voice spoke again.

"Gerry knew everything," Carolyn said.

No family. The rest of the knowledge came to her. "Gerry was afraid you'd become concerned about the child's future, and it would cause you to turn against them."

"So just like that he decided the solution was to kill my wife?"

"Yes. Is that what they did with Shelly? Did you kill her? If you think Gerry shouldn't have killed your wife, what does that say about the things you've done in their name?" she said.

"I didn't kill Shelly. Torque didn't either. It was what it appeared to be: a mugging. You've said it yourself." Michael lowered his head, avoiding her eyes. "They had you all flagged as traitors to your country."

"Is that what they told you? How are we traitors? Arnie and I are abductees. What were we doing that makes us traitors?"

He didn't reply. Instead, he pulled her to him, his grip firm. "Quiet," he whispered in her ear. "I can't let Torque know I'm talking to you. We've already taken too long. He knows the second we stepped out the front door, and he's watching for us. Our instructions were to take you in, not kill you."

"Take me in where?" she asked. "Where Arnie is? You didn't kill him, did you? He didn't kill himself."

"Never mind that," he said. "Just do whatever I tell you. If you don't listen to me, then he'll kill me and take you in. Do you understand?"

She stared up at him. His eyes were intense. She could smell sweat on him and his grip on her arm was moist and slippery.

"You believe me? You believe we're communicating with your wife?" she asked.

"Yes," he answered.

"Do you still think I'm a traitor?"

"I was finding it hard to believe you were a traitor a long time ago," Michael said. "He's seen us. When we get to the car, do what I tell you."

Carolyn nodded and let him lead her down the rest of the way.

CHAPTER 31

J ust before they reached the car, Michael waved to Torque, indicating he should pull in closer. The car backed into the driveway, all the way off the road. Michael banged on the trunk and it popped open. He pulled Carolyn behind the car, using the trunk lid to shield her body.

He leaned around the car and gave a low shout. "Grab the cuffs for me. I don't have mine here." To Carolyn, he whispered, "Stay out of my way. I gotta do this fast, so no sudden moves." He shifted his gun to his left hand and waited.

She heard shuffling and the car door opening.

A male voice said, "Not cool. You're supposed to have these things on you all the time. She should already be cuffed."

Torque appeared around the side of the car.

Carolyn recognized the other man in her dream and her fear intensified.

He held a pair of handcuffs out. Instead of taking them, Michael grabbed Torque's wrist and yanked him forward, simultaneously swinging the gun at his head.

Thrown off balance, Torque ducked the blow by a hair's breadth. He shoved Michael away, knocking the gun from his hand.

"What the fuck are you doing?" Torque shouted.

"You killed her, you son of a bitch," Michael hollered back.

Torque reached for the gun in the holster under his arm. Michael lunged at him, and they both went down onto the asphalt, struggling.

Carolyn grabbed the gun Michael had dropped and pointed it at the two men. "If this fires, I don't know who it'll hit. I've never used one before. Stop fighting now."

She had a sudden, insane urge to giggle. *I sound like I'm talking to a couple of little kids.* She hoped they didn't see how badly her hands shook.

The two men, looking startled, froze.

"Get his gun, Michael," Carolyn said.

He snatched the weapon from Torque's holster.

"Now get up and take over. I don't know what I'm doing, and if anyone makes a move my way, I might fire. No one wants that to happen." She took two steps back to give Michael room to stand.

He levered off the pavement and waved the gun at Torque. "Get up."

Torque rose.

"Put the cuffs on."

"What are you doing, Mick? What happened up there? Whatever she told you, it's a lie. She's a traitor. You'd be crazy to trust her. Take the gun out of my face. We're partners, for Christ's sake."

"You killed Jess," Michael said. "You found out she was pregnant, and you killed her without even considering alternatives."

"Is that what she told you?" Torque nodded at Carolyn. "If she did, she's lying."

"I don't think so. You were there. You watched her die."

Torque started, and then his face went cold. "I told you, I was following up on a suspect. It was near our office. I was sitting in traffic when she got hit."

"If that's true, then why didn't you tell me? Why keep that from me? Why wouldn't you have tried to help her or call 9-1-1? I'm the 'suspect' you were following up on, aren't I? What's waiting for me at the end of this ride, Torque?"

"She's lying to you. She's a traitor," Torque insisted. "Why would you believe her?"

"Your response tells me all I need to know. Put the cuffs on." Michael raised the gun, aiming it at his partner's face. "I won't tell you again."

Torque cuffed his hands in front, taking his time.

"Take the key," Michael ordered Carolyn. "But first, give me my gun before you hurt yourself."

"I'll get the key," she said, "but I'm keeping the gun." She strode over to Torque and raised her left hand. She held the gun in her right hand away from Torque. He fished the key from his pocket and dropped it into her outstretched palm.

"Get in the trunk," Michael ordered.

"What are you going to do?" Torque asked. "They'll know. Whatever you do to me, they'll find out. You won't get away with this. They'll track you down. You're a traitor now too."

He turned to Carolyn. "Did he tell you how he killed your husband? Did you tell her, Mick? He zapped John with the death ray. He killed him, and then we went for lunch, didn't we, Mick? Veal sandwiches, if I recall correctly."

She stared at Torque, horror in her eyes. "The ray. That's the same ray you used to kill Jessica?" She turned from Torque to Michael. "You killed John? You did it yourself?" Her voice rose, a shriek of pain.

She pointed her gun at Michael. Her hands trembled, but still she held it, aiming at his face. She gritted her teeth and sweat trickled into her eyes, stinging them. She squeezed one eye at a time, and tears and sweat trickled down her cheeks.

"Don't listen to him," Michael said. "He's only interested in saving his ass right now. Get in the fucking trunk, Torque, or I'll shoot you and put you in there myself."

Put the gun down. Carolyn wasn't sure if the thought was her own, a directive from her guides, or communication from Jessica, but she lowered her gun.

Torque steadied himself on the bumper of the car and climbed into the trunk. "You'll regret this."

"Shut up. Lie down." Michael's face was livid. "Carolyn, there's a black bag in the back seat of the car. Bring it here."

She went to the back door of the car and opened it. She picked up the medical bag and carried it back to Michael.

"Set it down next to me and open it."

She did.

"Now take out the syringe that's in a tin in the top pocket of the bag. It's already loaded."

She removed the tin and opened it. Inside rested a syringe with needle. She picked it up.

"Was this meant for me?"

"Give it to me." Michael held out his hand, gaze fixed on Torque, the gun trained on him.

She surrendered the needle to Michael.

He drew closer to the trunk of the car. "Make one move, and I'll shoot you." He jabbed the needle into Torque's neck and hit the plunger.

Torque stared at them a moment and then collapsed.

"If it was set up for me, how is it that it would knock him out? He's bigger than I am," Carolyn said.

His tone puzzled, Michael said, "That's your question?" He shook his head.

"You had enough in there to knock him out, even though it was meant for me."

"Get in the car."

She hesitated.

He slammed the trunk closed and picked up the medical bag.

"Please. Get in the car. I don't want a Mexican standoff. You'd find it's easier for me to pull the trigger than it is for you. We can't stay here.

If you go back into your house, they'll know something went wrong. The whole house is bugged. If I let you go, someone else will hunt you down. We have to get far away from here now."

Carolyn tamped down the urge to argue. She went to the passenger side of the car and climbed in, setting the gun down on the floor between her feet.

Michael slid in on the driver's side and started the car. He leaned over and, before she could react, picked up his gun.

"I'll take that."

She blushed. "I couldn't use it if I had to."

He smiled and his face softened.

"Where are we going?" she asked.

"First, we'll get my bug-out bag from my home in Aurora. Then we'll find a place away from here to hole up for the night."

"Are we going to find Arnie?"

"I can't help you get Arnie back. They had us stage his death, and he's in, well, let's call it custody." Michael pulled out of the driveway and headed back toward town and the highway leading to Aurora.

CHAPTER 32

They were on the highway, driving south along the 404 toward Aurora.

"What do you intend to do with me?" Carolyn asked.

Michael ignored her question.

She tried another one. "Why are the aliens abducting us?"

"Because you're more intuitive than the average person. The aliens are experimenting with it. So is the Agency."

"You work for the Agency?"

"Yes."

They rode in silence, Carolyn trying to think of something to say that wouldn't anger him. She searched for Jessica's presence, but felt nothing. She closed her eyes. The inside of the car was chilly. She was barefoot and in shorts and a tank top. Goose bumps prickled on her arms and legs, and she shivered.

Michael must've noticed because she heard him fiddle with the controls on the dash, and the cold air blowing on her diminished.

"Sorry. I should've at least let you get your shoes," he said.

"Yes. I hate walking around in bare feet."

"I thought you tree huggers loved going barefoot?"

"Not me." She opened her eyes.

He stared ahead, not sparing her even a glance, so she looked out her window.

"When can I go home?" She knew the answer, but wanted to make him say it.

"You can't. I doubt you'll ever be able to go home. If it's any consolation, I can't either."

"My husband's funeral is on Saturday."

"You'll miss it. My wife's funeral is tomorrow. I'll miss it. Nothing we can do about that. If either of us shows our face now, we're dead. At least, I'm dead and you're locked up. Our best chance is to get you away from the Agency and the aliens so they can't abduct you again. The alien base in Algonquin Park might give us a way to accomplish that. Either way, we have to disappear."

"How do you know about Algonquin?"

Again, he didn't reply.

She faced him. "Why won't you answer me? How do you know about the base?"

"I have Drummond's map."

The map Beth had turned over to the government agents. Michael had it. Should she be relieved or frightened?

"I can't do this," she said.

Michael met her gaze. "You have to." He returned his focus to the road.

She fell silent. Should she tell him Sam knew about the base? No, she wanted to keep Sam off everyone's radar.

Twenty minutes later, they turned into a long driveway that led to a large two-story home on a fair-sized lot. He stopped the car halfway up the drive and lowered the windows. He opened the caddy between their seats and handed her a cell phone.

"Torque's cell phone. If you hear or see anything suspicious, hit three on the speed dial. That's my cell number. No other calls. Don't try Brent; don't try your daughter. As far as everyone is concerned, you've disappeared. The last thing you need to do is put your daughter in danger. Is that clear?"

She nodded.

He handed her a gun. "If Torque wakes up, shoot him. Point it at him and pull the trigger. Make sure you put direct pressure on the trigger or it won't fire. It has a suppressor, which is why the barrel is so long. You don't have to do anything else. It's already cocked."

Her eyes went wide, and she made a choking sound of protest.

"It's fine. I'll get the bag and come right out. The gun's probably unnecessary, but if you need it, it's better to have it than not."

"Michael?" she said in a timid voice. Her heart pounded; her pulse thudded in her ears. Now that he planned to leave her alone, she didn't want to let him go.

He looked her in the eyes. "I'll help you; I swear. No one will take you again."

She swallowed. All she could do was nod.

He stepped from the car and closed the door. When he neared his front door, a motion sensor detected his presence, and a light flicked on. He unlocked the door and disappeared inside.

Carolyn hunkered down, feeling exposed even though Michael had parked in the shadows. In front of her, light splashed on the ground. She hoped it extinguished soon.

Head angled to the left, she listened for any sound from the trunk.

If he wakes up and pounds on the lid while I'm sitting here by myself, I'll have a heart attack without the help of the ray. She picked up the cell phone and toyed with the idea of turning it on and calling someone. She sighed and put it down. She wouldn't be that stupid.

That Michael had left her alone, had trusted she'd be waiting for him when he came out, told her a lot. She could run right now and he'd have difficulty finding her, especially if he was exposed as a traitor to his agency. If she ran, though, the Agency would find her. Her only chance was to stay with Michael and hope he'd protect and not betray her.

She checked the time on the phone. How long had he been gone? It was 7:48 PM. She thought at least ten minutes had passed. How long should she give him before she started to worry? She'd give him another ten minutes before deciding there was a problem. Carolyn sank lower in her seat.

* * *

Inside the house, Michael headed to his bedroom. He grabbed Jessie's pack for Carolyn. His pack contained a two-person tent and his military gear, which made it heavier. He lifted his wife's pack with one arm, testing the weight to decide if Carolyn could carry it. She was lean but not muscular. The bag weighed about thirty-five pounds. She'd have to manage.

While he was in there, he paused long enough to dig in the back of the closet and remove a plastic storage container that held photo albums. He opened one and peeled a picture of him and Jessie out of it. They'd had it taken the weekend they went to Jessie's sister's cottage. They stopped at a restaurant on the way up north, and Jess asked the waiter to take their picture. She printed it up when they got home. He'd thought it cheesy, but went along with it.

She'd probably gotten pregnant that weekend. He was glad they'd had that one last weekend together and she'd taken this photo. It didn't seem so cheesy now. He stuck the picture into his backpack. If he couldn't go to her funeral, he at least wanted something to remind him of her.

He snapped himself out of it. Torque might wake up at any moment.

Michael headed out of the bedroom without a backward glance. He checked his watch. Time felt as if it had sped up. He rushed down the stairs. When he passed the kitchen, he realized they'd want some small bottles of water. He went to the kitchen to get them. It would only take a moment.

CHAPTER 33

C arolyn checked the time again. She'd start worrying in five minutes. It was silly, putting her worry on the clock like that, so she tried to relax by slowing her breathing.

It occurred to her she hadn't investigated what was in the car. She tried to open the glove box, found it locked, and glanced at the ignition. No keys. So, he didn't trust her that much. She lifted the lid of the caddy between the seats. Empty. She looked in the back seat and reached for the medical bag.

This proved more interesting.

It held a variety of drugs, syringes, and first aid paraphernalia. These guys had their own little mini hospital going for them. They even had surgical tools. She shuddered. What kind of surgeries might they want to perform and on whom?

On the edge of perception, she heard a scraping sound.

She dropped the scalpel she was holding back into the bag and snapped it closed. She set the bag on the floor behind the driver's seat and listened. A glance at the door to the house showed no sign of Michael.

The car jostled and she spun around in time to see the back seat fold forward. Torque's feet and legs thrust through the opening.

She gave a small shriek and frantically looked for the gun, in her panic forgetting where it was. There, on Michael's seat.

As Torque moved to crawl out of the trunk, she grabbed the gun and pointed it at him.

"Don't move. I'll shoot." It wobbled in her shaking hands. She wasn't capable of pulling the trigger.

Torque's forehead was wet with sweat and his hair spiked up. He grimaced.

"You dumb bitch. Get that gun off me."

He lunged at her and, afraid he'd get the gun, she tossed it out the window. It hit the ground but didn't fire.

She cried out again and grabbed for the door, but Torque had her by the hair. He yanked her head back, swung his manacled arms around her chest, and pulled her into the back seat. She clawed ineffectually at his hands.

"Where's Mick?" he demanded. "I'll fucking kill you." He wrapped his hands around her throat, squeezing off her air supply.

Carolyn's legs kicked. She tried to brace her feet on the dash and shove herself into him, away from that strangling grip. Her fingers clawed at his hands. He was too strong for her. The world spun. Her vision blurred, and her consciousness swam into darkness.

Before she was completely lost, the hands relaxed. She was thrust aside, and her head hit the window. There was a new struggle behind her, and while she reoriented, the sound of Michael's voice cut through the haze. She gasped for breath, trying to get air flowing normally through her windpipe. She collapsed onto the seat.

A muffled shot reached her ears, then another. Not knowing who had fired the gun, she dragged herself to the open car door. She tried to focus her eyes, but for a moment saw only black spots and blur.

Her vision cleared. One man stood over the body of another man, and she gratefully noted that the man who was standing was Michael.

He bent down to pick up the bags he'd dropped and ran to her. He pushed her aside while he shoved the seat back up into position and threw the bags into the car. The door slammed in her face when she tried to speak.

He hurried to where Torque lay, grabbed him under the arms, and dragged him back to the car. Michael grunted, and the car jostled as he stuffed Torque into the trunk and slammed the lid closed.

Without a word, Michael jumped into the driver's seat, started the car, and threw it into reverse.

Carolyn held herself steady in the seat while he backed out of the driveway.

"Torque," she said. "Is he ...?"

"Dead? Likely. I didn't verify."

When the car pulled onto the road, Carolyn climbed into the front, taking care to stay out of his way. "Shouldn't we check? He'll need medical attention."

Michael frowned, opened his mouth, and then closed it again.

She stared at him, not understanding.

At last he spoke. "He's likely dead, and we have to get out of here. Don't think about it."

Horrified, she dropped her eyes. What kind of person could shoot his partner and feel nothing? He could kill her without remorse too. She tried to make her voice sound normal and keep him talking.

"Did you get everything you needed?"

"Yes. I had the bags ready a while ago. I lost my faith in the 'Project' weeks ago. That stuff you said was from Jess? That's how they operate. They tell you enough of the truth to make the lies sound believable, but I never would've believed Torque had it in him to kill my wife." He fell silent.

Carolyn filled the void. "What are you going to do about Torque? If he's not dead, then he's injured."

"If he's not dead, then I'll kill him."

"No. Please, no more killing."

"He'll come after us."

"Then we'll be careful. Please, haven't you killed enough people in your lifetime? Aren't you sorry? Don't you have any regret?"

Michael didn't respond.

She stared at him, waiting for some kind of response.

He frowned. "I was trained to do what I was told without question, for the sake of the Agency. No remorse."

"And now?"

"Right now, if I have to kill Torque to protect us, I'll do it."

"I can understand self-defence. I can't conceive of killing someone in cold blood. It's wrong."

"That's what you've been trained to believe."

She fell silent and stared out the window.

After what seemed hours, she looked at the clock. It was 8:51 PM—earlier than she'd expected. Few cars were on the road. They were well away from Aurora.

Carolyn gazed out the window as they passed fields, forests, and the occasional house.

When she looked up at the sky, she saw a faint spattering of stars and no clouds. The moon was a crescent. How long would they drive before they stopped? She was tired, but she'd never be able to sleep with this trained killer sitting next to her, no matter how much he promised to help her.

Interrupting her thoughts, Michael said, "What's your shoe size?"

She looked up, confused, but answered the question. "Nine. Why?"

"My wife's survival bag has a pair of hiking shoes in it. I hoped they'd fit you, but she's a size eight."

She considered whether she should ask him where they were headed and decided she had a right to know. She cleared her throat and said, "Where are we going?"

"Peterborough. We can get a room there for a few hours and get some rest."

"What about Torque?"

"They'll find him eventually."

"What if he's alive?"

"If he's still alive, it's a miracle. I'm using hollow-point bullets, and I capped him twice in the chest. If I hadn't shot him, he'd have killed me. You'd be with him, and he'd be carrying out our orders to take you in. He'd set it up to make it look like you were dead so no one would ever look for you again. That's what we did with Arnie. His family will believe they're burying him, and that's the end of that."

"And what happens to Arnie?"

"He spends the rest of his life, however long that might be, locked up where no one will find him except the extraterrestrials. The aliens will always bring him back where they found him, so he'll be there until he dies. If, or when, the extraterrestrials have no more use for him, he'll be executed."

"We can't let that happen."

"I can't do anything to stop it. They have him. They'll have you, too, if we don't get where I want to go."

"To Algonquin?"

"Yes." Michael glanced at her and then put his eyes back on the road.

Carolyn stared out the window and thought about Torque in the trunk of the car. The least she could do was help him by sending him some Reiki.

She put her hands together and mentally went through the process of sending distance Reiki to Torque. She caught Michael staring.

"Are you praying?" he asked.

"No. If you must know, I'm sending distance Reiki to Torque."

"Dare I ask?"

"Ask away. Reiki is a universal life force energy. It's intelligent and goes where needed. If Torque isn't dead, it'll send him healing energy. If he's dead, it'll help his spirit."

Michael didn't comment.

"You think that's crazy, don't you?" Carolyn asked.

"I didn't say that."

"But you think so, don't you?"

"I don't buy into this new-age stuff. Sorry, but it's illogical and no scientific research validates it."

"Actually, studies do exist. I don't care if you approve. It's something I can do."

"Why didn't you use the phone and call me when he started moving around?"

She blushed. "I wasn't paying attention, and when he pushed his way into the back seat, my first thought was to grab the gun. I just couldn't shoot him."

"You might have to learn to do that. If anything happens to me, you're on your own, and they'll keep coming for you. At some point, I want to show you the map. You should know where this base is in case I don't make it."

Dread speared through her. "What do you mean 'in case you don't make it'?"

"These people are ruthless. When they realize Torque and I are AWOL, they'll come out in full force to track us down. We have a limited amount of time before they start the hunt."

His words terrified her, and she fell silent. She peered out her window at the darkness over Scugog Lake while they passed over it. She looked up at the sky. Were the aliens out there, and if so, would they come for her?

"Can they abduct me while we're driving?" She shuddered.

Michael glanced at her, and his face relaxed. "No. You're not scheduled to be picked up by the aliens again this soon."

She frowned. "They have a schedule? If I wasn't going to be abducted, and I wasn't doing anything wrong, why did you kidnap me tonight? Why'd you people take me away from my family now? Couldn't you at least let me bury my husband who your agency killed?"

Her voice rose when she remembered what they'd done, what they wanted to do. "I was trying to stop Arnie from posting those entries. If you were eavesdropping on us, you knew that. Why did you need me to disappear?"

He didn't answer her.

She glared at him. She refused to let him stay quiet on this one. The longer the silence dragged on, the more she wanted an answer.

At last, he cleared his throat and spoke, his voice so low she had to strain to hear him. "I don't know. That's the last thing you want to hear, but it's the truth. I understand why they locked up Drummond and Griffen, but I couldn't figure out why they want you. That's one reason you're not in the trunk right now, though if you hadn't talked to me about Jess, you would be."

"You'd have gone through with it if I hadn't connected to Jessica?" she asked, her voice shaking. "The way you were at my house, you had a gun to my head. You threatened to shoot my child. I don't know what to do. I'm afraid of you, and you want me to trust you. The worst part is, I don't know what'll happen to me now. I don't know if you're my enemy or not."

"Sorry about what I did at your house. You have no idea ..." He exhaled loudly. "It's important that you trust me, so I want to make sure you're clear on where we stand. Do you understand I won't turn you over to them? If you have any doubts, you'd better tell me now. I don't want to have to constantly wonder whether you'll try to sneak away while I'm not watching you. So, do you understand I won't turn you over to either the Agency or to the aliens?"

His tone was firm, confident. He made her believe what he said was logical and she should trust him. Her uneasiness dissipated while he talked. Alarmed at how easily he was able to placate her, she nodded.

"Don't nod. I want to hear you say it."

"Yes, I understand."

"Do you understand if you leave me, if I lose you, you won't survive for long on your own? They'll come after you, and they'll find you. I want to make sure all this is clear in your head. Do you believe you're safer with me?"

She considered what it felt like to be by herself, without Michael. A shudder went through her, as did a surge of fear. A drowning sensation had her gulping for air. She then considered what it felt like having him by her side, trusting him, and depending on him. Warmth flooded her, and in her mind's eye, she received an impression of a shield and a flaming sword.

"My head tells me I shouldn't trust you, but my intuition tells me if I don't trust you, something awful will happen to me. I guess until that changes, I'm better off with you," Carolyn said.

"Okay. That's good. I'm trained to deal with this and you're not. I know you don't like it, but some things will be out of your control."

She sighed. "You're not the first person to tell me that."

CHAPTER 34

They left Highway 115 outside of the Peterborough city limits. Michael drove for ten minutes and then turned onto one of the many dirt roads they saw. This led them to a forested area, where he drove onto a fire route. When he spotted a clearing along the side of the road, he pulled into the small meadow bordered at one end by swamp and on the other sides by forest. He parked close to the swamp.

As soon as the car stopped, Carolyn jumped out and slammed her door shut—a little too quickly. He didn't blame her for being nervous. She was in the middle of nowhere with the man who'd kidnapped her.

He opened his door and the interior light flicked on. He glanced out into the field on his left. The ground was damp, which reminded him Carolyn was barefoot and probably uncomfortable. He'd have to do something about that soon, but at least the night was warm. He stepped out of the car.

Carolyn waited, her hands balled into fists at her side, her posture tense. When he went behind the car, she joined him, but kept some distance between them and stared pointedly at the trunk.

"I'm going to open the lid. If he's alive, which I doubt, he might try to get up. You let me deal with him. If I have to shoot him, I don't want you to try to stop me. Is that clear?" He stepped close to her.

She nodded, a haunted look in her eyes.

"Answer me. If he makes a move and I pull a gun on him, you can't interfere."

"I won't," she said, her voice barely a whisper.

He studied her for a moment. All he saw in her face was fear. "Go sit in the car."

She frowned and chewed her lower lip but then turned away and got back in the car.

He pulled his gun from its holster, held it ready, and opened the trunk with the other hand. The slight but foul odour that wafted out of the warm trunk told him Torque was indeed dead.

Michael stared down at the body of his partner.

This man had brought him into the Agency. From the moment Michael had started his training, Torque had mentored Michael and helped to make him a killing machine.

He grimaced, recoiling in pain. For a moment, he wished he'd found Torque alive so he could shoot him again.

Michael strode to Carolyn's side of the car and opened the door.

She stared at him, face pale and eyes wide. "You didn't shoot him."

"I didn't have to."

She hung her head.

He crouched down next to her.

She kept her face angled down.

He might as well tell her straight out. "Torque has a tracking chip in his neck. I'm going to remove it, and I want you to watch me do it."

She kept her head down, but shook it. "I can't."

"You have to." He hesitated, charged on. "I have a chip in me, too. You'll have to remove mine. It'll buy us some time if I take out his chip and keep it with mine. And it'll be easier for you to remove my chip if you've seen it done."

A tear dripped onto her thigh, but she nodded. "Okay." She said it so softly he almost missed it.

He reached out, wanting to touch her hair, but caught himself and lowered his arm. She wouldn't want him to touch her.

He stood, opened the back door of the car, and picked up the medical bag. He removed a flashlight, a scanner for detecting the chip, a scalpel, and a pair of surgical gloves, and returned to the open trunk. His partner stared out from it, unseeing.

Michael tried not to think about how supportive Torque had seemed after Jess's death. He needed to focus on the necessary task and feared what he'd do with that scalpel if he thought too much about the last few days.

"Carolyn." He waited, hoping she wasn't going catatonic on him. When she appeared at his side, he exhaled, relieved.

She stared into the trunk, tried to speak, but only emitted a strangling sound. She closed her mouth and looked away.

He set his tools down in the trunk next to the body, and this time, he did touch her. He put a hand under her chin and lifted her face up to his. "Torque was my partner. My friend. This isn't what I want to be doing right now. Do you understand? We have to do this to survive."

She was shaking.

He ignored an urge to put his arm around her. Afraid he'd add to her panic if he continued to touch her, he removed his hand from her face. "Can you focus on what I'm doing? I need you to pay attention."

"Yes. I feel sick."

"Anytime you want to pull away, tell me, and I'll stop."

She nodded and wrapped her arms around her body, hugging herself.

The urge to take her in his arms grew stronger. He turned back to the body in the trunk, put the gloves on, and leaned in a little to get a better view.

Since Torque lay on his back, Michael had to haul on the body and yank it into place. It required some effort to position him since rigour had already started to set in.

At least Torque had short hair, so his entire neck was exposed.

Michael used his finger to find the spot he needed, explaining each step in the process to Carolyn, whose gaze remained riveted on his hands. With the scanner, he located the chip, which hadn't migrated far from its original location.

He sliced into Torque and opened up a cut large enough to see the chip. He used the edge of his blade to pop the chip out. Next, he showed her how to stitch up the wound.

When he was done, Carolyn turned away and threw up.

"Go sit in the car. There's water in the bags. Help yourself. You don't have to watch anymore," Michael said.

She wiped her mouth with her hand and stumbled back to the car. Her sobs drowned out the cricket sounds around them.

He set his tools aside and leaned into the trunk again. He grasped the body under the arms and dragged it out onto the grass. At least they wouldn't have to drive around with a corpse in the trunk anymore. He glanced around and then dragged Torque to the swampy area, into the bulrushes and tall grass. He shoved the body into the water amongst the reeds and returned to the car.

After picking up his tools, Michael slammed the trunk lid down and sat sideways in the back of the car behind Carolyn, his feet on the grass. With the open medical bag resting on his lap, he tucked Torque's chip into a plastic bag. He then set about cleaning and sterilizing everything, preparing the things Carolyn would need to remove his chip.

He peered over at her. Sweat rolled down her temples and a spot of dampness grew on her tank top under each arm. A fingerprints-shaped bruise decorated the outside of each of her upper arms. He'd been rough with her when he'd dragged her out of her house. He turned away, ashamed.

For a moment, he considered leaving her there, letting her take her chances on her own. He could easily disappear. He'd get her to remove his chip, drug her, and leave. Without anyone to slow him down, he'd be far away by the time the Agency found the car.

He looked up at the sky. It was clear, dotted with thousands of stars visible to the naked eye in this remote area. Michael shook his head. He wasn't going anywhere without Carolyn. He looked at her again and had an urge to comfort her. His hand reached out, but he stopped himself.

Confused, he wondered where all this concern for her came from. Why should he care what happened to her? A month ago, he'd have death-rayed her without hesitation. Maybe it was her connection to Jessica. Was his wife with them now?

"Jess?" He whispered it.

There was only the silence of the night, broken by cricket song and woodland sounds. Carolyn had ceased sobbing. She stared at him. Maybe she'd heard him. Or maybe she sensed the emptiness inside him. A lump grew in his throat, and he scowled. He checked the time. Almost ten-thirty. He closed the medical bag.

"Carolyn." His voice sounded brusque.

She glanced at the medical bag in his lap. "You want me to remove your chip now." Her eyes widened, and she covered her mouth with a fist.

"Yes."

"I don't know if I can do this." She snatched up her bottle and swallowed some water, coughing when it went down the wrong way.

He waited for the coughing spell to subside. When she was quiet, he said, "I could try to do it myself, but it would take a lot longer. You have to do this for me."

"It was bad enough watching you do it. What if I make a mistake?" Her voice trembled.

"I'll talk you through it. It'll be fine. I've prepared everything."

He saw how pale she was. She didn't feel fine.

"What if I throw up?"

"Lean out of the car and throw up. Sanitize your hands and carry on."

"What if I pass out?"

"I'll wait until you come to and then you'll carry on."

"It's too dark. How am I going to see properly?"

"We'll leave the car light on. I have a flashlight, too. Quit stalling."

"Okay," she whispered. "Let's get this over with."

***

For Carolyn, the next twenty minutes seemed like hours. When the bandage was on Michael's neck at last, she climbed out of the car. She took a few steps away from the car and sank to her knees, shaking. Would she ever find her way out of this nightmare?

She heard footsteps and turned to see Michael holding out a bottle of water. She accepted it, rinsed her mouth, took another swig, and swallowed it. It was better, but she could feel the water pooling in her stomach.

He crouched next to her. "You okay?" He sounded concerned.

She thought, *No, I'm not okay. I'll never be okay.* She said, "Yes. I'll be fine."

He stood and held out his hand. She took it, and he pulled her to her feet. When he let go of her hand, she had to stop herself from grabbing him. His touch had been comforting. She took another swallow of water instead.

Michael held the baggie with the chips in it. She followed him around to the passenger side of the car. He opened the door, sat in Carolyn's seat, and unlocked the glove box. She noticed a small plastic folder in the glove box but nothing else. He set the baggie on top of the folder, closed the glove box, and locked it.

"We have to get moving," he said.

CHAPTER 35

Back on the 115, Michael left the highway at the Lansdowne exit and pulled into a gas station. The parking lot was busy, considering the hour. He parked the car between two transport trucks, the drivers nowhere in evidence. Michael turned off the car and removed the baggie with the tracking devices in it from the glove box. He also took out his and Torque's cell phones and dropped them into the bag.

After stepping from the car, he went around to the back and opened the trunk. Carolyn couldn't see what he did, but in a few seconds, he closed the trunk and disappeared behind one of the trucks. He returned minus the bag of tracking chips and holding a roll of duct tape in one hand.

"Did you just duct tape those chips and cell phones to that truck?" she asked.

"Yes. That should confuse them for a bit."

She didn't ask who "them" was. He probably wouldn't tell her anyway.

Michael started the car again and drove out of the gas station. They pulled into a nearby plaza with a twenty-four-hour pharmacy. He parked on the side of the parking lot farthest from the store.

"Wait here." He climbed out of the car and hurried across the pavement and into the store.

A phone booth stood next to the store. The sight of it brought on an urge to run over and call the police. Her hand reached for the door latch, but she didn't touch it. If she ran now, would she be risking her life, as Michael insisted? What would happen to him? He'd murdered a man. In self-defence, yes, but only in Torque's case. How many other people had he killed? He might've killed John. Her hand touched the door latch and, weakly, she tugged at it. The door opened. The interior light flicked on.

Startled, she jumped from the car and shut the door.

She stared at the phone booth. She'd promised Michael she wouldn't try to run, but she was here because of him. No, that wasn't quite true. Someone had told him to kidnap her. According to Michael, getting the police involved wouldn't keep her safe—if he told the truth. She'd felt intuitively before that she should stay with him. Despite the overwhelming urge to call the police, the thought of going through with it made her uneasy. Her intuition suggested that would put her in greater danger than staying with him did.

"Carolyn? What are you doing out of the car?"

She jumped. He'd approached her, and she hadn't even noticed he'd left the store. She'd make a lousy spy, agent, whatever Michael was. "I had to stretch. I couldn't bear sitting in the car anymore," she said.

He glanced at the phone booth and then met her gaze. He held up the bag he carried. "I hope you don't mind going brunette. We'll have to colour our hair. Also, they didn't have sneakers. Flip-flops. Better than nothing, for now."

When they'd both settled in their seats again, he turned to her and put his hand on her arm. "You can't call the police no matter how tempting. I appreciate you controlled the urge, but if you call them, you'll get us killed. No protective custody anywhere can keep you safe. If you get the urge to run, tell me. Believe me, if calling the cops was an option, I'd call them myself."

She hung her head, avoiding his eyes. He'd known what she wanted to do. He put his hand under her chin and tilted her head up. "It's understandable you'd want out of this, but we have to do it my way if we want both the Agency and the aliens off our backs forever. Okay?"

She nodded. "Yes. Okay." She changed the subject. "How's your neck?"

"Fine. It's as if you've performed surgery before." He put the car into drive and headed out of the parking lot.

"Very funny."

"That wasn't sarcasm. I'll heal fine."

"I hope it doesn't get infected."

"It won't. You worry about everything, don't you?"

"Not everything. The important things."

"Let me guess: everything's important?"

Carolyn smiled. "Okay. I worry too much. Just one more thing?"

"Yes?" Michael glanced at her and raised his eyebrows.

"Why didn't we ditch the car in Aurora?"

"Because they won't be looking for us until morning. They expect us to get to the base outside Peterborough sometime during the night. If they've checked on us during the night so far, using the tracking devices, they'd have seen we were en route. No one will notice something is wrong until the early morning when we haven't shown up, and my boss finds out we never checked in to say we delivered the package."

"You mean me. I'm the 'package.' "

"Yes. Sorry."

"It hurts to be referred to as an object, like I'm a thing to be couriered somewhere. I can't believe our own government is able to treat its citizens like this."

"They're not. Our agency doesn't officially exist, but some powerful people are involved, and they can make things official."

"I don't understand."

"I hope you never have to."

She thought for a moment, then said, "Wouldn't they have suspected something if they saw us stopped for hours?"

"They might. Or they might give us the benefit of the doubt. They likely won't figure it out until later in the morning, but we're running out of time. If they check all tracking simultaneously, they'll know something's wrong."

They drove for another few minutes, and Michael pulled into the parking lot of an inn. He drove around to the back, where there was additional parking, and parked the car.

"We're leaving the car here. Grab everything." He exited the vehicle and hefted his backpack onto his back. He picked up the medical bag and turned to Carolyn.

She stepped onto the pavement and tried to struggle the backpack onto her shoulders.

Michael chuckled. "Let me help you."

She flushed. "I guess I'm a bit of a princess. I'm going to slow you down, aren't I?"

He paused for a moment and then said, "We'll manage." He took the pack from her and set it down on the ground. "Put the flip-flops on."

She took the flimsy pink sandals from the bag and slipped her feet into them. They fit fine, but she could tell it wouldn't be long before the rubber thong between her toes started to chafe.

He opened her pack and removed Jessie's hiking boots, tossing them into the car. "One less thing to carry," he said. He closed and locked the car and helped her set the straps of her pack more comfortably on her shoulders. "Can you walk with this?"

I doubt it. "Yes."

Michael looked around.

She followed his gaze. No one was in sight.

"That way," he said, pointing. He started walking, and she followed. They headed for the tree line.

CHAPTER 36

Carolyn sat on the edge of the king-sized bed in the hotel room. She alternated between staring at the television and at her hair in the mirror above the dresser across from the bed. She couldn't get used to seeing herself with short, dark brown hair. Michael had assured her it was "cute." She'd told him he looked cute too, but she was being a smartass. He looked the same even with his black hair dyed light brown. Of course, he hadn't had to cut his hair. Every time she looked in the mirror, she saw a stranger looking back.

It was 1:18 AM, and neither one of them had suggested going to sleep. The TV had been playing since they walked into the room. Michael had tuned into a Toronto news channel, and the reel had looped around three times already, but they left it running. A particularly disturbing development was the disappearance of a popular horror writer and well-known alien abductee.

When the announcer reported Jason Meacher was missing, a chill went through Carolyn. As the clip about the writer began again, she turned her gaze on Michael. He sat at the table cleaning the guns, something she found unnerving though she understood the necessity.

She glanced at the television again, which continued to display Meacher's picture with "missing" flashing across it in large letters. She turned back to Michael.

"Do you think this is happening all over, to all abductees? You said you kidnapped us to silence us for what we said about the government. This guy wasn't saying anything about the government. He talked only about his abduction experiences."

"I don't know. Perhaps he was becoming too public."

She scanned their honeymoon suite. The clerk had told Michael it was the only room available. The fireplace, which was reflected in the mirror next to the heart-shaped whirlpool tub, gave off light, but not heat.

They'd turned off the blower.

It had been Carolyn's idea to start it up. She found it comforting, but it was too warm to turn on the heat. They'd argued a little about the air conditioner. She wanted it off and Michael wanted it on. They'd set it to twenty-three Celsius.

The tub reminded her of her last anniversary. She and John had rented a room at a bed-and-breakfast with a similar tub in Niagara-on-the-Lake. They'd spent an hour sitting in the swirling water, enjoying champagne and chocolate-covered strawberries, laughing at themselves for being so cliché.

If she'd known it would be their final anniversary together, she'd have savoured the time. Now, here she was in a honeymoon suite with a complete stranger. A bottle of sparkling wine and two glasses perched on the edge of the tub, complimentary with the room. She considered opening it and drinking it down to smother her memories.

It would be John's funeral the morning after next. Sam would have to bury her father without her mother there to comfort her. What if the Agency caught her, and she never saw Sam again? Panic flared up, and Carolyn had a wild urge to pick up the phone and call Sam. Instead, she said, "Michael, if something happens to me, promise me you'll find Sam and make sure they don't hurt her."

"I won't let anything happen to you." He finished cleaning the guns, which lay, reassembled, on the table next to him.

"But what if they get me? When Torque jumped me, I didn't stand a chance."

"Let me show you some self-defence moves. I can't teach you anything fancy, but I can show you how to hurt someone enough to allow you to get away."

"Only if it doesn't involve killing."

He grinned. "No problem. I'm just happy you'd be willing to hurt someone."

"I don't want to, but I think I can fight back."

"All right. Stand up."

They both rose.

"First thing I want you to understand is you have to be pre-emptive. It's better to avoid getting too close than it is to have to fight your way out. The second thing is you have to be okay with inflicting pain and injury. When you're attacked, it'll be you or him. Your best bet is to hurt and run. Okay?"

She nodded. "This feels so surreal."

"I know. It's okay. Pay attention to your surroundings. Make note of anywhere someone might hide and avoid walking there. Keep your head up and your eyes moving. Use store windows for reflections to see behind you. If you have a makeup mirror, you can use it to see behind you. If you see an attack coming, try to escape."

He continued. "Use anything to put a barrier between you and the attacker. Grab a chair if one is handy. You're using it as a shield. If someone attacks you with a knife, wrap your jacket around your arm to protect yourself, while you use the other arm for more offensive moves. When you're cornered, you have to do whatever you can to protect yourself, fight off the attacker, and leave."

Carolyn was uncertain. She envisioned grabbing her end table and confronting Michael in her den. She still thought her best protection was a working phone and enough time to call 9-1-1.

"Be willing to fight for yourself. Get angry if that helps. Action is quicker than reaction when it comes to fighting. It's okay to defend yourself, and it might make the difference between getting away and getting captured. At least it'll buy you time."

"I feel so weak and helpless."

"You won't if you know the things you can do to protect yourself. Never let anyone closer than two arm lengths. Let me show you how to stand."

He posed, feet hip-width apart, one foot back, his body turned at a forty-five-degree angle. Elbows close to his body, he held his fists up. "This pose gives you stability. It lets you stand strong. Your hands protect your body." He relaxed his arms. "You try it."

She tried to imitate his stance, feeling self-conscious as she raised her hands into the defensive position he'd demonstrated. He swung his arms up and shoved her. She stumbled back a few steps.

"Plant your feet. Stay firm. I didn't shove you hard. I can help you with the techniques, but you'll have to work on your confidence."

She nodded and planted her feet more firmly. When he shoved her again, she stayed in place.

"Much better," he said. "Remember, it takes time for a person to react. Do you understand?"

"Yes." Her own reaction time was slow, she knew.

"If an attacker gets closer to you than two arm lengths, don't hesitate. Use your palm to strike. Using a fist can get your hand hurt. If your hand isn't conditioned, punching someone in the skull can break your fingers. The heel of the palm is best for striking. Smash him right in the nose using the heel of your hand. His eyes will water, and you can use that moment to get out of there."

They spent the next hour practicing a variety of techniques that made Carolyn sick to consider executing. Her movements were at first hesitant and fearful, but Michael made her practice each one repeatedly until the motions became more fluid.

He removed the ammunition from his gun and showed her how to snatch a weapon from an opponent and to run away in a manner that reduced the risk of being shot. When they finished, he said, "I feel better knowing you can defend yourself a bit. Now, I think you should get some sleep. You look beat, and we have to leave early."

She wasn't sure she'd get any sleep with him in the room. "What about you?"

"I'll nap on the couch in the living room."

"Take one of these pillows with you. I saw a spare blanket in the closet by the door. I feel bad taking up an entire king-sized bed and making you sleep on the couch."

He smiled. "I've slept on worse." He stood and looked out the window, something he'd done with alarming regularity since they arrived. Carolyn had asked him if someone was out there, but he'd shaken his head and didn't comment. He went into the other room.

She peeled off her shorts, leaving on her panties and the T-shirt from Jessie's backpack she'd put on after her shower.

I'm wearing another woman's clothes—a dead woman's clothes. She pushed the thought away. At least they fit, though loosely. Jessie's feet may have been smaller, but she wore approximately the same size clothes as Carolyn.

The bed welcomed her, and she snuggled into it and pulled the sheets up to her chin. She turned off the television and lay on her back, staring up at the ceiling. Her mind didn't want to shut off, and she tried to relax and stop the thoughts.

The room was dim, not dark. Michael still had a light on in the living area. Sounds of movement reached her, then there was a click, and the fireplace in the mirror went dark. She heard more shuffling, and in the mirror Michael removed his pants. She turned her head away, prudishly, though part of her was tempted to watch him undress. She shifted onto her side, facing away from the living room.

The clock on the bedside table read 2:16 AM. She closed her eyes. Michael shut the light off in the other room, and the room grew dark and quiet. Her thoughts wandered randomly while she drifted off.

***

Jim Cornell stirred, the fragments of a dream dissipating until he had no recollection of it. A ringing he'd thought was part of his dream continued, and he realized it was his phone. He answered with an abrupt "hello," his voice gravelly with sleep. He glanced at the clock. It was 3:47 AM. This couldn't be good.

A voice on the other end acknowledged the early hour and apologized for waking him. "It's Traegar, sir. I'm calling from Peterborough Compound. We've been expecting your delivery since oh-two-hundred, but nothing has arrived. We checked the tracking, and it appears the car is sitting in a hotel parking lot in Peterborough. Both agents are on the highway heading toward Ottawa. The woman appears to be in another hotel in Peterborough."

Cornell shook his head, trying to process what he'd heard. None of it made sense. He didn't respond, trying to think of a way to handle it.

"Sir?" Traegar persisted. "What would you like us to do?"

Cornell suggested the first thing that came to him. "Send a couple of guys to retrieve the car. Monitor Fairchild's movements and the movements of the two agents. I'll contact Muniz and Valiant and figure out what to do when I know what happened. If something went wrong, they'd have contacted me. Thanks for your call, Agent. I'll get right back to you."

He hung up the phone without saying goodbye. He had a sinking sensation in his gut. What if Valiant had lost it? Torque had been assuring Cornell he could handle Michael, and Cornell had given Torque free rein with that situation, but Cornell had always had his doubts.

He dialled Torque's number. Voicemail picked up immediately. That meant the phone was either dead or off. He dialled Valiant, and that phone also went into voicemail. He grimaced and called Traegar back at Peterborough Base.

"Traegar."

"Yeah, it's Cornell. Listen, I can't reach Muniz and Valiant. Send two agents after them. Monitor the woman. Don't lose her. We can't have her running around out there. Call me when you have the car and let me know what you find. When you catch up with Muniz and Valiant, call me immediately."

"Yes, sir."

Cornell hung up the phone. He checked the clock again: 3:52 AM. He got out of bed to start his day.

CHAPTER 37

*J*ohn *and Carolyn drive along the ocean in a cab. It heads for a pier and drives onto it. John protests, telling the driver to stop the car.*

They yell at the cab driver, while the car gets closer to the edge with no indication the driver intends to stop.

The cab flies off the end of the pier and into the water.

Somehow, Carolyn finds herself outside the car, swimming for shore. John is with her. There's no sign of the driver. When they drag themselves up onto the beach, she realizes the agency she works for is trying to kill them. They're also trying to kill her mother. Her whole family has become expendable and is to be erased.

They go to the hotel to check out, but they've left their suitcases in the room and Carolyn insists they go back for them. When she steps out of the elevator, John is no longer with her. She panics.

She wants to run to her room but can't remember where it is. The elevator opens and agents step out. They're coming to kill her. She tries to run, but they grab her. She screams and struggles, grabbing at their hands, trying to get them off her. The terror intensifies. They're smothering her. She can't breathe and opens her mouth to scream again
...

"Shh. It's okay. It's only a dream." The voice was Michael's. He sat on the bed, holding her, his body pressed against hers.

"Don't let me go." She wrapped her arms around him, pressing her head against his hard chest. Its solidity reassured her. "I dreamed agents were trying to kill me."

"You're having a nightmare." His hand stroked her hair.

"They were coming after me, off the elevator. I was lost and alone."

"You're not alone."

"Please don't go." Need for him pushed aside everything else, and she didn't care who he was or why they were there. She wanted his body next to hers, on top of hers. She wanted him to take her.

Carolyn lifted her face up and kissed his lips. He hesitated, but it was only for a moment. His lips responded, and he returned the kiss. His tongue parted her lips, while his hands went to her hair, to her back, to her breasts, first over her T-shirt, then sliding under it to her bare skin.

She gasped when his hands slid over her nipples. Desire flamed through her from deep in her belly. She ran her hands over his arms and then stroked his back and stomach too. He wore only his underwear, and she wanted that off him, so she tugged at it until he nudged her hand away and removed it himself. She ached to touch every part of him, and her hands roved everywhere at once.

He grasped her T-shirt and pulled it off over her head. Then it was his turn to tug at her panties and her turn to nudge his hand away and strip. When they were both naked, she pressed the length of her body against him, savouring him with every part of her. His skin was soft, but his body was hard, and his perfection drove her to blissful madness. His breathing came in quick gasps that matched her own.

Neither said a word. They made love silently until the moment when they could no longer hold back. Michael's body melded with hers. She fused with him. It was more than physical. She experienced all of him. She received him, and he gave himself to her.

When they were done, they lay together, limbs still entwined. Carolyn laid her head on his shoulder. She ran her hand along his chest, tracing her way down from his heart chakra to his sacral chakra.

He stopped her before she could go any farther. He gently took her hand and lifted it to his mouth to kiss it. When he did, a surge, like an electrical charge, ran through her hand to her core.

"I don't know what happened to me," she said, self-conscious. "I couldn't stand it if you weren't touching me."

"Are you sorry?"

"No. Are you?"

"No. Surprised, maybe, but not sorry."

She looked into his eyes, seeking. "I felt close to you. It was overwhelming."

"For me, too. It might be a way of off-loading what's happened over the last couple of days."

She didn't reply. She wanted to hang onto the experience for a while longer, and analyzing it would spoil it. But Michael was back to reality, and she caught him checking the clock. She turned her head to see what time it was. The clock read 6:31 AM.

Michael spoke first. "God, I don't want to get up, but we need to leave. It's best for you to wear long pants even if it's hot. I expect to go into Algonquin today, and we should dress for it."

Carolyn went into the washroom, going through the routine of using the toilet, washing her face, showering, and brushing her teeth. She hadn't been with anyone other than John for over twenty years, and what had just happened confused her.

Michael was a killer, a kidnapper. She didn't want to feel anything for him. She gasped. *Is this what they mean by "Stockholm Syndrome?"* Was she experiencing something psychological that had nothing to do with who he was but grew out of the situation she was in?

Carolyn dressed, putting on the pants she'd fished out of the backpack. They were a little loose. Evidently, she was slightly thinner than Jess around the middle. How much longer would she continue to compare herself to Jessica?

She put on her bra—her own—she'd noted with some satisfaction her breasts were larger than Jess's, so Jess's wouldn't fit. As she picked up a clean T-shirt, there was a knock on the bathroom door. She slipped the T-shirt on.

"Come in."

Michael opened the door and stepped inside. "I've packed everything."

"I'm finished in here if you want to take your turn in the shower." She went to walk past him, but when she did, her hip brushed against his and a thrill surged through her gut, making her feel as if the wind had been knocked out of her. She tried to ignore it, but he put his arms around her and held her.

He pressed his lips to the top of her head. "I wish things weren't this way," he said.

"If things weren't like this, we'd have never met."

He let her go. "It's Jess's funeral today. I don't know if I'm betraying her. When you touch me, all I want to do is grab you."

"I don't know what this means either. Could be the stress from the situation. We both lost our spouses to it. Perhaps it's natural to turn to each other for comfort. We've got no one else. I can't even call my daughter to tell her I'm alive." Her voice broke.

He put his arm around her waist and pulled her into an embrace. "I'll fix that. You'll see her again, I promise."

"All right." She hugged him back, not wanting to let go, but knowing they should hurry.

Her head was fuzzy from lack of sleep. She couldn't think straight, and being near him made it worse. She extricated herself from his arms and stepped away.

He went into the bathroom and closed the door. Water ran in the tub, and then the shower started. She glanced at the clock: 6:44 AM. He'd better hurry.

CHAPTER 38

The phone rang. Jim Cornell snatched it up. It was 6:45 AM, and he'd already heard back from one team. They'd found Muniz's car abandoned in the parking lot of a hotel in Peterborough. He continued to call Valiant's and Muniz's phones, and each time he'd connected immediately with voicemail. This had better be news about them, or, better yet, one of them calling to explain.

"Cornell."

"Traegar here. We found the chips."

"You mean you found Valiant and Muniz?"

"No, I mean we found their tracking chips. They must've removed them. They were in a plastic baggie, along with their cell phones, duct taped to a transport truck heading to Ottawa."

"Son of a bitch. It's Valiant, I'm sure of it, but why would Muniz go along with him?"

"Sir?"

"I'm thinking out loud. What about the woman?"

"Her tracking chip indicates she's in a hotel in Peterborough. We've located the room she's in. Two agents are watching the hotel. Do you want us to move on her?"

"If Muniz and Valiant have removed their chips, they're likely with her. They probably don't realize she's been chipped too. See if you can find an opportunity to get her alone. If you can snatch her when she's away from them, we can deal with them later. I don't want anything to happen to her."

"Yes sir."

He hung up the phone. One way or another, Carolyn Fairchild would be locked up today.

***

The bathroom door opened, and Michael stepped out. He wore jeans and a T-shirt, and his feet were bare. Carolyn's gaze tracked him while he walked to his bag and put on his socks and running shoes.

He went to the window and peered outside. The room overlooked the parking lot at the back of the hotel. He spotted a man sitting in a car, watching the exits.

"We can't go downstairs for breakfast."

"They're out there, aren't they?" she whispered.

"Maybe."

"How will we escape if we're being watched?"

"I'll get us out. It might not be Agency, but I don't want to take a chance."

"If they know we're here, how will we get a car?"

"We'll figure it out. I don't understand how they found us so quickly. They knew right where to go. There must be another chip on me." Michael opened the medical bag and took out the scanner. "I'm going to strip down and I want you to scan my body. It'll beep if it locates a chip."

He removed his shoes and clothing and stood in front of her. He turned on the scanner and handed it to her.

She inspected his entire body, starting at his head. After five minutes, she finished. "There's nothing on you."

He stared at her, thinking. "Maybe it's you."

"I guess it could be. Aliens abduct me regularly. Would they have put a chip in me the government could use as well?"

"The aliens don't need to use chips to track you, which is why I didn't think of it. They have other ways, but there's no telling what arrangements they made with the Agency. Let me check you out."

Michael dressed while Carolyn stripped down. He then picked up the scanner and searched her body. Her eyes went wide and she recoiled when he scanned her nasal area.

"What's wrong?" he asked while the wand swept silently over her face.

"I get nosebleeds sometimes, and I was afraid that's where they stuck it. I don't want to think how we'd have to remove it from inside my nose."

"It's okay. I didn't find a chip, but they might have put something there this wand can't pick up."

He moved around behind her. The wand beeped when he scanned across the back of her right shoulder.

"There it is," he said. "You understand we'll have to remove it?"

Her face went pale, but she nodded.

"They're probably waiting for you to leave the room. I'll remove the chip and we'll get out of here." He opened the medical bag while Carolyn dressed. He watched her, unable to take his gaze off her body.

She glanced up while she pulled on her track pants and caught him staring. She smiled.

Michael blushed. "Sorry."

"It's okay." She left her bra and shirt off. "I'm ready. Where do you want to do this?"

"Lie face down on the bed. Give me a few seconds while I wash my hands and get ready." He went into the bathroom and scrubbed his hands and arms up to the elbows. He returned to the bed.

She lay face down, a pillow under her chest elevating her shoulders.

He sat beside her. "The procedure is exactly the same as when you removed my chip. It'll be okay." Michael put on a clean pair of surgical gloves. He removed some alcohol wipes from the bag and cleaned the area where the chip was located.

She stiffened.

To distract her while he worked, he talked to her. "You'll be fine. Tell me about how you can talk to spirits. Could you always do that?"

"I was a little girl when it first started. I was close to my grandmother. When she died, I saw her in a dream. She came to me when I was sleeping and told me she wasn't sick anymore. She said I shouldn't cry or feel sad because she wasn't going to be too far away. I could always connect with people who passed, but that one really opened me up. Spirits seem to know when you have the gift, and they come around."

She stopped talking and flinched when he slipped the hypodermic into her and pressed the plunger. He touched her shoulder and leaned closer to her.

"It's the local. We'll give it a minute." He paused. "I dreamed about my wife after she died. Was that really Jess?"

"Yes. It's common for people to dream about their departed loved ones. It's the easiest way for spirits to communicate with those who can't see spirits when they're awake. You're more open when you sleep, and it's easier for them to get through to you. I saw John, too, but not in my dreams. I was awake. He didn't say anything, but I knew he was okay and he loves me."

"Why can't Jess come to me when I'm awake?" He felt cheated she hadn't appeared to him after that single dream. Didn't she know how much he wanted to see her again?

"She might if you worked at being open enough to feel her around you. If you practice raising your vibration, you'll be able to connect with her. You can also ask her to give you signs she's around. Spirits can reveal their presence by leaving coins in strange places around the house, or they mess with electronics or with the lights. If the TV suddenly turns on by itself, that could be your departed loved one."

"I'd like to see her again. My dream ended so abruptly that I didn't get to hug her or even go near her."

"That's common too. I think it has to do with their energy and how much it takes out of them to visit you like that."

"Three men in robes were with her. They looked like monks. Who were they? Or was that symbolism in the dream?"

"Some people think they're spirit guides. Others think they help everyone who passes make the transition. Was she in a hospital bed when you saw her?"

"Yes. How did you know?"

"That's common too. It's as if they have to rest for a while when they first cross."

His voice changed, becoming lower and gentler. "Stay still. I'm going to get started. Tell me if you have any discomfort and I'll stop."

"Okay."

He noticed she was holding her breath. "You can breathe."

"Sorry." She exhaled. "I'm nervous."

"It's okay. I won't hurt you."

It took Michael ten minutes to remove the chip, stitch her up, and bandage the wound. When he finished dressing the small cut he'd made, he considered what they could do to distract those agents. He assumed there were two. They couldn't watch all the exits. One was probably the guy in the car at the back of the hotel. The other could be at the front or in the lobby.

"I have an idea," he said. He dropped the chip into the pocket of his jeans. "Don't move from this room and don't open the door unless it's me."

"Where are you going?" Her voice rose with fright.

"I'm going to take care of these guys so they can't follow us."

"Don't kill them."

"We can't debate that right now. Latch the door when I'm gone. Torque's gun is on the table. If you need it, use it." He went to the table and picked up the gun. "Aim and shoot; put direct pressure on the trigger. Don't hesitate. If you do, you're in trouble."

"Is the safety off?"

He shook his head. "It has internal safeties. That's why you have to put direct pressure on the trigger. Come here. I'll show you how to hold it."

Carolyn stood and picked up her bra and T-shirt, and he helped her put them on. She flinched when the material touched her shoulder.

"Are you okay?" he asked.

159

"Yeah. It feels weird."

She turned to him and frowned at the gun in his hand. He pulled the slide back to cock it and then held it out. She hesitated but took it from him.

"Use two hands, one to hold the gun, and the other to steady it. When you fire, it'll recoil a bit, but you should be able to keep it steady. This is an easy gun to use."

He helped her position her hands. "When you want to fire, put your finger here, right on the trigger, and then press on it like you mean it. It won't be loud, because the suppressor is on it, but it won't be silent, either."

She nodded.

"If I'm not here and something happens, then you'd better be prepared to use this. They're here to take you back with them. Understood?"

"Yes."

He released her hands, and she set the gun back down on the table. She frowned, her eyes wide, but he turned away. He'd have to trust that if things became critical, she'd use it.

Michael put on his shoulder holster, screwed his suppressor on the gun, cocked it, and placed it in the holster. He put a jacket on to conceal the weapon and pressed his arm against it. When he stepped into the hallway, he put the "Do not disturb" sign on the outside of the doorknob. He pulled the door closed and Carolyn latched it behind him.

CHAPTER 39

Michael went to the stairwell and headed down the stairs, stopping at the second floor. The door at the bottom of the stairwell creaked as someone opened it. Michael slipped into the hallway, pulling the gun from his holster and using his jacket to conceal it.

He pressed his ear to the door. Someone coming up the stairs abruptly stopped. The agent in the car likely tracked his movements using a receiver and communicating with his partner over a wire. They were expecting Carolyn to be on the other side of the second-floor door.

The door eased open.

Michael smashed his body into it. A grunt of pain followed a thud, and the door slammed shut. Michael raised his gun and shoved the door open, jumping onto the landing.

The agent staggered back, raising his gun and aiming at Michael, who fired into the agent's chest blowing him backward. Michael shot him again, this time in the face, blood and brain matter splattering around him.

He removed the chip from his pocket and dropped it in the pocket of the agent's pants. He checked the man's ID. Robert Cunningham. No one he knew. He removed Cunningham's jacket and wrapped it around his head so moving the body wouldn't leave a blood trail. Also taking Cunningham's gun, Michael slipped it into his own holster. The gruesome evidence would remain on the wall and stairs, but at least he could hide the body. Michael used the fireman's carry to take it down to the ground floor.

He dropped the body at the bottom of the stairs, shoving it under the stairwell out of sight. He opened the door to the main floor, peeked out, and scanned the area. Everything seemed quiet. He opened the door wider and looked down the hall to the left. It was empty, the hall stretching down through rooms on either side, with a break on the right where the entrance led to the lobby.

Gun raised and ready to fire, he stepped out, quickly turning right. He could see an exit to the parking lot a short distance away. He waited, expecting the other agent to appear from that direction. Nothing moved.

He walked down to the exit, alert for any sound or movement. When he reached the door, he stood to the side and scanned the parking lot. The car he'd seen earlier was still there, but the man in it was gone. Why wasn't he coming to find his partner? He should've been tracking both his partner's movements and the movements of Carolyn's chip.

Unless he knew it wasn't Carolyn using the chip.

Michael's gut did a flip-flop. He ran back to the stairs, taking them two at a time. He had to get back to their room.

***

Two minutes after Michael left the room, Carolyn was pacing back and forth through the bedroom and the living area. She was terrified he'd be killed trying to stop those agents, leaving her on her own. Then she was afraid her fears would manifest what she didn't want and visualized him returning to the room. She said a quick prayer for him and asked the angels to protect him.

She went back to watching the news, but couldn't bear sitting still and started pacing again. At one point, she paused to turn off the television. The noise was getting on her nerves. She tried to sense any spirits. She hadn't felt anyone around for a while. Nothing.

Michael had seen someone outside. If she looked out the window, would she be able to spot the agents? She didn't know what to look for, but she crept to the window, moved the sheers out of the way, and peered out.

Nothing moved. Then she noticed a car parked on the right side of the parking lot. Someone was sitting in it. She shielded her eyes, squinting for a better view. At that moment, the person in the car gazed up in her direction. Carolyn staggered back.

He has binoculars. He'd seen her and knew she hadn't left the room.

Cursing herself for going to the window, she considered what to do. If she stayed in the room, they might get to her before Michael realized she'd given herself away. She should at least leave the room and hide somewhere, but then, how would Michael find her?

The door's latched. They couldn't get in through a locked door. Could they?

She opened the door and peeked into the hallway. Empty. She closed it again and stuck her key card in her back pocket. She peered out into the hallway again. Still empty. She stepped into the hallway and pulled the door closed. She hesitated, trying to decide which way to go.

Carolyn fled down the hall toward the elevators, which were about fifteen metres away. The stairs should be nearby. Or perhaps there was a utility room or closet to hide in.

The elevator pinged and the doors opened. A man stepped out, did a double take when he saw her, and ran at her.

She realized she'd left the gun in the room, and her panic escalated. She spun around and retraced her steps. No choice now. The only place to go was back to her room. She reached the door, yanked the key card out of her pocket, and shoved the card into the slot. After a second, she slid it out. It didn't work. She'd pulled it out too fast. Frantic, she jammed it in again.

The indicator light on the door changed to green. She flung open the door and rushed into the room. She shoved on the door, but the man had reached it and pushed on it.

Somehow, with an adrenaline rush perhaps, she forced the door closed. She locked the deadbolt, flipped the latch, on and jumped back. To her horror, she heard a kick against the door. The latch rattled, and wood splintered. She ran to the phone to call 9-1-1. Instead of picking up the phone, she grabbed the gun from the table. She aimed it at the door with shaking hands.

Point and shoot. Don't hesitate.

Her heart thudded, and she thought her knees might buckle. The door shattered away from the jamb and the latch went flying.

The man burst into the room. He was big, shorter than Michael, but not by much, and he was stockier and more brutal looking. He lunged at her.

She pulled the trigger. The shot went wide. She swung her arm down again to take another shot, but he was on her.

He knocked the gun from her hand and punched her in the stomach.

Carolyn dropped to the floor and doubled over, tears leaking from her eyes. She couldn't breathe, and her mouth opened and closed, opened and closed, like a stranded fish. The dream she'd had this morning flashed through her mind. She was alone with this man, and he would kill her or take her away. Michael wasn't there after all.

CHAPTER 40

In a panic, Michael burst into the fourth-floor hallway. He raced around a corner and ran to the room. The door was ajar, the splintered jamb keeping it from closing. His heart in his mouth, he raised his gun and shoved the door open, afraid she was already gone. Relief flooded through him when he saw her.

Carolyn was curled up like a fetus, trying to suck air into her lungs. The agent hovered over her. He didn't even have his gun trained on her anymore. He went rigid and then lifted his weapon when Michael crashed into the room.

Gun already raised, Michael fired first. There was a muffled report, and the agent dropped from a bullet to the face. He wouldn't threaten them anymore. Half his head was gone.

Michael ran to Carolyn's side, pulling her to him. He stroked her hair, held her head to his chest. "We have to get out of here. That door breaking must have alerted someone. Can you get up?"

She nodded her head. When she tried to stand, she collapsed again, shuddering. Michael rose to standing and rushed to the door. He repositioned it, lining it up so the hinges and bolt were holding it in place. At least when it was shut, someone walking by wouldn't notice the damage. She'd need at least a few minutes to recover.

He scanned the room and spotted a bottle of water on the table. He retrieved it, uncapped it, and put it to her lips.

"Sip some water."

Her gasps were slower and quieter. She coughed, tried to take a sip from the bottle, and got some down her throat. As her breath became regular, the shock set in. She shook, and Michael went to the bed and yanked the blanket from it. He took it to her and wrapped her in it.

"You'll be okay."

He couldn't believe no one was pounding on the door. Had no one

164

heard the door smashing? Or were they all trying to stay out of what they assumed was a domestic dispute? Whatever the reason, he was grateful for the favour.

Michael held Carolyn in his arms, rocking her. Her gasps for air had turned to sobs, and she clung to him. Fear welled up, and he crushed it. He refused to think about what would've happened to her if he hadn't realized what had happened.

After a time, she stopped sobbing and looked up at him. He stroked her hair and kissed her forehead.

"Can you stand?"

"Yes." It came out as a croak, and she cleared her throat. "Yes."

He kissed her lips, softly. Then he stood, lifting her to her feet. She walked to the washroom, and he noticed she stumbled a little. When she was in the bathroom, he crouched next to the body of the agent he'd killed and searched his pockets. He opened the man's wallet. David Mathers. The name meant nothing to Michael.

He rose, picked Torque's gun off the floor, and put it into his pack. At least this time, she'd pulled the trigger. The other agents' guns went into his pack as well. He'd acquired quite an arsenal, but he didn't want to leave weapons lying around. He removed the suppressor from his own weapon, put it away, and put the gun in his holster, closing his jacket over it.

Carolyn reappeared, looking much better. He went to her. She stared at the body, her eyes going wide and her face turning green.

"Don't look." Michael turned her away. "Let's get out of here before the police descend on us."

After he helped get her pack on, he hoisted his own onto his shoulders and picked up the medical bag. He went to the door, and she stepped through the opening he created. He closed the door with difficulty, but he made it resemble a firmly shut door—if you didn't examine it. The "Do not disturb" sign lay on the hallway floor, and he hung it from the doorknob.

Carolyn automatically headed for the closest set of stairs, and Michael gently took her arm and turned her around. Not wanting to use the stairs with the body at the bottom, he led her to another set. He held the door open, and she entered the stairwell.

They made their way down, Michael keeping the pace slow so Carolyn could manage. She followed him without a word. When they reached the bottom, he motioned her to stay quiet. He opened the door a crack. When he saw the housekeeping trolley a few metres down the hall, he closed the door again.

"Housekeeping is nearby. Let me check it out. I'll come back for you when it's safe."

Immediately, her eyes registered fear and panic.

He brushed her cheek lightly with his fingers. "Don't worry. I'll only be gone for a moment."

She remained silent.

He turned and cracked open the door again. The trolley still stood in the hall. He stepped out, closing the door behind him. He strolled past the room with the trolley, glancing in through the open door.

It was a utility room. Someone was inside, but out of his view. He returned to the stairwell and waved her out. She slipped past him, and he took her hand, feeling her relax at his touch.

When they reached the exit, he motioned her to wait while he scanned the grounds. No one stirred. He checked his watch. Just after eight o'clock. They'd lost a lot of time. More agents would be coming soon.

"Stay close."

She nodded. The air felt hot already. The afternoon would be scorching. A slight breeze stirred the humidity, and Michael took a deep breath.

"Let's go." He walked with her out into the parking lot. He glanced around to make sure no one watched them from a distance, and when he was satisfied, he took Carolyn's hand and led her away.

CHAPTER 41

B y 7:30 AM, Jim Cornell had reached his office in Toronto. He checked his voicemail. Nothing from Valiant or Muniz, but Traegar had left a message stating things had moved forward at the hotel.

Cornell returned the call, and Traegar told him that the last report from the agents at the hotel said that Fairchild had left her room and headed down the stairwell. One agent went to intercept her.

Cornell booted up his computer, glancing at the phone every few seconds, expecting it to ring. He didn't know how this job got so screwed up, but when he got his hands on Valiant and Muniz, they'd have some 'splainin' to do, Lucy. He felt a headache coming on and buzzed Helen.

"Yes, sir?"

"Get me a coffee, would ya?"

"Yes, sir."

He opened his desk drawer and pulled out a chocolate bar. Breakfast. He'd wash it down with coffee whenever his assistant showed up with it. The phone rang at seven fifty-eight.

"Cornell."

"It's Traegar."

"Well, what have you got for me?"

"I'm sorry, sir. Muniz is dead. They found his body dumped in a swampy area along the route to Peterborough. According to the GPS data, the car stopped there for over an hour."

"Shit. How'd he die?"

"Gunshots to the chest, sir."

"Thoughts on who killed him?"

"Too early to say, but they speculate it was Valiant."

Cornell paused. Valiant and Muniz had been partners for what? Twenty years? What had made Michael turn on his partner and mentor?

The woman?

"Sir? You there?"

"Yeah. Anything else?"

"Yes, sir. We have a problem at the hotel." Traegar didn't pause to let Cornell respond. "Looks as if Mathers is in the hotel room alone. Cunningham appears to be in the stairwell with the woman. None of them are moving."

"Assume they're dead and the woman is gone. Get agents down there now to clean up the mess. Give the hotel manager a cover story that it was a domestic dispute and no one else is at risk. Don't let any cops near anything until it's been sanitized."

"Yes, sir. Where do we go from here?"

"Check surveillance cameras in the area. See if you can spot them anywhere. Find out what name he used from the guest registry. If you have anything to report, call me right away. I want them found. And Traegar?"

"Yes, sir?"

"We need Fairchild alive. I'd prefer to have them both alive, but use lethal force on Valiant if necessary."

"Yes, sir."

Cornell hung up the phone. A knock sounded on his door, and Helen appeared with his coffee. He nodded, indicating she should set it down on his desk. He grunted his thanks when she placed it on a coaster at the top of his desk.

"Will there be anything else, sir?"

"Yeah. I want the surveillance tapes from the Fairchild residence. Everything they have from last night to now. And have them monitor any calls in or out of the Fairchild place, anything from landlines and cells. Anything significant, they should notify me immediately."

"Yes, sir."

"Thanks, Helen." He watched her leave.

She'd been with them since they'd moved the offices up here five years ago. She was bright, all business. He'd found her to be a good listener, but not nosy. She was somewhat homely. With her short, mousey hair and her business attire, she resembled a librarian. He sometimes had the urge to get her a makeover, but it was none of his business.

Cornell was married, his wife and kids mostly living without his presence. He didn't think they minded too much. They had all the luxuries they wanted to compensate for that.

The phone rang and he snatched up the receiver.

"Yeah? Cornell here."

"Traegar again. As you guessed, they located Cunningham in the stairwell. Dead. Fairchild's chip was on him. She wasn't anywhere in the hotel. Mathers was in the hotel room. Also dead. We figure it was Valiant."

"Anything else?"

"No, sir. That's all for now."

Cornell ended the call. Where'd Michael go with the woman? What were his options? Disappear out of the country? No matter where he took her, the aliens would find them. Once they did, it would be easy for the Agency to reclaim her.

His phone rang again, and he answered. "Cornell."

"It's Helen, sir. I have the files you requested transferred to your network folder. They're in a folder with today's date."

"Thanks."

He hung up and logged into his computer. He navigated to the network folder, which contained hours of audio and video files. He transferred them to his external hard drive and opened up the video from the other night. He trolled through the footage and paused when he located a scene that showed Carolyn in the den.

She looked panicked and was trying to call for help on her cell phone. Valiant showed up before she could connect and chased her outside. Cornell couldn't hear their conversation.

When they stepped back into the house, the woman said, "Who is Jessica?" and he noted Michael's reaction. He dragged her back outside and closed the sliding doors. The camera stopped filming thirty seconds after the doors to the porch closed.

It picked up again when the pair stepped back into the house. At this point, it appeared as if someone, probably the daughter, entered the house. Michael held the gun to Carolyn's head and kept her from crying out. So far, it looked as if he was still in the game and on board with his mission.

Cornell continued to examine the footage until he'd reviewed everything. He found nothing in there to explain why Michael was helping Fairchild instead of delivering her to the Agency as he'd been instructed.

The one odd piece was her question about Jessica, obviously a reference to Valiant's wife. How did Carolyn know about Jessica? Her psychic abilities. She'd picked up the truth about Jessica's death and told Michael. That had to be it.

Cornell felt his ulcer burning a hole in his stomach. He had to get that woman away from Valiant. God knows what else she'd find out just by being around him.

His phone rang again and he picked up. "Cornell."

"It's Groser. I'm monitoring the surveillance on the Fairchild residence. I thought you might like to know the daughter is at home. The main phone lines are still out, though she's called the phone company for service using her cell. She also contacted the neighbours and Brent Morgan, looking for her mother. She established no one saw her last night, and they don't know where she is."

"Has she notified the police yet?"

"No, sir. She called a friend. This same friend dropped her off at home this morning. They decided she should wait since they aren't certain the mother's missing."

"Anything else?"

"Yes, one thing. The daughter suggested to the friend Fairchild might have tried to go to Algonquin Park because of something Drummond told them. Does that mean anything to you?"

"No, but maybe I'll head over there and question the girl myself. Thanks." He hung up the phone and dialled Helen.

When she picked up, he told her he would be stepping out and to forward any calls from Traegar or Groser to his cell phone. All other calls should go to voicemail. He put his computer in "sleep" mode and made a note to get an unregistered gun on his way out. Cornell wasn't expecting to use it on the daughter, but he wanted to have it ready.

He unlocked a drawer on the bottom left of his desk. A small box in it contained various badges and identification cards with his picture on them. Today, he'd work for the RCMP. He took out his wallet and slipped the relevant ID card and badge inside.

Cornell nodded to Helen on the way out of the office, feeling optimistic for the first time since he'd been awakened with the news his agents had gone AWOL. By the time he reached his car, he was whistling.

CHAPTER 42

A black Mercedes rolled up to the Fairchild's garage, Sam tracking its progress from the living room window. A man she didn't recognize got out of the car, and she crossed her arms and hugged her chest while he climbed the stairs. When he knocked on the door, she opened it.

"Carolyn Fairchild?"

"No." She hesitated. "That's my mother."

She studied him carefully, but he wasn't familiar. He was overweight, balding, and his large, round eyes reminded her of an owl, but his face seemed kind. He was probably a lot older than her mom.

"My name is Jim Cornell. I work for a branch of the government that investigates UFO sightings." He held out his identification.

"I thought the government denied having anything to do with UFOs?"

"We investigate certain events that come to us through military channels. Many times, it has more to do with investigating the people who report the events than with the possible existence of extraterrestrials. I'd like to talk with your mother. Is she available?"

"I'm sorry. She's not here right now."

"Do you know a man named Ralph Drummond?"

"He's a friend of my mom's. Has something happened to Ralph?" She tensed. If something had happened to Ralph, something terrible might have happened to her mother.

He frowned and then shook his head. "No. Nothing's happened to Ralph. I'm investigating his involvement in a cult. They recruit people who believe UFOs are abducting them and send them to their camp up by Algonquin. I'm tracking down anyone he's had any affiliation with for questioning. It would help me reunite many people with their missing loved ones. Once they get involved with this cult, they cut off all connection with their families. It's heartbreaking the pain this group causes."

"Oh, my God," Sam said. "My mother might be going there. We visited Ralph the other day, and he told my mom to go to Algonquin. He sent her there. Please, come in."

Cornell smiled and stepped inside.

"Can I make you a cup of tea?" she asked.

"Yes, that would be nice."

"Please, come into the kitchen, and we can talk while I put the kettle on."

"Thank you, dear." His voice was kind. "Where's your mother now?"

She picked up the kettle from the kitchen counter and filled it from the water purifier. He sat on a bar stool at a counter along the side of the kitchen.

"I don't know. Maybe she went to Algonquin." There was panic in her voice. "Ralph said there are aliens helping abductees in Algonquin Park. My mom believed him. He said he had a map."

"Did you see this map?"

"No. We went to Ralph's to get it from his wife, but she said she gave it to the government people. Was that you?"

"Perhaps. I'll investigate. If you didn't get the map, why would she go to Algonquin now?"

The water boiled, and the kettle shut off. Sam went through the motions of preparing the tea, which reminded her of her mother, and she thought she'd go crazy with worry. She was silent for a moment, trying to collect herself so she wouldn't cry in front of this stranger.

When she could speak without her voice breaking, she said, "Ralph's wife said he gave Brent a copy of the map. My mom was trying to get it from him. I can't reach my mom though. She was supposed to spend the night at a neighbour's last night, and the neighbour said she never did. I'm worried. Should I call the police?"

"I'm sure nothing has happened to her. Perhaps I can help you find her. Let me make some calls, and I'll verify for you she's okay. If we haven't located her by tomorrow, I'll contact the authorities myself."

"Her purse and all her things are here. She wouldn't leave without her wallet and everything. I'm afraid something has happened. She even left a duffel bag with her clothes and personal stuff in it sitting on the floor in her bedroom."

"I see. Was there anything in the house to indicate a struggle?"

"No. Everything looked fine. A note I wrote to her was gone. When I came in last night, she wasn't here, and I left her a note telling her where I was going. After I left, she must have come in, picked it up, and then left again. It doesn't make sense. Her car is still here. Unless she left with someone else, I don't know what could have happened. I don't

172

understand why she wouldn't have left me a note to say where she was going, and I don't understand why I can't get her on her cell phone."

"Perhaps she's somewhere with limited cell service."

"I guess, but she wouldn't have gone away when my dad's funeral is tomorrow."

"I'm so sorry. This must be a difficult time for you."

"How will I get through it without my mother? I want my mother." Her voice sounded shrill to her ears.

He took a gulp of his tea and stood up. "Before I go, would you mind giving me this Brent person's contact information? I'll talk to him and see if he can shed some light on what's happened to your mother. Don't worry, dear. We'll find her." He patted her hand.

Thank God someone would help her. "Thank you so much."

Cornell reached into his shirt pocket and pulled out a card. "Here," he said, handing it to her. "If anything comes up, please call me. If you hear from your mother, or you find out anything else, call me. Anything I learn about your mother, you'll be the first to know."

"Thank you." Sam smiled at him. She turned and headed for her mother's office to get Brent's contact information.

CHAPTER 43

Cornell pulled up in front of Brent Morgan's home in Bradford at 10:15 AM. He strode up the cobblestone walkway to the door of a large, ranch-style bungalow. Brent's practice obviously did well. The property was professionally landscaped. Cornell rang the bell and waited. Footsteps approached, and the door swung open.

"Brent Morgan?"

"Yes?"

"I'm Agent Jim Cornell, RCMP." He flashed his badge. "May I come in? I'd like to ask you a few questions about Ralph Drummond."

Brent allowed Cornell to step inside.

"Has something happened to Ralph?"

Cornell shook his head. "Nothing like that. Are you aware he checked himself into a psychiatric hospital?"

"Yes. What's this about?"

"Mind if we sit down? This could take a few minutes."

"Come in." Brent led Cornell into an immaculate living room, painted white and sparsely furnished.

What, no plastic on the couches? He listened for the wife's presence. No one else seemed to be in the house, but he'd better make sure. He noted Morgan didn't offer him anything to drink.

"Is your wife here? She might help."

"No. She's at work."

"I'm not keeping you from a client, am I?"

"No. What's going on?"

"We believe Drummond was working with a cult located near Algonquin Park. They scam UFO abductees, making them believe they can help them."

"I've never heard of this." Brent's voice was guarded. He wouldn't be as easy to convince as Fairchild's daughter.

"Carolyn Fairchild may be involved with this group at Drummond's suggestion. Has she contacted you in the last two days?"

"She left me a phone message yesterday. I tried to call her back this morning, but she didn't pick up."

"Can you tell me what she said in her message?"

"That she needed to talk to me."

"Did she say what it was about?"

"No. Has something happened to her?"

"We're not sure. Her daughter fears she's missing. We suspect she might be headed to Algonquin."

"Why? Her husband's funeral is tomorrow."

"She was in an agitated state after visiting Mr. Drummond yesterday. A map with the cult's location exists. Drummond would've given it to you for safekeeping. Samantha said her mother wanted to get it from you."

Brent's eyes narrowed.

Cornell tensed. If Morgan saw through this, he'd have to be eliminated.

"What branch of the RCMP are you with, exactly?"

"We investigate UFO-related events. Mostly incidents involving people who claim sightings or encounters, or who fall victim to people exploiting experiencers."

"May I see your badge?"

Cornell retrieved the badge from inside his wallet and held it out.

Brent still looked dubious. "I'll just call police dispatch and verify this." He reached for the phone.

Cornell was faster. He pulled his gun and pointed it at Brent. "Stop."

Brent froze.

"Where's the map?"

"I don't know."

"Did you give it to Carolyn?"

"She was never here. I told you that. And I don't have any map."

"You do. Drummond's wife said you do. Where is it?"

"I don't know what you're talking about."

"Where are Drummond's backup files?"

"I don't know what you're talking about."

Cornell decided he didn't have time for this. "Have it your way." He shot Brent in the stomach.

Brent collapsed to the floor, hands pressed to his abdomen, blood trickling from between his fingers.

Cornell aimed the gun at Brent's heart and put another bullet in him. He went limp.

Cornell took a pair of gloves from his jacket pocket and went to search the house, starting with Brent's office. He found memory sticks and an external hard drive he took to review later.

He pulled open a filing cabinet. He found some UFO-related documents, but no map. Perhaps the map was hidden in a safe deposit box. If so, it would take a while to get access. Somehow, he didn't think Morgan would've gone to that much trouble.

Cornell used his cell phone to call the office.

"Helen, send two agents to the address I'll give you. They have to do a cleanup. I'll wait here for them and explain everything when they get here."

He gave her the information. When the team got there, they could go over the house a final time and make sure he hadn't missed anything. He'd also instruct them to call the local police and tell them and Morgan's wife that Brent had been the victim of a robbery and it related to his involvement with Ralph Drummond.

Cornell collected the items he'd retrieved from Morgan and went to the door. He'd been careful not to touch anything with his bare hands during his search of the place. Anything he'd left on the door or in the living room was fine. He'd claim to be the one to have found the body. Next, he wiped the unregistered gun free of prints and dropped it in the trashcan in the kitchen.

He took one more look around the house. Satisfied, he went outside, leaving the front door closed but unlocked, and went back to his car. He was anxious to get to his office to examine the files he'd found. If some of the aliens were interfering with the experiments, they'd have to be stopped.

He pulled out his cell phone and dialled his office again.

When Helen picked up, he said, "Can you check for me the next scheduled abduction for Carolyn Fairchild?"

"Yes, sir." There was a pause while she searched her files. "End of May."

He considered. "Send in a request to change that to tonight and specify we need four agents to be there when it happens. I want two of the agents returned with her to the Peterborough compound. The other two should be left where they pick up Fairchild so they can acquire Valiant."

"I'll do that right away."

"I also want ETAP military personnel ready to go into Algonquin. When we locate that base, they have to be ready to go in and clean it out."

"Yes, sir."

He disconnected. He had a solid action plan now. They could still get to Fairchild.

The aliens working with the Agency would find her location and, likely, Valiant as well. If she was picked up in Algonquin, they might even nab her near the rebel alien base. In the meantime, he'd take what he'd found at Morgan's and see if he could find that map.

His optimism from earlier returning, he smiled. Perhaps he'd take Helen out to lunch tomorrow to celebrate when it was confirmed they had Fairchild.

A van and a car approached. The team had arrived. Cornell stepped from the car to greet them.

CHAPTER 44

Carolyn shifted in her seat to better observe Michael, who stared straight ahead, focused on the road. He glanced often into the mirrors, probably to make sure they weren't being followed.

They'd rented a car and cleared out of Peterborough. He'd made her wait in a nearby coffee shop while he went to the rental place. The forty-five minutes she'd sat with her head down staring into her coffee and pretending to read a newspaper had felt more like forty-five hours, but at last, she saw him walking up to the door.

He'd come in long enough to tell her everything was fine and order the egg sandwich. She'd only been able to stomach a fruit muffin and coffee, though she questioned if the fruit was real and assumed the muffin was made with genetically modified ingredients.

Michael insisted they make only bathroom stops along the way, and she was sure he'd expect her to go into the bush to do it. The rations in the packs and wild edibles he foraged at the park would have to keep them going once they left the coffee shop. At least the wild edibles would be healthier than the food at the coffee shop.

The one exception to his "no stopping" rule was a pause in the town of Bancroft to get her a pair of hiking shoes. He found a shoe store with a decent pair and allowed her to enter the store to try them on. She'd felt like a kid let out of detention. While she'd enjoyed the little outing, Michael had acted the entire time like a cat in a room full of sleeping dogs. He'd remained tense until they were back in the car and away from the town.

Carolyn softened. When things were most terrifying, he came back for her. She ached to hold him but settled for running her hand through his hair.

He turned to smile at her. "What's up?"

"I'm happy to be with you."

"Are you crazy?"

She laughed. "No. I'm not happy about the circumstances, but I'm happy you didn't leave me. I was afraid that guy at the hotel would take me away forever."

"I would've hunted him down and taken you back. Don't dwell on it. It didn't happen."

"I'm still happy you came back."

He frowned. "I hope you didn't think I'd abandon you."

"No," she said quickly. "I knew you'd want to come back, but you didn't know he was after me, and I didn't know where you were." She paused, thinking about it, reviewing the sequence of events in her head. "Did he want to kill you?"

"His orders were probably to take me alive. I, however, was under no such restrictions."

Carolyn fell silent again. She had difficulty thinking of Michael as a killer, but since she'd met him, he'd killed three people, seemingly without remorse. To him, it was simple necessity. Could she become the type of person who'd choose to kill? Perhaps if Sam was in danger. It was different when you were protecting someone you loved. Did that mean she didn't love herself enough to protect herself?

"How many people have you killed?"

"I can't discuss that with you."

"Was it a lot?"

"What do you think is a lot?"

"Well, for me, one would be a lot, and you topped that in the last two days, so I guess I have my answer."

"I won't justify anything to you. You can't possibly understand."

"No, probably not. Was it all just for the money?"

Michael glanced at her. "What do you want me to say? If I hadn't agreed with what I was doing, I wouldn't have been doing it."

"I'm trying to understand how you could take a life and feel okay with it. I can't comprehend that."

"Would you have preferred I let Torque kill me and take you in?"

"Of course not. Why didn't you just tie him up and leave him? You didn't even flinch."

"I can't afford to flinch. Are you forgetting he had a tracking chip in his neck?"

"No, but you could've removed it. You removed it when he was dead."

"A much easier procedure to do when the person is dead."

"Do you have a license to kill?"

That made him smile. "You've seen too many movies. There's no such thing. It's not as if they issue agents a hunting license."

"Not even in the British Secret Service?"

"I doubt it. I'm sure that's just in the movies."

"Do you like to kill?"

"No. I do it because I have to."

"That's debatable. You didn't have to kill John." There it was. Now she'd said it, she couldn't take it back.

He looked at her again, and his expression told her he'd been there. Uncertain if he'd been the one to do it, but he was a part of it.

Michael didn't respond immediately but drove in silence for about a kilometre. He turned onto a dirt road and pulled over. Agony on his face, he took both her hands in his and cleared his throat.

"I was ordered to do it, and I even started to. My hand was on the button, but I didn't press it. When I hesitated, Torque put his hands over mine and forced my finger down. I'd give anything to change what happened. I go over it in my head. There are things I could've done, and John wouldn't have died that day. He didn't deserve that. I can't expect you to forgive me. But understand, I'll have to live with that for the rest of my life, and I'll regret it for at least that long. I'm truly sorry. I questioned it, but I didn't take a stand, and John died."

She hung her head. Numbness spread through her. She thought she should be crying, or on the verge of crying, but she was too numb even for that. She pulled her hands out of his. He didn't stop her.

"They said it was a heart attack. How is that possible?"

He remained silent for a long time. He stared at her, frowning.

She waited, trying not to interrupt whatever mental gymnastics executed in his head. Hopefully, his conscience would win.

Finally, he said, "A weapon referred to as the Tesla Ray. It uses directed energy. It can make someone's heart explode, and it'll look like a heart attack. The coroner can't tell the difference." He paused and then said, "Knowing that, are you still happy to be with me? Do you hate me now?"

She sensed fear in this man who wasn't afraid of anything, but she refused to ease his conscience. Not yet. It felt too much like betraying John. Or was it too late for that? Could she forgive Michael for the role he played in John's death? If not, was it wrong to accept his help? Would that make her just as evil?

If she escaped from Michael, agents would hunt her down. He risked his life by helping her. If all he wanted was to get away from the Agency, he'd have a better chance without her slowing him down. She looked up at him. She refused to believe he was evil. His gaze met hers, unwavering.

"I'll do everything to make up for what I've done. I swear to you. I swore before I wouldn't let anyone take you again, and I meant it," he said.

They stared at one another in silence. Carolyn wanted to touch him, to take him in her arms and tell him it was okay. His regret eased her pain, but it didn't eradicate it, and it didn't change that he was a killer. It showed he was capable of remorse, which helped.

"Did you love your wife?"

"Yes, of course I did."

"Did she know you killed people for a living?"

"No."

"Then she thought you were someone you weren't. You were living a lie."

"I was protecting her."

"It didn't work, and she never knew who you really were. In the end, keeping her ignorant didn't help her."

"Don't talk about my wife. They're burying her today, and I'm not there." It came out an agonized shout. The anger in his voice frightened her. His pain flowed through her.

"Michael."

He waited.

"I don't know what to do," she said at last.

He started the car again. "Then do the practical thing. We have to get to Algonquin. If you don't let me help you, you'll never be free of either the Agency or the aliens. They'll hunt you down and take you. You'll live out your life in their cages. I'll never do anything to hurt you again. I'm not asking you for anything except to let me help you."

"Okay. That much I can do."

She fought the urge to touch him. She wanted to tell him she'd forgive him. They drove in silence, neither looking at the other.

***

Jim Cornell stared at the diagram on his computer screen. There it was: Drummond's map. It was on Morgan's hard drive and had been scanned in from a hard copy. How had there been no trace of the map amongst the items retrieved from Drummond's home? They'd collected everything. Drummond's wife had said agents had taken everything, and she'd personally given them the map.

So, why wasn't it in the storage room?

Cornell could come to only one conclusion: someone had removed it from the evidence room, and he had a feeling he knew who. It couldn't be a coincidence Valiant disappeared with Fairchild headed in the direction of Algonquin. He picked up his phone and had Helen connect him to Folliott down in Evidence.

Folliott was on the line within seconds. "You wanted to speak to me, sir?"

"Yeah. I want you to check the sign-in and sign-out data for the evidence room and review the footage from the cameras. Focus on the items brought in from the Drummond house the day our guys searched it. I think there might be some evidence missing. See who went in and out of there and who handled it before it was catalogued. Notify me if you find anything suspicious."

"Yes, sir."

Cornell hung up.

Valiant, you son of a bitch, if you removed evidence, you're fucking dead.

He was sure Michael had been turning before he'd vanished with Carolyn. All Cornell needed was some proof, and he'd justify having Valiant terminated. If only he hadn't let Muniz handle it. He'd been too close to Valiant. They were partners for so long he'd been blind to the signs indicating Valiant had cracked.

Cornell would be blamed if anyone found out he knew an agent was a potential problem and hadn't removed him from the Project. He had to clean it up now. If Valiant caused them to lose Carolyn Fairchild, it would be even worse. Cornell tried to push that thought away and failed.

He realized he should consider the possibility the two would make it to the base before it was cleaned out and get help. Would the aliens accept Sam as a subject in Carolyn's place? They often abducted members of the same family. He hoped he'd be able to work something out if Carolyn escaped. He'd have to keep a close eye on Sam and make sure she didn't disappear as well.

Cornell checked the time. It was 2:00 PM. The aliens wouldn't be coming for Carolyn until tonight. He couldn't wait to get his hands on Michael. It'd be satisfying to drag him back to the Agency.

Hatred and rage welled up. No one betrayed the Agency. Valiant had been handpicked to survive, and this is how he repaid them for their generosity? He'd suffer for it. In the meantime, Cornell would send a copy of this map to Peterborough Compound and get the military unit out to Algonquin. He grabbed the phone, wondering how many helicopters he could commandeer.

CHAPTER 45

They rode in tense silence. Carolyn lost herself in her thoughts, and she assumed Michael did the same. Perhaps he, too, feared another argument. He turned on the radio, and it was a blessed distraction, putting a wall of music, news, and commercials between them.

They drove along Highway 60, approaching Algonquin Park. Michael had explained they'd enter the park through the East Gate. To her surprise and puzzlement, though, he pulled the car into a secluded area before they reached the gate. He turned to Carolyn, and his expression told her she wouldn't be happy to hear what he had to say.

"Get out of the car." He opened his own door and stepped out.

She exited the car, fear rising through her gut.

He didn't waste any time. "I want you to get in the trunk."

Her stomach lurched, and the blood drained from her face. "Michael …"

He approached her, and she backed away. His hands brushed at the air, the gesture placating. "It'll be okay. I don't want anyone to see us together when we enter the park. Any agents looking for us will ask about a couple. If I go in alone, it'll help keep us off the radar. I'm sorry. I don't know of a better way."

She took a step back, away from him. "Please. No." She whispered it, begging. Her thoughts went to Torque, locked in the trunk, dead in the trunk, of their abandoned car. The day was hot, and the trunk would be stifling. The fatigue and stress backed up on her. She cried, her body shaking as she pictured herself in the trunk and something preventing Michael from letting her out again.

He rushed to her and put his arms around her. She let him pull her to him. Her arms went around his waist, and she pressed herself tightly against him. One of his hands cupped the back of her head, and he stroked her hair. His lips pressed the top of her head. The gestures of compassion from this hired killer frightened her more than if he'd tried to force her into the trunk against her will. The sobs came unrestricted. He let her cry, holding her until the weeping subsided.

She took a deep breath to steady her voice. "What if something happens, and you can't get me out?"

"I wouldn't let anything happen. I'll show you how to get yourself out. Would you like to see? The car has a lever in the trunk."

She lifted her face to look up at him. "I'm sorry. I understand what you're saying, but I can't stop thinking about Torque. What if I suffocate?"

"You won't suffocate. It's not airtight. Let me show you how it'll work."

He took her hand and led her around to the back of the car. He popped the trunk using the remote. "There are two ways you can get out. One, you can do what Torque did and kick the back seat down. Then you'd be able to crawl out into the car. Two, use the lever at the bottom of the trunk. Look."

Michael pointed to a handle near the trunk latch. "This handle should glow in the dark. It'll be easy for you to turn it and open the trunk. We can test it out before we get back on the road so you know you can do it."

She nodded, tension easing. "Okay. Yes, I'd like to practice opening it."

He helped her get into the trunk, and she held her breath as he closed the lid. Eyes squeezed shut for a moment, she opened them again and saw the handle, a faint firefly glow in the dark. She jiggled it, not knowing which way to turn it. The trunk lid yanked up, and she lost her grip on the handle, letting it slide out of her sweaty palm.

"It's okay, right?"

She nodded.

He helped her climb out again. Retrieving her backpack from the back seat of the car, he stuck it in the trunk. He opened her pack, removed a bottle of water, and handed it to her.

"You'll need this. Do you want to take your pants, shoes, and socks off? It'll be hot in there for you if you don't."

Carolyn smiled. "You're just trying to get me out of my clothes." But she did as he suggested.

Michael returned the smile. "If I'd known it would be that easy, I'd have told you it was hot in the front, too."

She giggled, self-conscious. Tension eased. She placed her things into the trunk and gripped the car. He held her arm, steadying her as she climbed in.

When she was settled, he said, "It won't take more than about ten minutes to get there. We're close. When you hear me turn off the radio, you'll know I'm through the entrance. Stay quiet and stay hidden. Don't panic. Once I have the map and the permits, I'll drive to a secluded spot to let you out."

"Okay," she said, resigned. As he moved to close the trunk, she called out, "Michael."

He halted, puzzled.

"Why didn't Torque use the handle to open the trunk and get out? Wouldn't that have been easier for him than crawling out the back seat?"

Michael took a moment to answer her. Finally, he said, "The handle in Torque's car was disconnected. It didn't work."

Before she could respond, he closed the lid. The car jiggled as he opened the driver's door and got in. The realization sank in that the handle in Torque's car had been deliberately disabled because they used it to transport kidnap victims.

Carolyn rested her head on her arm. The trunk was warm and close. She gripped her bottle of water. What would it have been like to travel from Newmarket to Peterborough in the trunk of Torque's car? Then she remembered she would've been drugged and handcuffed, and unaware of most, or possibly the entire, journey.

Arnie had endured that. The thought of her missing friend brought tears to her eyes again. John, Arnie, and Shelly were all gone. As far as everyone else was concerned, she was gone too. She closed her eyes, trying to sense anyone with her. There was nothing.

Why couldn't she feel anyone?

Guides and angels, please give me a sign you're around. She needed something to help her spiritually connect. The lack of presence made her feel separate and alone. It was as if closing her in here had cut her off from the unseen world as well as the physical world.

She tried to recollect how long it had been since she'd connected with anyone: John, her spirit guides, Jessica. She'd connected with Jessica the night before. It seemed a lifetime ago. Since then, she'd slept with Jessica's husband. Guilt welled up. She hadn't meant to. It had just happened.

Were John and Jessica aware of what had occurred between Carolyn and Michael? Were they angered by it even though they were now in the spirit world and outside of what transpired on the earth plane?

It bothered her she'd compromised her values. She didn't know Michael, and what she knew of him should have made him despicable to her. But when she thought of him, when she looked at him, all she wanted to do was touch him and be with him. Was she going crazy? She closed her eyes and clung to the bottle of water as if it were an anchor to reality.

CHAPTER 46

Michael approached the East Gate. The sun blazed in a clear sky, the highway stretching ahead through a valley of evergreen trees rich with needles in varying shades of green. Wildflowers lined the edge of the road, filling the culverts. The recent drought left some of the grass scorched and brown, but the beauty of the natural wilderness still shone through.

It wouldn't last much longer. Whatever they did to put a stop to the Agency's plans, this would still all be doomed to disappear. If only he could stop time for a moment, sit with Carolyn in his arms, gaze out over the land and just be. When the end came, this would be a better place than most to face it.

Michael drove up to the arch of the East Gate and veered right, taking the road leading to the information centre. He turned off the radio, signalling to Carolyn they were through the gate.

The Information Centre included the Parks Store and a separate building with washroom facilities. He pulled up across from the washrooms, parking the car as far from the buildings and other cars as possible. On one side, a field of grass stretched about fifteen metres to the forest beyond. On the other, about five parking spots away, was an RV.

He hurried into the information building and got a permit for the Source Lake access point to the backcountry. He had a tense moment when the grey-haired woman behind the counter insisted he should've made a reservation by phone two days ahead of time, but since the park wasn't booked up, she let it slide.

Once back in the driver's seat, he stuck his permit on the dashboard and drove the car onto the highway. He continued along Highway 60 until he left the parking area out of view. Pulling over at the first spot that offered some cover off the side of the road, he got out and looked around.

Nothing moved. It was hot—at least twenty-five Celsius with the humidity. Carolyn must be stifling. He hurried to the trunk and popped it open. Dyed-brown hair plastered to her face with sweat, Carolyn sat up, blinking in the sunlight. Her water bottle was empty.

"Come on out."

She nodded, looking too hot and miserable to reply.

He picked up her pants and handed them to her. "Much as I admire the view, you should probably put these back on."

She gave him a slight smile.

When her pants, socks, and shoes were back on, he opened the passenger door for her.

"Climb in. It's cool in there."

She started to get into her seat, but paused, startled. She reached down and picked something up.

"How did this get here?"

"What have you got?"

"This." She held up a small, white feather.

He shook his head. "I guess it must've floated in from somewhere when I opened the door."

She grinned. "I was looking for a sign. This is it."

"A sign of what?"

"You'll laugh at me."

"Try me."

"White feathers are a sign of angelic presence. When I was in the trunk, I asked for a sign from my guides that I wasn't alone. You might think it's a coincidence, but it's a strange place to find a white feather, and I'm taking it as the omen I asked for."

"I'm not laughing. This time yesterday, I wouldn't have expected to ever hear from my wife again, and you've convinced me she was with us last night. Nothing is too weird for me anymore."

She climbed into the car with a pleased expression that lightened his heart.

When she'd settled in her seat, he handed her a bottle of water; she opened it and took a long swallow. He shut her in with the cooler air and got back in the car.

"Are you okay?"

"Yes."

"I'm sorry you had to do that."

"I know."

He pulled onto the highway. "We can drive on for a little while, but then we have to ditch the car and cut across the park toward the north. The base is somewhere beyond Sunny Lake if that map is legitimate.

We'll break all kinds of rules and regulations, veering off accepted routes, and we have to keep you out of sight as much as possible."

"How long to get to the base?"

"At least two days of hiking. Maybe more. It depends on how fast we can get through the underbrush. There are no trails where we're going. Also, we can't have any fires. Much of the area is probably dry from lack of rain. Though it would take a longer drought to completely dry up some of the soil here, we have to be careful."

"This weather is frustrating. A few years ago, roads were closed and bridges were flooded out at this same time of year. Now, there's a drought and spring feels like summer. I can't believe there are still people who deny climate change," she said.

Michael didn't respond. He wondered if he should explain to her what was happening. He decided it wasn't the right time. If she knew what was coming, she'd panic and want to get back to her daughter. He couldn't risk that. He'd have to tell her sometime, but not until she was at least safe from the aliens. If they kidnapped her again before he could get help ... At the thought of losing her, he unconsciously reached out his hand and took hers.

She stared at him; her brows furrowed, and then she squeezed his hand.

"I'm sorry. I did that without thinking." He released her hand though he didn't want to.

"I don't mind. I find it comforting." She took his hand again.

They drove in silence for a while. Where did this ache for her come from? He hadn't felt anything this strong before, not even when he'd dated Jess. He'd definitely had a physical attraction to Jess, and they were compatible, but with Carolyn, it was as if he'd found something he hadn't known he was looking for. Now, when she wasn't with him, or when she was with him but not touching him, he felt like a piece of him was missing.

He glanced at her. He sneaked peeks at her often.

Her slightly greasy hair hung limp around her face. Her sweat-damp shirt clung to her body, and she wore a pair of track pants slightly too big for her. She'd never looked more appealing.

"It's beautiful here." She turned to catch him staring and smiled. "Eyes on the road, pal."

He laughed and released her hand to put his back on the steering wheel.

She placed her palm on his thigh. "Does that bother you?"

"No, but we might crash if you keep it there."

Carolyn blushed and laughed softly. She moved her hand away, and he felt a piece of him go with it.

***

Cornell cursed under his breath. Folliott, standing next to Cornell's desk, waited. Cornell paused the video. He'd seen enough. The footage from their surveillance cameras not only showed Michael Valiant breaking into the storage area to steal evidence but continuing the theft while the security guard slept on the couch in the reception area.

He couldn't immediately get his hands on Valiant, but he could take care of the security guard. He picked up his phone.

"Helen, get the security manager up to my office right away. We have a problem."

"Yes, sir."

He hung up the phone and turned to Folliott. "Good work. You can go on back to what you were doing before I pulled you away."

Folliott nodded and left.

Cornell again called Helen. When she answered, he cut her off before she could speak. "Get me the Peterborough commander. What's his name?"

"Weeks, sir."

"Oh yeah. Weeks. Thanks. Get him on the line for me."

He hung up the phone. He needed to hear back on those choppers. If they beat Michael to the base, they could clean it out, leaving the two fugitives trapped with nowhere to go.

The phone rang. He snatched it up. "Cornell here."

"It's Weeks. I know what you're going to ask. It's been done. We sent five choppers out to Algonquin. We have enough personnel on board to clean out a small base with due force."

"Thank you. I look forward to hearing from you when the mission has been accomplished."

"Will do."

Cornell set the phone back onto its cradle. He looked at the clock. It was 4:09 PM.

CHAPTER 47

They'd hiked since early afternoon. It seemed as if they'd walked for hours, but Carolyn suspected less time had passed than she thought. Ahead, coniferous trees grew in clumps. Mushrooms and ferns sprang up from the dark soil. Evergreen needles, leaves, twigs, rocks, pinecones, and a variety of buggy, yucky, mouldy-looking things she didn't want to examine carpeted the ground. Black flies tortured them at every step.

Michael had wanted to spray her with chemical bug spray, but she refused until she thought she'd go insane from the constant buzzing and biting. Then she'd yielded and let him apply whatever he wanted. It helped, a little, but the longer they walked, the more she wanted to snap. Worst of all, everything looked the same, and for all she knew, they wandered in circles. Michael stopped every once in a while to pick a plant and shove it in a plastic bag he carried. So far, she hadn't summoned the nerve to ask what he'd saved.

Once, she almost stepped in a pile of dung that looked as if the world's biggest St. Bernard had deposited it—a vegetarian St. Bernard, judging by the berries in it. Her stomach lurched at the sight, and she almost tossed what little she'd eaten that day. Michael identified it as bear scat, which made her draw closer to him. After that, Carolyn kept silent, focusing on walking and keeping an eye out for more bear pies. She also didn't want to distract Michael. He led them by using the map, a compass, and, apparently, the sun.

At last, he called a rest. Grateful, she sat on a log, verifying first there was nothing too icky on it. Michael checked the map, the compass, and the sun. She fished a protein bar from her pack and broke her silence. "Everything okay? Are you lost? I'd say 'we,' but I know I'm lost. I hope you're not, but the amount of times you've checked your bearings concerns me."

He dropped next to her and gave her a look as though he was wondering if he should be insulted or not. "No, I'm not lost," he said without rancour. "I admit, though, a GPS would be great right now." He opened his pack and retrieved a protein bar.

"How much longer must we walk?" she asked.

"Until almost dark. Not sure how long we have. If they send the aliens to track you, we may not make it." He ripped open the wrapper and bit into the chocolate-coated snack.

"How can they track me? You removed my chip."

"That was an Agency tracking device. The aliens use a mode of tracking I'm unfamiliar with. You said you've had regular nosebleeds?"

"Yes." She remembered the one after her most recent abduction and felt sick.

"They probably inserted a tracking device into your nose. Or it could be anywhere on your body. Do you have any scars you can't explain?"

She nodded. "On my thigh. I had a bruise after Friday night. I have a scar on my arm, too. I found a small lump under the skin, and the doctor removed it in the office. When I asked him what it was, he said he didn't know and threw it into the garbage."

"He didn't speculate on it at all?"

"No. He barely looked at it. I expected him to want to send it for testing, but he didn't. He gave me a couple of stitches and sent me on my way."

"Alien trackers are organic and difficult to locate. If you try to remove them, they burrow deeper into the tissue."

"That didn't happen. It was close to the surface and looked as if it could be organic. It was white." Carolyn popped the last bite of her protein bar into her mouth and stuck the wrapper into her backpack.

She looked up and caught Michael watching her. He appeared on the verge of speaking, but when he remained silent, she said, "What? I hope you're not going to suggest stuffing me in the trunk of a car again."

"No." He laughed. "It's nothing like that. I'm curious about angels."

"You don't believe, so it must be my imagination or superstition, right? And you're wondering how I could be so gullible?"

"Not quite. You believe you have angels around you, protecting you?"

"Yes."

"Everyone does?"

"Yes."

"Even Jess?"

"You're wondering why Jessie's guardian angels didn't step in and save her from Torque?"

He nodded.

"It might have been her time. Wait," she said, when he opened his mouth, probably to argue. "Let me explain what that means, or what I believe that means, based on my experience and the studying I've done."

"You can study this?"

"Yes. Let me explain?"

"Okay."

"It's possible she had uneasy feelings that might've helped her avoid what happened, but most people are oblivious to the guidance they receive. As well, you must be aware angels are around you and then ask for help. Angels can't interfere with free will to help you unless you request it, or unless it's not your time to pass.

"Sometimes, people who have near-death experiences say they were told it wasn't their time to go and were sent back. Some people believe we create our life path before we're born, and that major events, particularly death, are predetermined. Perhaps it's true, and I keep an open mind about it, but I've seen no evidence to verify it."

"You don't believe in fate?"

"I don't believe the future is set, but you can be directed toward something, arrive there, and fulfil an intention. Whether you set that intention prior to your birth or whether some divine force sets it, I don't know."

"How do you explain Hitler? That's a lot of people to have intended to die. Some divine force wanted that?" Sarcasm tinged his voice.

"What happened with Hitler had to do with his vibration. It aligned with enough people who also vibrated at that resonance to cause the Holocaust. As well, too many people missed the warnings that something was spiralling out of control. It didn't need to happen to propel humanity forward spiritually, and I don't think anyone agreed to be a victim. You can progress more through joy than from sorrow."

"I hope you're right. We'll need all the joy we can get real soon." Michael put his arm around her. "If they find us, if we get separated, no matter what happens, I'll find you again."

"Michael …"

"Listen to me. The aliens could come, and they'd take you. If they do, I want to make sure you remember that I won't leave you. I won't give up. I'll find you and rescue you."

"You mean at the Agency?"

"Yes."

"I don't understand. Isn't the Agency what they call the CIA? That's American, not Canadian. How can they be here?"

"I'm sure they can be wherever they want, but this isn't the CIA."

"Then what is it?"

"I can't tell you. The less you know, the better."

"That's not fair."

"It's safer. Trust me. What's important is I know where they'll take you, and I'll come for you no matter what. Okay?" His eyes grew intense, worried.

She frowned. "You said that couldn't be done."

"I'll find a way. Even if they kill me, I'll come for you." He smiled. "Luckily, you can talk to the dead."

"Please don't say that. I've lost John. I can't bear to lose you, too. Don't joke about that."

"I'm not joking. I'm trying to tell you there are no guarantees. If the Agency finds us, they'll want you alive, but I doubt they'll care if they kill me to get to you."

"Then you'll have to let them get me. I'd rather be captured than watch you die. Promise me if it comes to that, you'll let them take me." Then it occurred to her that if she disappeared, Sam would never know what happened to her. On impulse, she removed her engagement ring and wedding band and offered him the band.

"If something happens to me, give this to Sam and tell her what happened."

Michael frowned. "That's not necessary. You can tell her yourself when we're sure the aliens can't get you anymore."

"Please. This is proof you were with me. She might not trust you otherwise."

"Keep it. It'll be okay. I don't want to take your wedding ring. Go ahead. Put it back on." He leaned in and touched her forehead with his. It was a gentle touch, but a powerful surge of energy flowed into her from Michael.

She gasped and had to steady herself as a wave of dizziness hit her. Then his lips pressed against hers, and instinctively, she put her arms around him, holding him, running her hands through his hair.

He slowly pulled away. His breathing was shallow. "I'm sorry. I don't mean to …" His voice broke. "God, I want you so much."

Carolyn tried to speak, but he stopped her, pressing his lips to hers again. They kissed, losing themselves for a moment, forgetting everything for a brief, blissful, precious moment. But Michael wouldn't let them forget for long where they were and why. He pulled away and took her hands in his.

"We must keep going. If we don't, they'll find us. We only have until nightfall. Then we'll have to stop whether we like it or not. Go ahead. Put the ring back on your finger." He watched her while she did that, then pulled her to her feet, hugged her, and released her.

That's when she heard the sound of helicopters.

CHAPTER 48

Michael grabbed their packs and threw them into the underbrush. He pulled Carolyn after him into the cover of some trees.

"Don't move. Military choppers."

Frightened, she clung to him. They huddled, waiting. Through the trees, three helicopters flew in from the south.

"It looks as if they're heading in the same direction we're heading. They've discovered the base," he said.

"What'll we do? They'll destroy it, won't they?"

"I'd have to assume so. All we can do is carry on and hope we find something that'll help us, even if they beat us to it."

"Could we go somewhere else? There might be other bases."

"If so, the only way to find them is through this one."

They continued to stare up at the sky. Carolyn glanced occasionally at Michael, but she couldn't read his expression. Suddenly, she sensed a presence. She reached out with her psychic senses to figure out who it was.

Torque.

"Michael," she said.

He looked at her.

"Torque is here."

Michael's body went rigid. He looked around as if trying to see the spirit. "Why do you think that?"

"I feel him. He wants to tell you something."

"What about Jess? Why aren't you connecting to her? Why him?" Hurt permeated his voice.

"You said her funeral is today. She's probably there."

His jaw dropped. "You're joking. That's more important than anything else?"

"In the grand scheme of things? Yes. She has grieving family. You're

194

not the only one who lost her. She'll be there for all her family. She's already connected with you. You've had more communication than anyone else who loved her." Her voice gentled. "The failing could be mine. I've been under stress. It blocks me. That I can sense Torque at all is a relief, but it means he needs to get through to tell you something important, like Jess did before."

"What does he want?"

She closed her eyes. Pain. There was a flash and an image of Torque's body by the car in Michael's driveway. The pain vanished, leaving only surprise. Michael stood over Torque's body, now a shell. She viewed the scene as if from above.

"You shot him in the chest. It hurt, but the pain was fleeting. He saw a flash, and he was above the scene, out of his body. You stood over him."

"I know what happened. So do you. You were there." He sounded irritated, impatient.

"Usually a spirit will tell me how it died. I was there, but I didn't see what happened. I heard the shots and then saw you standing over him. For most spirits, their death isn't only the last thing they remember from the physical plane, but also, for obvious reasons, it's one of the most important events in their lives. They start there when they begin communication. At least, that's my experience."

"I'm sorry. It's hard to accept. I had to do it, but it doesn't mean that's how I wanted things to play out."

True. "He knows." She paused, trying to pick up anything else. There was sadness. Regret. She had a flash of a spacecraft. "He's making me feel sad ... He's sorry ... I don't know for what, specifically, and I won't speculate ... He's showing me a spacecraft."

Faster. "Something about going faster. Any idea what that means?"

"Does he want us to move faster?"

Accelerating. "I hear the word 'accelerating.' Does that mean something to you?"

"I don't understand. Can you get him to explain?" He sounded frustrated.

"It's difficult. All I can tell you is what I get. He's trying." She got a flash image of a spacecraft again. It grew larger in her mind's eye, as though coming at her. "I see a spacecraft coming at me."

He cursed, his eyes betraying a sudden realization. "They're coming. He's telling us they're coming for you. You're not supposed to be abducted again this soon, but that's changed. I expect they'll come tonight."

Terror overwhelmed her, and it escalated as she pictured herself floating away from Michael, leaving him, maybe forever. Then she received an impression of two men pulling guns on him, shooting him.

"They want to take me and shoot you."

When she said that, she no longer felt Torque's presence. "He's gone. I think he wanted to tell us that, and then he left."

"Can't he help us?"

"I think spirits do what they can, when they can, but they're still only human. He hasn't been in spirit long, and he had a violent and traumatic death. He probably had difficulty coming through with just this much."

Michael rolled open the map and studied it, motioning her to look. "Here's the base." He pointed. "This is where we are." He pointed again to another spot southeast of the base. "We're too far to get to the base today, but other places near here might offer shelter amongst the rock. We need to reach something before nightfall."

"Will that help?"

"It might. This entire area is part of the Canadian Shield. If we get underneath, it could help to conceal us. The rock itself might prevent them from picking up whatever signal you're giving off."

"What makes you think so?"

"This rebel alien base is underground. Without the map, the Agency never found it. The only thing I can think of is that it's something about the composition of the earth here. They built a base in a provincial park, and no one ever found it. There must be a reason they chose this location. That's my best guess."

"How do we find somewhere to hide?"

"Some lakes around here likely have rocky nooks or places to hole up in. There's a lake close to us, and we can try that. We'll stick to the trees in case those helicopters come back. It's okay. We'll find something." He hugged her. "They won't get you, and they sure as hell won't shoot me."

He pointed to a lake on the map.

"Here," he said. "That's where we're going. The shore will be all stone. There's a lot of granite and gneiss here. The granite would contain quartz."

Carolyn grabbed his arm. "Quartz is an amplifier."

Michael arched his brows. "It's mostly smoky quartz."

"That's grounding. It can raise your vibration, which will help me. Granite and smoky quartz are protective."

"I don't know about that part of it. It should interfere with their tracking devices."

"Yes, that makes sense energetically."

He smiled. "Then let's go."

He led her in the direction she guessed was northeast. They'd been heading north. At least, that's what Michael had told her when they'd first headed out, though she'd quickly become disoriented. The helicopters were circling in the direction she and Michael had headed. The closest lake, according to the map, was away from their original destination.

In the distance, a loon cried out. The sky was cloudless, the air still and close. Shadows lengthened though the humidity continued unabated.

"What time is it?"

Michael checked his watch. "It's just after six o'clock. We have two hours of daylight left. I don't think they'll come right at nightfall, but it would be dangerous to keep hiking in the dark."

"If all this is Canadian Shield, aren't we walking on it already?"

"Yes, but we need to at least have it around us. Under it would be best."

She nodded, hurrying to keep up with his long strides.

He took her hand and pulled her after him. In the distance, they heard explosions.

Carolyn threw a terrified gaze at Michael.

"They're blowing it up."

"Possibly," he said.

"Won't that attract park rangers and harm campers?"

"No. They would've radioed park officials and had them block off the area. Hikers and campers aren't supposed to venture into that area anyway. Anywhere near that base is off the accepted routes. We're doing it, but most people play by the rules when they vacation here. Besides, this is a government agency backed by private funding. They can get the cooperation of local law enforcement anywhere without having to explain anything. That's one reason we can't call the police. We're fugitives from the law as far as the police are concerned. If they take us in, we'll be handed over to the Agency. They'll simply follow orders from their superiors and no one will ask questions."

She didn't reply, but tried to walk faster. Michael would've been running if he didn't have her to slow him down. The pack on her back grew heavier the faster she tried to go, but she didn't complain. Michael's pack was heavier, and he was moving quickly without breaking a sweat. She asked her angels and guides to help them find cover before nightfall. It was the only thing she could think of to do.

CHAPTER 49

Samantha Fairchild stood in Ralph Drummond's room and stared at him in disbelief. Ralph sat on his bed, head down, avoiding her eyes, either from shame or fear.

"What do you mean, 'go away?' " she asked him. "My mother is missing. They found Brent shot to death. Help me. Please. Tell me something I can do. I don't know what to do."

"I can't help you. Get out of here. Stop talking to me." He lurched to his feet and lunged at her. Taking her by the shoulders, he guided her to the door. "Go away." His voice was rough, desperate.

He shoved her into the hallway. "If you don't leave now, I'll call security. Stay away from my family, too."

She spun around to face him and struggled to push the door open as he tried to force it closed.

"Please. Don't do this. I have no one else. They took your map. They killed Brent before we could get the map from him. Please. Help me."

Ralph's eyes went wide. She couldn't tell if it was fear or horror.

"Shut up." It came out as a snarl. "Get out," he bellowed. He gave the door a final shove that made her stagger backward, and the door slammed in her face.

Sam stumbled along the hallway in a daze. She noticed a ladies room on her left, went inside, and leaned against the wall, shaking. Ralph had refused to help her—had actually pushed her away. Why had he turned his back on her?

At the sink she examined herself in the mirror. Tears stained her cheeks, so she turned on the water and rinsed her face. She searched for paper towels but found only a hand-drying machine. Frustrated, she pressed the button to turn it on and dry her hands. She used the bottom of her blouse to pat her face dry.

A wave of longing and sadness for her lost parents flowed over her.

Tears threatened again, and she choked them back. She reached into her purse and took out Jim Cornell's business card. Should she call him and ask for help? He'd tell her what to do. She had no one else she could turn to, and he'd been nice to her. He seemed to care about her mother. So far, he was the only one who'd shown any interest in finding Carolyn.

Sam left the bathroom. Yes, she decided, she'd call him from her car. She stuck the card back in her purse, walked to the elevator, and pressed the "down" button.

A flurry of activity made her look up. Orderlies ran past her. She turned her head and was shocked to see them run to Ralph's room.

Heart in her throat, she followed them. Behind her, the elevator pinged, signalling its arrival, and the doors swished open. She ignored that and walked to Ralph's door, which gaped open. She stared, wide-eyed, into the room.

At first, she didn't comprehend the scene. Ralph hung from the light fixture, his body swaying as an orderly struggled to cut it down.

She screamed.

Someone said, "Get her out of here now." A man blocked her view and pushed her away from the door. The man handed her over to a nurse, who led her down the hall.

People tried to talk to her, but she ignored them. The nurse led her to an office. The doctor there asked her about Ralph. He seemed to care if she could get herself home.

"Do you have someone you can call?"

She nodded, not bothering to explain the someone was a stranger. Briefly, she considered calling Vanna or one of her other friends, but she wanted to call Jim Cornell.

How could Ralph be dead? She had to hear it. "Is Ralph dead?"

The doctor stared at her, puzzled. "Yes. I'm sorry."

Then terror overwhelmed her, as the reality sank in, and what if it was her fault? What if the people here had killed Ralph? They might try to kill her, too. She had to get away.

Sam jumped up. The doctor stood and tried to grab her arm. Terrified that he wanted to hurt her, she leapt back.

"Don't touch me!"

He dropped his hands, shock crossing his face.

As she ran from the office, he picked up his phone. She ran faster, blindly, her one thought to get to the car, her mother's car, and call Cornell.

She raced past security. The guard stared at her but didn't stop her.

Out in the parking lot, she automatically scanned the cars to see if anyone was watching her. Nothing moved, and she didn't see anyone.

She hurried to the car, climbed inside, and locked it. After retrieving her cell phone and Cornell's card from her purse, she dialled his number.

"Cornell."

She cleared her throat. "It's Samantha Fairchild."

"What can I do for you?" He sounded delighted to hear from her.

"I didn't know who else to call. Sorry to bother you."

"Not at all. How can I help?" Genuine concern laced his voice.

She relaxed a little. He'd fix everything.

"Some terrible things happened."

"Tell me."

She exhaled her relief. "The news said my mom's friend, Brent, was shot."

"Yes. I'm sorry about that. I can't comment on what might've happened. We're investigating. We'll catch whoever did it. Don't worry. I'm sure you're okay."

"No, I'm not. I went to see Ralph because I was scared and didn't know what else to do. I'm at the hospital now."

"Yes? Have you talked to him?"

She thought she detected a note of alarm.

"I tried. He told me to get out. After I left his room, I guess he … I don't know. He … Maybe it's my fault for going there. He hanged himself. They said he's dead." She burst into tears.

His voice broke through her sobs. "Listen to me."

She fell silent.

"Are you okay to go home?"

"Yes. Do you think someone will come after me?"

"No. Not at all." His confidence put her at ease. "I'll come over and make sure nothing happens to you. Will you go straight home? Don't call or talk to anyone. Do you understand?"

"Yes. Thank you." She opened the glove box and pulled out a tissue.

"I'm going to hang up now. Go home and wait for me. Is that clear?"

"Yes, Mr. Cornell. Thank you."

"Sam?"

"Yes?"

"Call me 'Jim,' " he said, his tone kind and reassuring.

"Okay, Jim."

There was a click, and he was gone.

Sam grabbed a tissue from the glove box, wiped her eyes, and blew her nose. She started the car. Everything would be okay now. She had help.

CHAPTER 50

They found refuge along the shore of the lake and were inside, as far away from the entrance as they could go, in what was an opening in the stony shoreline. A rivulet of water flowed up into its bowels, and Michael said it would be safe to have a small fire for warmth, cooking, and light. The energy of the rock, powerful and ancient, surrounded them. Outside, the air was hot and humid, but inside their shelter it was cool and damp. They collected enough tinder and pieces of wood to keep a fire going for a while. Seated on Michael's sleeping bag near the flames, they ate salad made from the plants he'd collected.

"What's in this?" She scooped another mouthful from her bowl. "It's tasty."

"Dandelion leaves, garlic mustard flowers, pigweed, some lamb's quarters, a little bergamot, and wild grape vine leaves—whatever I could find in prime condition for eating. You can even eat bulrushes, roasted, if you're desperate."

"I ate pigweed?"

"You might be more familiar with its other name: Amaranth."

"I've heard of that. It's a nice change from the protein bars, but bulrushes sound gross."

"You can get used to anything if you have to." Michael filled a stainless steel pot with water. He went to the shore, collected some flat-topped rocks, and set them in the fire, which had burned down to coals. He set the pot on top of the stones and threw in some herbs.

The aroma wafted through the enclosed space as the water heated and then bubbled. Carolyn inhaled deeply and let it refresh her.

Michael carefully poured some of the herb-infused water into two mugs and handed her one.

She let it cool for a minute, breathing in the delicate aroma. She blew on it, took a small sip, and raised her brows in surprise. "Nice." She set the mug next to her, and, pulling her knees up, rested her chin on them.

He built up the fire again while she watched. His face was so serious. His wide mouth and full lips made her think of someone ... She had a revelation.

"Torque called you 'Mick.' That's because of your lips, isn't it? You kind of resemble—"

He cut her off. "I try to ignore that. It started during training. Guys always make up nicknames for each other. That was a long time ago, but it stuck. Even my boss calls me that. My family doesn't use it. They call me 'Mike' or 'Michael.' "

"Why do you call Gerry 'Torque'?"

He grinned. "That didn't start with me. When he first joined the Agency, he got a reputation for being a 'twisted force,' and someone started calling him Torque. I'm not sure what they meant; I think it had to do with his enthusiasm for carrying out his orders."

They both fell silent. Talking about Torque reminded Carolyn of when Michael broke into her house and dragged her out into the night, away from her family and her life.

Michael drew inward as well. He fiddled with the fire even though it didn't appear to need tending.

She stared into the flames and sipped her tea. When she finished, she said, "I'm going to wash up in the lake."

"Stay close to the rocks. Don't swim out into the lake. You're not protected out there."

He pulled out a bottle of biodegradable liquid soap from his pack. "Here." He tossed it to her. "This will be fine for your hair and body. Take this pot and use it to rinse yourself away from the lake. Don't go too far up on the shore. I'd rather some soap went into the lake than you risk exposure."

Carolyn stripped off her clothes and made her way to the water, climbing over the stones around the shelter's edge. She washed the sweat from her body and out of her hair, then moved from the water onto the rocks to lather up and rinse off.

Done, she placed the soap and pot at the cave's entrance and returned to the shallows. She paddled around, enjoying the cool water. She glanced up to catch Michael watching her.

"You look like a mermaid." He grinned.

"Come and join me. It's way warmer than it usually is at this time of year."

He removed his clothes and walked toward her.

She picked up the soap and the pot and motioned him over to the shore. She poured some soap into her hands.

"Let me wash you." Her voice came out low and husky. She stepped close to him, offering her soapy hands.

He accepted her with a nod.

She placed her hands on his shoulders, massaging them and rubbing soap onto them, mindful of the bandage on his neck. When she finished washing his body, she helped him clean his hair. She could feel and see his desire for her, but he didn't touch her, and it made her want him more.

When she finished rinsing out his hair, he clasped her hand in his and led her back into their nest. She hurried to him, unable to endure another moment without his body touching hers. They sank to their knees, lips pressed together.

His hands on her body at last, she, in turn, stroked him, running her palms over the hard muscles of his arms, belly, and thighs. He released her mouth from his lips and kissed her forehead, then bent his head down to her throat.

She moaned. Time seemed to stand still as she let him engulf her.

After, when Carolyn allowed herself to wonder about mundane matters, she looked toward the entrance to their little cave and realized she couldn't see it. Darkness had fallen outside, and she saw only velvety blackness and the sparkle of stars.

"It's okay," Michael said.

"I do feel protected in here." She shivered, finding the air chilly though his body next to hers was warm, and the fire beside her lapped heat onto her bare skin.

He sat up and grabbed her pack. Retrieving the other sleeping bag, he draped it over them.

"Is that better?"

She nodded, and her breathing shallowed as desire for him flooded through her once again.

His face hovered over hers, and she looked into his eyes. It was like gazing into the eyes of an old friend.

"I didn't realize I was missing you when we hadn't met, but I feel as if you've returned to me after a long absence."

He stroked her cheek. "Every time I look at you, it's like I recognize you from somewhere. At first, I thought it was because I'd seen surveillance photos, but it's more than that. You always seemed familiar."

She remembered the dream in which Michael, a witch hunter who wanted to burn her, had captured her. She wondered what it meant. He'd come for her but hadn't harmed her.

Then she realized what he'd just said.

At first, I thought it was because I'd seen surveillance photos. And he knew the layout of her home and the things she'd said in private conversations. He must also know she was infertile—he wasn't just assuming she was on the pill.

She gasped.

"What's wrong?" He frowned.

"You know I can't get pregnant, don't you?"

"Yes. I'm sorry. It must be hard for you."

"Can you tell me why?"

"I don't know. I didn't know you had a problem until your sky watch last Friday. Then you talked about it with Shelly."

"You were listening?"

"Not then. I listened to the recording after."

She put her head on his shoulder and draped her arm across his chest. She stroked his hair, his cheek.

"Are you okay?" he asked.

"Yes. You know so much about me. I guess that includes how many men I've been with too?"

"Carolyn."

She smiled at his worried tone to show him she wasn't angry. "It's okay, but if you have information about me, tell me the truth about it. After all we've been through together, be honest with me."

"When I started investigating your group, I looked for everything we had on all of you. The file on you is extensive."

"Why can't I have any more children? Is it something the aliens have done?"

"I didn't find that information. What the aliens do to you and why wasn't in there. Files on that must exist somewhere, but they weren't where I could find them."

"Promise me you won't keep things from me."

Michael gently nudged her off his chest and propped himself on one elbow, facing her. "I promise. I told you before I don't want to hurt you ever again." He bent down and kissed her forehead.

"What will we do now?"

"Well, we have all night." His lips puckered, and he nuzzled her neck.

She laughed. "That's not what I mean, and I hope we have all night, but what if they find us? We can't stay here forever. How can we get away from them?"

His face fell.

She regretted breaking the spell, but the fear had returned.

"We'll figure something out by morning. We have to," he said. "But let's forget about everything for a little while longer." He leaned down to kiss her, and she let him.

CHAPTER 51

*S**he's with Ralph. It's so good to see him again. She steps into the room, and there he is. He's not in bed, and he's alone, standing in front of her, waiting. When he sees her, he smiles. She should give him a hug, but her body won't respond, so she sits on the chair she finds next to her.*

"Oh, Ralph, I've missed you so much."

"I've missed you, too, Carr." He sounds happy to be with her, but his expression is worried. He has something important to tell her.

"Sam's in trouble."

The words pierce her heart. She's allowed herself to be distracted from her child. "Where is she? I'll go to her right away."

"It's not that simple. She's with someone."

"Who?"

"He means you harm. He's searching for you."

"Why are you telling me this? It sounds like a Catch-22."

"It is. Choose anyway."

"Tell me."

"I'm not permitted to give you the answers."

"You're dead," she says, realizing in her heart it's true.

"Yes."

"How did you die?"

She feels it—the noose tightening around his neck. It is quick. Sam stares in through the open door, face blank with shock. "No."

Ralph nods. "If you don't go, they'll hand her to the aliens."

"What about Michael?" He's there, sleeping, at peace.

"That's up to you."

"You're telling me I have to leave him and let them take me or they'll take Sam."

"No. You can choose to stay with Michael and tell him."

205

"Will he believe me?"

"That's his choice." Ralph meets her gaze, pity in his eyes. *"I'm sorry. I should have done more for you and Sam, but I was afraid and wanted to save myself."*

"We're all afraid, and we all want to save ourselves," she says.

"They want you to go now."

"No, Ralph. Wait. Tell me what to do ..."

Carolyn woke. The fire was out. Everything was black, except the slight glow from the fire's embers and a faint grey space that told her she was looking at the cave entrance. She savoured the warmth of Michael's body next to her. God, she'd miss him. Her heart despaired at the thought of leaving him. He wouldn't know why, but if she woke him and tried to explain, he wouldn't let her go, and her only thought now was to keep Sam safe.

She groped around for kindling and placed the twigs on the embers, then blew on them. When they caught, she had enough light to see her pack. She hunted in it for some clean clothes. Carolyn wanted to leave something for Michael as a message, but she had only her wedding band. She removed it from her finger and placed it into a zippered pocket of his backpack. He'd take it to Sam and rescue her.

She dressed, making as little sound as possible. When she was ready, she slipped on the shoes he'd bought her. It almost made her cry. She wanted to hug him, kiss him, and touch him before she left, but if she did, she'd certainly wake him, so she took one step away from their bed and then another. If only she'd hugged him more—she should've caressed him more, kissed him more. Now it was too late. She could have said the same for the last time she'd hugged John, or Arnie, or Shelly, or Ralph, too. They were all lost to her now, but Sam was still out there. She had to give herself up so they wouldn't start in on Sam.

She reached the mouth of the shelter and stepped out into the moonlight. When the night breeze hit her face, she realized her cheeks were wet. She wiped the tears away and climbed up and away from the cave. She'd have to walk as far away from Michael as possible. If she were near here when the aliens came, they'd get him, maybe kill him.

Carolyn left the shore and walked into the forest. Were bears nearby? *Who cares?* Let them come.

She found a stick sturdy enough to use as a walking stick, and she walked. Since the direction didn't matter as long as it was away from the cave where Michael slept, she headed into the trees. Using the stick like a blind person using a cane, she slowly made her way through the forest.

Time passed. She sensed no one around her. If spirits accompanied her, she didn't feel them. It seemed she walked for hours, but the moon had moved only a little way through the sky, so perhaps it hadn't been that long. Somewhere, an owl called out. The air smelled fragrant.

Where were they? When would they appear? *Soon.* She didn't need precognition to know they drew close. Something in her besides her innate abilities responded to their proximity. It was almost time.

Carolyn halted and waited for them to find her. Tears continued to pour down her face. She'd just found Michael and now she had to give him up. An ache to hold him again overwhelmed her. Why hadn't she told him she'd forgiven him when she'd had the chance? He'd told her how sorry he was, and she hadn't given him absolution. She'd made him suffer, punishing him.

Ashamed, she recalled how she'd told him he'd failed his wife. Now she would never get the chance to tell him how sorry she was that she'd thrown that in his face.

She wished, too, that she'd told him she loved him, and that she wanted to be with him. It might have made their separation more bearable. Even if he found her now, she wouldn't be able to go with him—not while the possibility existed that the aliens would abduct Sam. Regret begat more regret. She should've told him what a good heart he had. He needed to hear it.

She covered her face with her hands and cried.

After a while, she controlled the sobs, stilled the tears. The ache became a dull throb. She'd always have the memory of their time together. No one could take that away. In that way, they'd always be together. It comforted her, a little, and she could face them now. She thought about Michael's strength and courage, and it made her stronger and more courageous. She forced herself to stand tall.

The ship, when it appeared, came suddenly. She looked up at a star-filled sky, and then the stars were obliterated and brilliant light engulfed her. As she rose, she saw two men on the ground where she'd stood. Agents. They expected Michael, but he wasn't there.

Her heart gave a lurch of fear as she realized that if they had any tracking skills, they'd be able to backtrack her trail and find him. One of them looked up at her, and she met his eyes. It frightened her to know that if she had a gun, she could bring herself to shoot him. Rage surged through her when she realized he'd hunt down Michael, and she knew she would do anything to stop him.

She pushed the violent thoughts away and replaced them with more helpful ones. She silently asked her angels and guides to protect Michael. For a moment, she saw the trees below her, and she thought she felt him waking up. He was such a part of her now she could feel his despair at her absence. Afraid they'd read that from her, she struggled, knowing her struggles would cause them to knock her out. As blackness took her, she smiled.

CHAPTER 52

Michael woke with a start. Even before he opened his eyes, he knew she was gone. He felt the void—a void he'd had all his life though now he understood her absence caused it.

Dull dawn light poured in from the direction of the opening of their small cave. In the dimness, he discerned the pile that was his clothes and the two lumps that were their packs. She'd left her pack behind. She'd gone out to meet them.

An urge to scream grew unbearable. How could he have slept through that? His life had walked out into the darkness, and he'd slept on, oblivious. He dressed in military gear and strapped on a belt with a sheathed knife. When he put his holster on, he verified his gun was loaded and cocked.

Michael doused the fire and threw his pack onto his shoulders. He went to the mouth of their shelter and gazed out over the lake. A light mist covered everything. She'd have left an obvious trail—she was a city girl all the way, and tracking her would be easy.

He climbed above the shoreline and headed into the trees, alert to any sounds. When he reached the trees, he searched for the point where she'd entered the forest. Easily found as he'd expected. She'd left a track a blind, scent-deprived dog could follow. He shook his head, loving her for being so careless.

Michael pulled out his gun and screwed on the suppressor. He stepped to the side of the trail to find a place to hide. Two agents likely headed this way. All he had to do was wait.

He moved into the underbrush and crouched behind a copse of fir trees. The air wasn't as heavy as it had been the last few nights, and a slight breeze rustled the trees. It occurred to him that he acted under the assumption that they'd already retrieved her. Without knowing how, he was aware they had.

Why had she left? Something must've triggered it. Had she received a message during the night that made her conclude sneaking away was her only option? Her disappearance had to be a reaction to something. But what? Worry about her daughter? If so, then why didn't she wake him and tell him? He shook his head. Speculating was useless.

As he stared at the trail, he realized he waited here only to get revenge. Killing these agents wouldn't help him get Carolyn back, and she wouldn't want him to kill them. He could interrogate them to try and learn where they'd taken her, but these men wouldn't know. Their orders would be to either take him in or kill him. Where Carolyn ended up didn't concern them.

The more Michael considered it, the more he realized he could walk away, continue on to the alien base, and find help. The two agents would follow Carolyn's trail. They'd discover the cave, which now contained only Carolyn's backpack and sleeping bag. They'd see no trace of Michael and report the two hadn't been together.

He put away his pistol and hoisted his pack onto his back. Leaving no trace of his passing, he crossed Carolyn's trail and headed away from it toward the alien base they'd originally sought.

As he walked, the sky brightened. It would be another sunny day.

Were any spirits around if Carolyn wasn't there? He'd found it fascinating to watch her communicate with Jess. The thought of his wife aroused guilt. Carolyn was a stranger to him, but he felt her absence in his core. He missed Jess, loved Jess, but he didn't feel as if she was a part of him.

Maybe he was going crazy. Perhaps he should ask for a sign from the spirit world as Carolyn had.

Couldn't hurt. Self-conscious, he thought, *If I have guides out there, give me a sign I'm not alone.* He looked around, wondering if something was supposed to happen right away or if this would be a process. He remained still, listening. Nothing.

He removed the pack from his shoulders and set it on the ground. As he did, he noticed the front pouch, the one containing his wallet, was slightly open. He went to close it but took his wallet out instead and shoved it in his pocket. Something popped out with the wallet and dropped to the ground, landing next to a small white feather. Startled, he picked up both the feather and the item and examined the item first.

A woman's wedding band. It had no markings, save for a single, tiny diamond in the centre of the band. He recognized it from when she'd tried to give it to him the day before. *Carolyn's.* She'd left it for him, probably so he'd find Sam and give it to her, and it had landed next to a white feather.

Give me a sign I'm not alone. Perhaps this was it. He put the ring in

209

his pocket and released the feather, letting it drift to the ground. He'd keep the ring for her and give it back to her when he found her again.

As he walked, he reached into his pocket to touch the ring, and it reassured him and gave him faith they'd meet again. Confident he'd find what he needed at the base, he quickened his pace.

***

Cornell sat in the Fairchild's living room, his cell phone pressed to his ear, listening to an update from Weeks. Finally, he'd received the message for which he'd waited all night. They had her. They didn't have Valiant, but they had Carolyn Fairchild. Her death had already been staged. All that remained now was to wait here until the cops arrived and then deliver the news to Sam.

He thanked Weeks for the information, hung up, and looked toward Sam's bedroom. She'd gone to bed late, expressing gratitude that he'd stayed to watch over her and guilt that she'd kept him from his family. He'd assured her it was all in the line of duty.

Poor kid. She'd now have to suffer through the loss of both her parents so close together. At least he wouldn't have to hand her over to the aliens now in lieu of her mother.

Of course, she wouldn't last long on her own. When the crisis hit, she'd be wiped out along with everyone else, and it might be a protracted death—a slow slide into sickness and starvation if one of the natural disasters didn't kill her.

Should he take her with them? She'd be like a daughter to him and help his wife with the kids when they went underground. It would be one way to make it up to her. He'd have a word with his wife. Sam was a sweet kid, and she thought the world of him. It might be nice to keep someone like that around, and, of course, he could use her as leverage with Carolyn, who'd do whatever he wanted if she knew her daughter's life was at stake.

Noise from outside alerted him to an approaching vehicle. Cornell looked out the window. A police car. He checked his watch: 8:06 AM. He rose and walked to the door. Show time.

CHAPTER 53

The helicopters' appearance three days before warned Michael he was probably too late. His fears were confirmed as soon as he drew within eyeshot of the point on the map indicating the base. The area surrounding the base and what was marked on the map as the entrance were a smouldering ruin.

He withdrew and monitored any activity for a day, trying to gauge the risk of going in there—the place might be radioactive or otherwise contaminated. Agents entered and exited the building without protective suits, so he was sure now that wasn't a concern.

Thoughts of Carolyn intruded constantly, making him want to throw caution aside and just get in there. He forced himself to put her out of his mind. She couldn't afford for him to get reckless.

A man in military gear hovered near the rubble, guarding access to the base, which had been reduced to a gaping hole leading into what resembled a mineshaft in a cave. The man wasn't Canadian or even US military. He was Agency personnel. The FN Herstal assault rifle gave it away.

The sun was setting, the coming darkness providing extra cover, so Michael observed and waited. Silently, he backtracked ten metres to where he'd stored his pack in the shelter of some bushes.

He loosened the knife in the sheath at his side. Besides the Glock he held in his hand, he had another one strapped to his leg. That he'd have to kill to get into the base wasn't an issue. He saw this as his only option. He put on a pair of night-vision goggles and crept closer to the base.

The guard hung out near the entrance. He'd lit a cigarette and stood smoking, his gaze roving the surrounding area.

Michael inched nearer but froze at a shout from his left, and, more disconcertingly, a dog bark. Another Agent, leading a German shepherd on a leash, approached the man guarding the entrance.

"Find anything else?" the smoker asked as man and dog reached him.

"No. They're dead or gone."

Another man appeared from the cave entrance. The man with the dog shouted to the newcomer, "All clear, Captain Trecartin."

Trecartin gave a nod and strode to the guards.

Smoker dropped his cigarette and put it out with his boot.

When the captain reached his men, he said, "I'm going to head back to the chopper. You two will be relieved in four hours. No one goes in or out; is that clear?"

"Yes, sir. What about the other entrance?" Smoker asked.

"Guards are posted there as well. Right now, I want this sealed off until Cornell gets here, which ought to be by morning. He doesn't want anyone tampering with anything. Don't get curious. Got it?"

"Got it, Captain."

Trecartin took the dog's leash and walked along the treeline, but paused as the dog stopped and sniffed the air.

Michael raised his gun, aiming the barrel at Trecartin. The dog growled, and Michael ducked and watched from the ground as the captain scanned the bushes and trees, panning over Michael's hiding place.

"Something wrong, Captain?" Smoker walked over and stood next to Trecartin. All three men standing by the entrance wore night-vision goggles.

Michael kept still. If they caught the right angle, they'd spot him.

Then the captain shrugged and turned back to Smoker. "Guess it's nothing." He yanked on the dog's chain. The dog continued to pull in Michael's direction. It yelped when the captain tugged roughly on the chain again. He stared once more into the trees.

Trecartin gazed at a point beyond Michael's hiding spot. He allowed himself to relax.

The captain said something to Smoker that Michael couldn't catch. The guard nodded, and Trecartin led the dog past the trees on the right.

Michael continued to wait, listening for the sound of a helicopter taking off. Ten minutes later, he was rewarded and heard the chopper leaving.

If what he'd overheard was correct, only four men remained to guard the base, which had probably been cleaned out. He'd be lucky to find any survivors.

Smoker and the other agent raised their guns, holding them ready, both on alert.

Michael tensed. He sighted his gun on the two guards, targeting Smoker first. Before he could pull the trigger, he heard rustling behind him. He started to turn and felt searing pain as something struck the back of his skull. Everything went black.

***

The darkness faded, returning Michael to a throbbing headache. He lay face up, pressure on the back of his head causing him to feel sick as the pain lanced through him. He kept his eyes closed, reaching out with his other senses to get an idea of his surroundings.

Straps held his body in place—across his chest, his lower belly, and above his knees. It was cold. He was naked. He panicked when he realized they had Carolyn's ring. Anger followed panic. If it killed him, he'd get it back.

The chill struck him then, and his body shook, his teeth rattling together.

"Cap? He's awake." A woman's voice.

Michael opened his eyes.

A woman in army fatigues pointed an assault rifle at his head.

He winced. "I'm flattered you think you need that."

She didn't reply, but the gun barrel moved away from his face. However, she kept it levelled at him.

Michael sensed the approach of another person and tried to move his head in that direction. Another wave of nausea swooped through him.

Captain Trecartin appeared, and they stared at each other. Trecartin spoke first. "Glad to see you're awake. I was afraid I'd killed you. That would've been a shame. Cornell wants you alive though I don't know why."

"You gave me a fucking concussion," Michael said.

"You'll wish I'd killed you."

"Where am I?"

"In the alien base in Algonquin. Congratulations. You made it, but abductees will get no more help from this quarter, especially that little bitch you tried to save."

Michael grimaced and took a deep breath to calm down, refusing to take the bait. If he were going to get out of here and help Carolyn, he'd have to stay in control.

"You killed them all? I find that hard to believe."

"Oh, no. Not all. Some we saved for experiments of our own, as you'd see if you weren't restrained so well. The aliens working with us don't care. The ones who built this base were rebels. They interfered, sabotaging the experiments and helping the abductees escape. We were given carte blanche to use any prisoners as we see fit. They're traitors to their race as you are to yours." He leaned in close as though searching for something in Michael's expression. "They say you're special. I don't see it. Doesn't matter. You'll be part of the experiments now, too."

Michael averted his eyes, hiding his hope. If they turned him over to the aliens in league with the Agency, maybe he'd be transferred to the same holding cells where they kept Carolyn. They'd take him right to her.

As if reading his mind, Trecartin shook his head. "No, you're not going anywhere near Peterborough Compound. You're going up." He pointed at the ceiling, meaning into the ships. "And you ain't coming back down."

Footsteps approached, and the captain straightened and turned. "Welcome, sir."

"Thank you, Captain Trecartin."

Michael slowly turned his head and faced Cornell, who stopped about a metre away.

Trecartin and the other agent disappeared.

"Why?" Cornell uttered the one word.

Michael stared at him, amazed. "Why do you think?"

"You had it made, Mick."

"How did I have it made?" He almost said "Jim." He stopped himself. Fuck him. "You fucking killed my wife—you and Torque."

"What are you talking about? What do you mean we killed your wife?" His arms opened, palms out, a gesture of innocence.

"Don't play the fucking innocent with me. I know the truth. She became a threat to the status quo, didn't she? You couldn't let us be happy, have a family."

"She had an accident in the street. There were witnesses."

"Torque used the ray on her. Don't deny it. The two of you were huddled together, talking about how to get me back on side. He killed her, and when that made things worse, you planned to take me in. So don't look so surprised that I defended myself." The accusation that Cornell knew Torque had killed Jess was a wild guess.

"Very well. I won't deny it. I'm not here to 'get you back on side' anyway. It's too late for that. It was too late for that the moment you ran off with the Fairchild woman." He paused, smiled.

Michael's intestines turned to stone.

"I have her." The smile became a grin. His voice filled with glee. "The daughter, too. Neither one of them knows where the other is."

Michael tested the restraints, pressing on them with the side of his leg. He couldn't move. He forced his voice to stay even, confident, neutral. "Where are they?"

"The daughter is living in my family's guest house. I've convinced her to rent out her family home and stay with us as a live-in nanny. All the better to keep her safe, you see." He grinned again, baring his teeth this time.

"And Carolyn?"

"You know where she is. Safely locked up." Cornell took a step toward him, an eager glint in his eyes. "She's got a cell next to Arnie. Don't worry. I'll take very good care of her." He tilted his head to the side. "What's she like in bed?"

Michael's heart thudded against his chest. He couldn't speak.

Cornell licked his lips, leering. "I know you fucked her. They tested her. How was it? Anything I should know before I take my turn?"

"Keep your fucking hands off her. I'll kill you." He struggled against the restraints. They held him tightly in place.

Cornell chuckled. "Sorry. You'll never see her again, and if by chance you do, she won't even recognize you."

"What do you mean?"

"You know what's nice about revenge?"

Michael opened his mouth, but Cornell waved him down. "Don't bother. Rhetorical question. Everything is nice about revenge. In your case, I get to control what happens to you for the rest of your life, and I get to make you pay for what you did to the agency and to me."

Cornell's voice rose so he came close to screaming. "You betrayed the Agency, and that was bad enough, but you almost destroyed everything I built. You tried to steal one of our subjects. Fairchild was ours. You had no right to take her from us. Worse than that, I trusted you. Anyone else would've had you terminated when you started to crack, but I didn't. If they'd discovered I gave you that kind of slack, I'd have been ruined."

One hand stroked Michael's hair, a father, forced to chastise a prodigal son, desiring to forgive, but unable to do so. "Well, I guess it can't be helped now. You brought it on yourself. She'll never be yours. I'll make sure of that. We have ways to manipulate her mind. She'll think you're the enemy. She'll think I'm her lover. Whatever I want her to believe, she'll believe."

Michael remembered the reports he'd found in the evidence room. MKUltra. The mind control experiments. Had they succeeded? Was it possible to tamper with Carolyn's mind to the extent that she'd believe her abductor was her lover? Cornell had to be bluffing.

"The aliens won't let you. They're experimenting on her. They won't let you tamper with her." That had to be true.

"When they're done with her, they'll turn her over to me. I can terminate her if I want, or I can keep her for myself."

"You sick fuck. What about her daughter?"

"Sam thinks I'm a hero. I won't have to do anything to her. She thinks her mother is dead. The police gave her the sad news a few days ago. I was there to guide her through that tragic event. The funeral is tomorrow. Shame you'll have to miss it, but you'll be participating in some experiments yourself."

Horror swept over Michael.

Cornell smiled that big-bad-wolf smile again. He tapped Michael on the forehead with his index finger. "Don't worry about your mind. I want that intact. They'll just experiment on your body. I want you to be aware of everything that happens to you—and everything that happens to Carolyn—or what's the point? No. I need you of sound mind, but not sound body."

He leaned close to Michael's ear. "I'll let you in on a little secret. You're one of them."

Michael grew colder. "What do you mean?"

"The aliens. You have their DNA."

"You're lying. That's impossible."

"Not really. Your mother was part of the experiments. They allowed her to carry you to full term and keep you, but you have their DNA. Why do you think we cared so much about what happened to you? Why do you think we recruited you?"

A door opened, followed by the sound of footsteps. A woman in a lab coat appeared next to Cornell. She carried a clipboard. More footsteps. A man appeared—Smoker.

"Ah. I see they're ready to start work. We want to run a few tests on you before the aliens take you. Nice chatting with you. I'm heading to the Peterborough compound now. Shall I give Carolyn your regards?" Cornell flashed his teeth once more.

He turned and walked away, Michael's curses following him out.

CHAPTER 54

While struggling against the restraints, Michael lifted his head and peered into the dim light. The table on which he lay and the straps that held him down were all he could see. He slowed his breathing and relaxed his muscles. A vision of Carolyn in bed with Cornell popped into his head, but he pushed it away.

Never. Not on my watch.

The woman in the lab coat drew close. She looked him over, made some notes on the clipboard.

"You a doctor?" Maybe if he got her talking, he could convince her to remove the straps.

She ignored him. The guard didn't. He punched Michael in the jaw, snapping his head back onto the table, smacking the bump Trecartin had gifted him with.

Michael gritted his teeth against the pain, refusing to give the fucker the satisfaction of hearing him cry out.

"You'd be wise to keep your mouth shut and cooperate," the guard said.

Michael resisted an urge to struggle again. He was worse off than an animal in a leg trap—at least trapped animals had the option to chew off the leg and escape.

"I'll need the cart." The doctor pointed in the direction from which they'd come, and the guard walked away.

Wheels squeaked and the guard reappeared, pushing a medical cart with various implements on it. Michael eyed the hypodermics and scalpels. In seconds, he scanned the entire tray, determining the best weapon. He only needed an opportunity.

The doctor picked up a tourniquet. She paused, staring at her subject, and then turned to the guard. "Remove the top strap. I have to take blood, and I need his arm free."

"Not a good idea," the guard replied.

"He's not going anywhere. I have to take a blood sample. You can hold him down or do whatever you want to restrain him, but I need his arm free."

The guard pointed a pistol at Michael and then unfastened the strap holding his chest and arms down. The doctor tied a tourniquet onto Michael's arm. She slipped on a pair of latex gloves and searched for a vein. She swabbed the inside of his arm and met Michael's gaze for the first time since her arrival.

"Make a fist."

He did and used it to punch the guard. Before anyone could react, Michael snatched the scalpel from the tray and slit the guard's throat. Blood spurted and Michael shoved the man to the floor.

The doctor shrieked and tried to back away, but Michael grabbed her upper arm, pulling her to him. He held her in a chokehold. Her legs kicked out, knocking the cart over. He tightened his grip, holding her until she was unconscious. He released her, and she slumped to the floor.

Michael removed the other two straps and lowered himself from the table. Blood covered him. A glance at the guard verified blood drenched his clothing. Michael bent down and picked up the pistol. A Glock. Perfect.

He went around the table, removed the doctor's lab coat, and used it to wipe the blood from his body. He made a move to scan the room and swayed a little on unsteady feet. The room tilted, and he grabbed the edge of the table. When the wave passed, he viewed his surroundings.

Emergency lights near the ceiling gave off a faint glow. He estimated the room was large, twenty metres by thirty metres. The walls were solid rock. He spied a vent close to the floor on one wall—too small for him to climb into. Other tables littered the room, ten or twelve of them. Most were empty, but five of them looked as if they contained an occupant. A sheet covered each body but left the head exposed. Aliens.

There was a closet next to the door, and he hurried to it, listening for any sound of approach. The closet door was unlocked. His clothes. *Thank God.* He dressed and checked his pocket for Carolyn's ring. Still there, and so was his wallet. His weapons and ammo were gone, but at least he had clothes and boots.

He cracked the door open, listened. Nothing. He was about to step out of the door when something made him turn back. He had to go look at the beings on the other tables. Even as he argued with himself against it, told himself how stupid he was and that he had to get the hell out of there, he closed the door again, locking it. He went to the closest table and lifted the sheet.

A Grey. He'd seen many of them during the years he'd spent with the

Agency. They were always around when people were abducted, mostly assisting the other beings in charge of the experiments.

The creature was strapped down. Did that mean they were still alive? He touched the alien's shoulder. Nothing happened. Had it died on the table? Another wave of vertigo hit him then, and he lurched into the table. The table rattled, and he gripped it, dropping the gun to the floor. He closed his eyes, hoping that would ease the dizziness. When he did, images poured into his mind's eye, then out again, like a slide show.

He tried to follow it. A giant crystal, clear as quartz, glowed with an orange light. That was replaced by an identical crystal, but smaller. Opaque eggs suspended from a ceiling. Growing fetuses. A cave.

Images rushed by. He felt nauseated again. The pictures flashed by so quickly he couldn't see them. It was like watching a fan spin. The faster it went, the more the blades blurred together until it looked like one solid plane.

The aliens weren't dead; they were dormant. He didn't know how he knew that, but it was true. He touched the alien again. More images poured in, but slower. Carolyn lying on a cot in a cell. Other people in other cells. The crystals again. They were showing him there was a connection between the crystals and the people.

He saw the base he was in as it had been before the Agency arrived to destroy it. Abductees arrived. The beings used the crystal to sever the connection the aliens had to the abductees.

The images stopped. Michael looked down. The alien opened its eyes.

CHAPTER 55

Michael backed away from the thing, regretting coming back. He should have left. He should leave now. When he tried to turn away, his body refused to cooperate. Instead, one by one, he removed the straps holding the alien down.

It sat up.

Michael stood, unable to move.

It raised an arm and touched Michael's head, which repelled him, but his arms hung uselessly at his sides. Frozen in place, he watched it, allowing it to do whatever it wanted. He had no urge to resist. Is this how Carolyn felt when they took her?

It cupped its hand around the back of Michael's head, and his headache vanished. The lump, too, was gone, though he couldn't lift a hand to check.

The alien placed its hands on either side of Michael's head, adjusted, and then pressed a finger on the space above and between his eyes. Holding the finger there, the being traced a line from that point to the back of Michael's head, along the left side of his head. Next, it traced another path along the other side of Michael's head, again to the back of his skull. Finally, it removed his hand from Michael's forehead and gripped his face between its palms. It leaned its own head forward so their brows touched.

Michael felt queasy, but he also noticed a heightened sense of awareness. He wanted to leave, to get out of here and rescue Carolyn, but he needed to find a way to sever her connection to the aliens, or they'd capture her again. The large crystal reappeared in his mind's eye. A sense of urgency prickled him. The thing was in his head, in his mind. He tried to move and couldn't.

It wanted him to go to Nahanni, in the Northwest Territories, to a place known as "The Valley of the Headless Men," after the decapitated

220

bodies of some prospectors were found there. Legend also had it that an entire tribe of Aboriginals had disappeared from that same area.

Michael thought again about Carolyn. He wanted to go to her, get her away from Cornell. When he turned his thoughts in that direction, pain and fear stabbed him.

"No." It came out of his mouth as a croak. Through gritted teeth he said, "I'm going to get her."

An image came to him. He saw himself in Nahanni, in a cavern with the large crystal. The image expanded, and he watched himself as if in a dream.

He creates a physical, mental, and spiritual connection to the crystal with his hands and then severs the connection between the aliens and the abductees. They're all freed.

"Why didn't *you* do that?" he asked.

The image flashed to a view of Algonquin Park. His vision flew to the entrance of the alien base within the park, then down, through tunnels, rooms, elevators, down through circular levels, into the depths of the base, where a smaller crystal, the mirror image of the large one in Nahanni, sat. He watched as Agents broke into the cavern. The next image showed the crystal in fragments, its glow extinguished.

His new awareness gave him comprehension. This was how things worked for Carolyn. She just knew things. Information burst into her mind, and she recognized it as the truth. He knew now, for instance, that the base in Nahanni wasn't a rebel base. It belonged to the hostile aliens in league with the Agency. The crystals were interconnected, like a communication link, but so much more than that. Nahanni's crystal was the master; the others, the slaves.

Only, the rebel group had managed to somehow hide that they were using this particular slave to free the abductees. He gazed down at the alien again and went cold. The pupils in the alien's eyes were gone, the eyes milky and clouded. He looked closer and exhaled in relief. The alien had a nictitating membrane—another eyelid that slid closed horizontally.

Afraid the alien was going dormant again or, worse, dying, Michael touched its shoulder. He swayed again as his own vision blurred. Urgency flowed through him. Get to Nahanni.

What about Sam? I can at least get Sam away from Cornell.

A searing flash roared through his brain. *Notimenotimenotimenotime.* At first, he couldn't make out anything in that slur of words, and then it slowed, and he heard it, *no time, no time, no time,* while the images in his head showed a spacecraft army sucking up people in droves.

So this was his choice: rescue Sam or help the abductees, Carolyn included. If he went after Sam, the abductees would be pulled onto the ships by the time he got to Nahanni to free them, and, if the images were correct, they wouldn't be coming down again. He remembered what Trecartin had said when Michael was strapped down on the table. *You're going up. And you ain't coming back down.*

They were planning to take them all. What would happen to them then, he didn't want to know. He'd have to go to Nahanni. Then he'd go straight to Carolyn and get her away from Cornell.

He left the alien sitting on the table and quickly released the one on the next table, not stopping to see if it regained consciousness. He released them all. As he freed the last one, he heard someone unlocking and then opening the door. He grabbed the pistol and ran for the door. The door swung open.

Captain Trecartin entered the room.

Michael was ready for him.

Trecartin's shocked face exploded when the bullet hit it. His body collapsed, the door hitting it on the backswing.

Michael raced to the door, aiming his gun at the gap, but Trecartin had been alone. Michael dragged him into the room, letting the door slam shut. He glanced back at the aliens. Three of the five still lay on their table, but the one he'd communicated with and another were standing.

"I'll go where you want," Michael said. "Then I'm going to find her."

He didn't wait for a response but took Trecartin's holster, which had ammo and a knife. He stuck the Glock in the holster, shouldered the assault rifle, and picked up the night-vision goggles. Thankfully, the man hadn't been wearing them when his face blew off. Michael put them on.

He listened at the door. All was silent. He opened it and stepped into the deserted corridor, swinging the rifle around. Nothing moved.

Which way? He had to get out without being detected.

Go down. He wasn't sure where that directive came from. His intuition? The aliens? He didn't care. He may as well see where it led him. It was better than blindly running around the base.

Which way was down? The corridor dead-ended on one side and led to a T-junction on the other. He headed for the junction, pausing before he reached it. The passageway on the left sloped down. He checked the tunnels. All were empty. He suspected the Agency had minimal personnel here. Cornell was confident they had the place secured. Michael followed the passageway on the left.

Up ahead, the light grew brighter. The tunnel opened again, and this time, the opening terminated in a deep pit. There was a rim around the pit, about a metre wide. Every five metres vertical rows of metal rungs, used as ladders, led into the pit. More alien bodies were scattered below.

This pit appeared to be some kind of storage area and the entryway into the rest of the base. There were three doors at the bottom of the pit, about ten metres apart, probably elevators to the levels beneath. All were blown open, and the shafts were dark.

Michael walked to one of the rungs and began to climb down. It was a deep pit and descending the ladder was a slow process. He wasn't afraid of the height, but he still didn't trust no one waited to ambush him when he reached the bottom.

At last, he reached the ground and put his back to the wall while he looked around. There were desks here, computers, and lockers. It reminded him of a military installation. He wondered what the aliens were doing with this stuff. Humans must've worked here.

Michael walked the perimeter of the pit, noticed a hatchway in the centre, and went to it. He spun the wheel, opened the hatch, and peered into the opening.

Rungs led down and he faintly made out the bottom. Everything looked empty. No sound from below, but sounds of activity from beyond the outer rim of the pit reached his ears. They must have found the Agents and doctor he'd killed.

He stepped into the hole and climbed down the rungs, pulling the hatch closed behind him. It wouldn't take them long to find the hatch, but if he was lucky, he could be well away before they did.

When Michael reached the bottom, he found a circular room. Corridors led in different directions. Which way? He waited, hoping whatever thought had been guiding him would voice an opinion again. When he started to think he wasn't going to get any help on this, it came.

Straight ahead.

He ran. The sense of urgency grew unbearable. The walls glowed a soft green. After half an hour, he was still running, but he'd slowed his pace. The corridor seemed endless. There had been no openings along the route, and no forks to give him pause. There was only the long, green glow of the corridor and the hard rock floor.

As he walked, his thoughts turned to Carolyn. If she was with the hostiles, they were doing tests, possibly hurting her. Arnie, and who knows how many others, were likely held where she was. He had no way to get them out without help. He was a wanted man, and if Agency grunts found him, they wouldn't hesitate to kill him. His only hope would be to get to Nahanni and remove the hold the aliens had on the abductees. Carolyn would have to wait though it tore him apart to leave her with the Agency. He'd have a hell of a time getting out of this place with agents hunting for him. He didn't think he could do this.

You're going to have to. He paused. Whose thought was that? He'd said the same thing to Carolyn once, what seemed like eons ago. Yes, he'd have to. Michael ran on.

###

NOTE FROM THE AUTHOR

Fiction often draws on real events or explores concepts drawn from reality. *The Valiant Chronicles* are no exception. For some interesting reading, investigate Rendlesham Forest in Suffolk, England, and the UFO sightings there; Nikola Tesla and his death ray; the StarGate project; and project MKUltra.

The reading list below contains some non-fiction books that offer a unique perspective on "life, the universe, and everything" (as Douglas Adams would say):

Chaos and Harmony: Perspectives on Scientific Revolutions of the Twentieth Century by Trinh Xuan Thuan

Communion: A True Story by Whitley Strieber

Life after Life by Raymond A. Moody, Jr., M.D.

Limitless Mind: A Guide to Remote Viewing and Transformational Consciousness by Russell Targ

The End of Materialism: How Evidence of the Paranormal is Bringing Science and Spirit Together by Charles T. Tart, Ph.D.

UFO's: A Scientific Debate edited by Carl Sagan and Thornton Page.

ABOUT THE AUTHOR

Val Tobin lives in Newmarket, Ontario with her husband, Bob, and Scully, their cat. She spends her days writing, reading, and searching for the perfect butter tart.

Her educational background includes a diploma in Computer Information Systems from DeVry Toronto, a B.Sc. in Parapsychic Science from the American Institute of Holistic Theology, a M.Sc. in Parapsychology from AIHT, Reiki Master/Teacher certifications, and Angel Therapy Practitioner® certifications.

CONNECT WITH VAL TOBIN

Facebook: www.facebook.com/valtobinauthor
Web Site: www.valtobin.com/

OTHER BOOKS BY VAL TOBIN

Paranormal Sci-Fi Thrillers
The Valiant Chronicles Series (available individually or as a box set)
Earthbound (prequel): A spirit becomes earthbound after refusing to cross over in order to solve her murder and prevent more deaths, some of which might be predestined.

The Experiencers (book one): A black-ops assassin atones for his brutal past by helping an alien abductee escape capture.

A Ring of Truth (Book Two): A rogue assassin triggers an apocalypse when he attempts to rescue a group of alien abductees.

Paranormal Romance
Walk-In: A young psychic woman fights an attraction to a handsome but sceptical novelist while she battles a power-hungry sorcerer determined to make her his next conquest.

Horror Suspense
The Hunted: A Storm Lake Story: A monster hunter revisits her terrifying past while helping a reporter uncover the origins of Storm Lake's creatures. A stand-alone sequel to the short story "Storm Lake," *The Hunted* takes place twelve years later.

Urban Fantasy

Tales from the Unmasqued World Series
The Fool: New Beginnings (book one): A newly divorced woman suffering a midlife crisis gets involved in the search for a missing half-vampire teen.

The Magician: Infinity's End (book two): After getting expelled for setting a demon loose on campus, a student mage searches for the real culprit and finds his troubles have only just begun.